PRAISE FOR

TIGER MOODY

"Having 'Induction of the Sycophant' next to 'The Red Book' of Carl Jung and the 'Codex Seraphinianus' by Luigi Sarafini completes my Trilogy of Insanity...in spades."
    —*Richard Lloyd, Television*

"Moody is the best thing to happen to writing since I figured out you can cop a buzz huffing correction fluid."
    —*Gillian McCain, Please Kill Me*

"Moody has the nerve to confront the reader with the notion that the old farts and witch hunters may have really been onto something, and that lives may have been ruined. Then he further goads the reader to perseverate over whether they should even give a shit."
    —*Adam Woodrow Nathanson,*
    Born Against

"A very good writer...I am happy that he doesn't DRAW cartoons! He doesn't, does he?"
    —*Arnold Roth, Trump/ Humbug/ Help!*

For Pearl.

INDUCTION
OF THE
SYCOPHANT.

a

fairy tale

by

TIGER MOODY.

KICKS BOOKS
NEW YORK, NEW YORK

Induction Of The Sycophant © 2015 by Tiger Moody
This edition © 2015 Kicks Books

Published in 2015 by Kicks Books
PO Box 646 Cooper Station
New York NY 10276

Printed in the United States of America

ISBN: 978-1-940157-13-9

Editor: Miriam Linna
Design: Patrick Broderick/Rotodesign

www.kicksbooks.com

FOREWORD

They are the lascivious stuff of dreams: graphic hallucinations of day, sweet, wet, riding the mare of night. Their yellowing pages lie between the golden and silver age of superheroes, in a midcentury when once-children's comics seemed to seize the moment from the waning pulp magazines, appropriating their rogue's gallery of the fiendish and fantastical, prurient to the point of provocative; the alluring lurid, emphasis on the id.

"We do mostly crime, romance, and the scary monster crap now," says Zach Kirby, in an alter-ego and not-so-secret identity that presages his Marvellian incarnation, disdaining the "pajama boy" do-gooders that were comic industries staples through World War II, when perhaps such caped crusaders were psychically necessary to preserve truth, freedom, and the star-spangled way. Now it's the post-war boom, television and space cadets and rock and roll on the horizon, and America is ready to indulge its collective fantasies.

As always, there are those who wish to clamp down on such unrestrained desire; even if depicting wish-fulfillments on a page allows the artistic distancing of subliminal transference. Such a thing happened in the fall of 1953, when Dr. Frederic Wertham began his campaign to convince a Senate sub-committee to look into the degenerate influence comics had on their supposedly underage target audience. Tiger Moody describes the world of pre-Comic Code comics with a fetishist's eye: his Times Square travelogues Nedick's, Jack Dempsey's, Chock Full O' Nuts; his characters reference famous illustrators and wily publishers (Wally Good, Millard Gaines of Exciting Comics), mixing fact and fantasy, much as the comics themselves. He has an insider's grasp of the cartoonist's tools-of-trade – their use of background and shading, the angle of their drawing boards, the lingo of "headlights" and "cross-hatch" and "swipes," their insecurities working the outlier borders of art, the internecine competitions and unlikely friendships. And that each ink-stained hand tightening on a pencil is attached to a human as strange as those that grow from the realms of imagination, life replicating art.

I only wish I could step off the page and go to the newsstand and pick up a few of the then-current issues. Perhaps I can. For, yes, over in the corner is a Pandora's box. I open it. I place my hand within a sheaf of plastic bags, each with their cardboard stiffening, preserved in the amber glow of a gathered collection, and randomly choose: *Weird Tales of the Future* # 2 with its Basil Wolverton cover of alien grotesquerie; *Web of Mystery* #8 with its helpless femme caught thrust-chested in a spider's spinning, surrounded by ominous skulls; *Crime Does Not Pay* #98, a gunfight erupting, a moll the prize.

And then, thinking of that six year old whom Dr. Wertham thought he was protecting, I have to hand it to him. He was right. I was corrupted forever, and been grateful ever since.

Lenny Kaye
February 2015

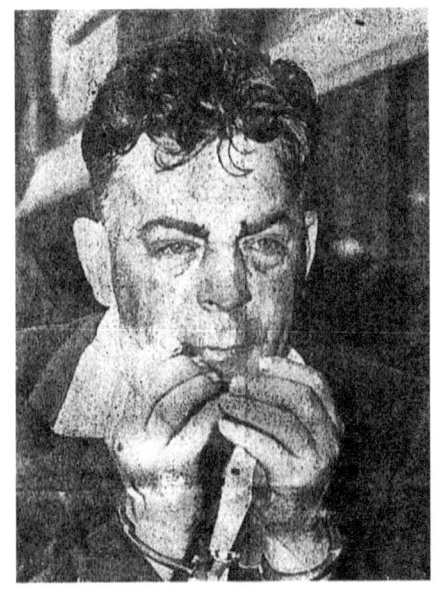

"And I verily do suppose that in the braines and hertes of children, which be membres spirituall, whiles they be tender, and the little slippes of reason begynne in them to bud, ther may happe by evil custome some pestiferous dewe of vice to perse the sayde membres, and infecte and corrupt the soft and tender buddes."

—Sir Thomas Eliot, 1531.

THERE was a chill in the air.
Jack Coal, a forty one-year-old comic book artist,
felt pangs of hunger as he watched an ocelot-wrapped
blonde carry a small child up the busy throng
of Third Avenue.
She was young, attractive, and bosomy; but
he failed to notice her good looks. He was too
absorbed with the tortured features of the little boy.
The child was crying, his face drawn tight,
twisted, and red with cold.
He wondered how salty the little boy's tears would
taste. He wanted to kiss them away. Then, he thought
of a sliced ham on rye, with plenty of mustard.
The tall, heavy, bespectacled man loved children.
He'd loved being a child himself. He'd had an idyllic

youth in New Castle. He'd loved his parents, his siblings, and his friends very, very much. More than anything, he wanted to begin this cycle anew. He wanted children of his own. To love, to protect, to feed, and to hold.

In fact, that was *all* that Jack Coal had ever really wanted.

Nothing else mattered.

And now, he was hungry again.

The young mother noticed Jack Coal's blank, languid stare and smiled back at him with a genuine warmth and sympathy.

Her eye-contact jarred him.

He glanced down to the rectangular, gold Elgin on his left wrist and picked up his stride without returning the woman's smile. The Meiser Studio didn't tolerate lateness, there were important deadlines to meet.

It was the Autumn of 1953.

It was Manhattan.

It was just below Thirty Third Street.

THE Lafargue Clinic was located in the basement of Saint Phillip's Episcopal church in Harlem, which had been handsomely re-finished into a small cluster of psychiatric offices. The clinic was headed by an aging doctor named Fredric Thaddeus Wertham.

The doctor was white-haired, short, and slight; but he was by no means frail. On the contrary, he was fueled with a youthful vigor that bordered on constant rage. This inner-fire had served him well at the front during the first World War, where Dr. Wertham had killed nine men, including five American Marines, in hand-to-hand combat.

He kept his medals hidden in the bottom left drawer of his massive, immaculate walnut desk.

Across this desk sat a small Puerto Rican boy, who looked nine but was actually twelve.

Julio, somehow remaining silent as he shivered with the violent restraint of tears, was suspected of shoving his younger brother Juan off the roof of a Lower East

Side tenement building the week prior.
There'd been a red towel tied around the corpse's neck.
Dr. Wertham's black horn-rimmed frames contained
thick lenses that magnified his ice-blue eyes to
Martian-like proportions and filled Julio with a
deep, lurking terror. That the old man spoke with
a thick German accent only served to heighten the
tension. Julio's father had been killed by Nazis in
France; and grotesque, bile-spewing Huns stormed
Julio's nightmares with unceasing regularity. Even
the sight of sauerkraut on a weenie was enough
to deeply upset him.

Dr. Wertham stood up and walked to the large
window. He brushed aside the thick, lemon drapery
and peered upwards towards the sidewalk traffic
along the busy avenue. A thin, elderly black man
wearing a gleaming platinum crown and a long
violet mink was walking his pet African serval on a
rhinestone-studded leather leash. The animal took
long, majestic strides.

Dr. Wertham pulled the drapes back shut.

"*Please*, Julio. What you must understand is that
I'm not here to hurt you, nor to make you feel badly.
I simply want to know *why* this happened. That's
what we *all* want to know. We want to get to the
bottom of this. We want to help you, so we can make
things all better. Not just for you...but for *many*
people. For *everybody*."

Julio remained quiet and stared at the dull red
industrial carpet. He focused on the bleats of the
horns drifting down from the street. He thought to
himself that when he grew up, he too would be a
taxi driver. He would honk his horn at everybody,
all the time. Julio had never been in a taxi before,
only on buses and subways. But someday,
things would be different.

Julio looked up towards the drapes, but the
German had vanished. Then, he felt a small,

4

rigid, claw-like hand settle upon his right shoulder
from behind and squeeze.
"Young man, I shall now read you some
of my research."
Dr. Wertham lifted a narrow, vertically-folding
notebook from his desktop, similar to the type
commonly carried by police officers. He placed the
heel of his small right fist over his mouth, and cleared
his throat with an odd phlegmless hack.
Julio had heard an ostrich make such a sound once
at the Central Park Zoo. He'd seen a chimpanzee
ejaculate that day as well. The Central Park Zoo was
very educational.

"1) A boy of six wrapped himself in an old sheet and
jumped from a rafter. His brother said he saw that
behavior in a comic book called *Jughead*.
2) A twelve-year-old boy was found hanged by a
clothesline tossed over a shower rod. His mother told
the jury that she thought he had re-enacted a scene
from Tarzan comic books, which he read incessantly.
The jury returned a verdict of accidental death and
scorned comic books and Tarzan.
3) A boy was found dead in the bathroom, wearing
a Superman costume. He had accidentally strangled
himself while trying to walk on the walls of the
room, like his hero.
4) A boy of ten accidentally hanged himself while
playing 'hanging'. He will never play that game again.
5) A fourteen-year-old boy was found hanging from
a clothesline fastened over a hot-water heating pipe
on the ceiling. Beside him was a comic book, open
to a page showing the hanging of a man. The chief
of police said, 'I think the comic book problem can't
be solved by just a local police ban. It will require
something bigger. This is why I voted for Eisenhower.'
6) A twelve-year-old boy was found hanging naked
from a door hook, suspended by his bathrobe cord.

On the floor, under his open hand, lay a comic book with this cover: a girl on a horse with a noose around her neck, the rope tied to a tree. A laughing man was leading the horse away, tightening the noose as he did so. The grief-stricken father said, 'The boy was happy when I saw him last. So help me God, I'll be damned if I ever allow another comic book in the house for the kids to read! They are the Devil's tennis-racquet, and the poor children are his unwitting balls.'

7) A boy of eleven was found hanged naked from a rope in the bathroom. He had the habit of acting out stories he had read in comic books. He had once lit his babysitter on fire while she had slept. He had been naked then too.

8) A boy of thirteen named Roy was found hanged in the garage. On the floor was a comic book showing a hanging. On the wall, written in chalk, was a crude self-portrait and the words 'Kill Roy Here.'

9) A boy of twelve was found hanging naked from a clothesline in a woodshed. On the floor was a stack of comic books and pairs of soiled girls' underpants.

10) A ten-year-old boy was found unconscious, hanging from a second-story balcony. He got the idea from a comic book he had been reading. When revived, he expressed genuine dismay that Captain Marvel had not rescued him, as he was the regional fan-club president.

11) A boy died after swinging in a noose from a tree. He had tried to show another boy 'how people hang themselves to get high.' The City Council denounced the 'mind-warping' influence of comic books.

12) An eight-year-old boy jumped from a second-floor fire escape 'like Superman' and broke both his wrists. His promising career as a violinist was also shattered."

Dr. Wertham set down the notebook upon his desk, wiped his glasses with a monogrammed

linen handkerchief, and looked back towards the
boy, who stared at the carpet.
"*So.* Does *any* of this sound familiar to you?"
Julio's tears were now flowing freely, though he
continued to remain silent. He'd seen enough James
Cagney movies to know how to handle this.
Deny everything.
Doctor Wertham handed Julio the linen handkerchief.
"My boy, as you can undoubtedly see, this is a
big, big problem."
Julio stared at the blue initials on the handkerchief.
F.T.W.
"My boy, *please.* I am here only to help. Together, we
will get you through this."
The doctor noticed that long, thin streams of
transparent yellow snot had begun to seep from both
of Julio's nostrils. The snot ran over the boy's lips,
down his pudgy jowls, and dripped slowly from his
cleft chin onto his atomic-flecked, pink and black
gabardine shirt; like the water from a leaky spigot.
The old doctor smiled at the boy kindly.
"You can keep that hanky if you'd like, Julio.
Think of it as a *souvenir.*"

THE first thing that Will Meiser did that
morning was to quietly announce the cancellation
of Elastic Man, and Jack Coal felt as though he was
going to have a stroke.
His blood seemed to seize in his veins and his testicles
tied themselves into a tiny, throbbing, white-knuckled
monkey's fist.
He slumped down unto the cracked wooden stool in
front of his ink-spattered drawing board, dropped
his faded brown Stetson to the dirty floor, and slowly
began to die.
Meiser, a paunchy, balding pipe-smoker in a rumpled
grey suit, tried to comfort Jack Coal in his best
fatherly manner although, at thirty five, he was a full
six years his junior.
"Jack, m'boy, look at it *this* way...you've had a terrific
run! Thirteen years is *nothing* to sneeze at. Nothing!
But...the times...the times they are a'changin'."
Jack Coal stared at last summer's dead insect

cemetery on the dusty corner windowsill ten feet from
his table.

Three years earlier, on a particularly brutal August
morning, he'd glued a homemade tissue banner to the
tail-end of one horse-fly's abdomen. All of the boys
had enjoyed a rousing laugh while the insect buzzed
angrily about the studio, espousing the message
'Drink Pepsi Cola!'

Even Will Meiser, a man of little personal humor,
had chuckled.

There'd been a tinge of general sadness in the room
when the furious unpaid pitchman finally sailed
through an open window onto East Forty First Street,
disappearing into the hustle-and-bustle beneath it.
Jack Coal wondered to himself where the horse-fly
had finally expired, he hoped it was over the river.

There was a somber dignity to the thought.

"Listen, Jack. Really. Don't look at this as the end...
look at it as a *new opportunity*! A new beginning.
A re-awakening of sorts! It's not like I'm canning
you, or anything even close to that. There's plenty
of other work. Elastic Man was truly great, but...
it's just...the kids...they don't *want* men in colored
pajamas anymore. That stuff's *had* its day. What
sells now is lust, blood, guts, *horror*! Science Fiction!
Flying saucers! Vampires! Ghouls! Thrills! Chills! *The
Unknown!* You know...that sort of blote."

Jack Coal stared at the veiny backs of his pale, liver-
specked hands, palm down on his knock-knees. They
already looked like his grandfather's. He was glad that
they weren't shaking.

He took a deep breath and held it in for as long as
he could until his blood slowly began to move again.
But his testicles still didn't feel right. No, they
didn't feel right at all.

The monkey still squeezed at them.

Jack Coal wondered what *blote* meant.

He wondered why Jews so often insisted on speaking

Yiddish to him. Did he look Jewish? Or was it just
because they're such a pushy race?

He looked up towards his boss.

"But, Will, I know all of that. I *do* pay attention, and
I've done everything you've asked. I've thrown in
every bloodsucker, dope-peddler, and white-slaver
that you requested. I've spiced things up *plenty*, and
I'm willing to up the ante even more, but Elastic Man
is the hero of millions of children. They still love him!
If *any* pajama-boy can survive this, then it's *Elastic
Man*. He's *elastic*, for Pete's sake! He can *literally*
change with the times! '*Chazzers in dreck*,' remember?
Think of the children, Will. The *children* will cry!"

Will Meiser realized he needed to soften the blow, but
something misfired in his brain and sent the message
to his hands instead of his heart. He patted Jack
Coal's back a few times and then began rubbing at his
shoulders like a dumb Swede in a Turkish spa.

"Jack, I hate to be blunt, but let's talk brass-tacks
here. Your book hasn't cracked two hundred K since
the war ended. Even the shtup books are outselling
Elastic Man now. More girls are reading just St. John's
romance stuff alone than *boys* are reading Elastic
Man and Captain Blammo combined. And let's face it,
Jack...the *boys* drive the business. You know that."

The seated man stared at his lifeless brown
Florsheims and nodded sadly.

"Yeah, I know."

Will Meiser removed his hands, shook his head, and
sighed sadly.

"*Heck*, man, If it makes you feel any better, I'm even
sending the Apparition into outer space! *Imagine that!*
It makes me sick – really it does – but I just don't know
what else to do. I've tried *everything!*"

Jack Coal looked up at Will Meiser with astonishment.
If comic books were the bin-liners of the art world,
then '*the Apparition*' was the field's one true ray of
hope. Meiser, a virtuoso cartoonist, had created

and drawn the series himself, and it was of an unparalleled quality. Unlike other comic books, the Apparition wasn't sold on magazine racks; it was distributed directly as a Sunday paper insert, which further contributed to its uniqueness.

Comic books were for children. The funny pages were for adults. This was a comic book in the *funny pages*.

A comic book for *adults*. The only one of its kind.

And now, Will Meiser was about to commit four-color Hara-Kiri.

No, it didn't make Jack Coal feel better.

Not at all.

This was bad.

After Meiser's drafting in 1942, Jack Coal himself had ghosted the Apparition for the duration of the war. Tacking on the assignment on top of his Elastic Man chores made for eighteen-hour workdays, and his wife had worried openly about his constant fatigue. A few weeks into the routine, he'd fallen asleep face-first into a plate of shepherd's pie, breaking his nose and shattering his lenses amidst the pile of mashed potatoes, chunks of carrots, and ground lamb. This had distressed Dot to no end, and she'd begged him to lighten his load.

But Jack Coal was a man of his word. He'd promised Will Meiser that he'd take good care of his baby, and he wasn't about to let him down. His complexion soon dulled to a translucent, bluish pale, the stoop in his spine sharpened, and his lamp required stronger bulbs. When his energy ran extra-thin, he'd drawn barefoot with a tin bucket of ice water beneath his table; shocking himself back to consciousness when his eyelids failed.

But it'd all been worth it. Working on the Apparition had been the proudest moment of Jack Coal's shoddy career. He'd taken great pains to capture, synthesize, and maintain the series' unmistakable shadow-drenched style, and he'd succeeded wildly. Only expert readers could spot any significant tonal differences.

It was as if Will Meiser had never donned olive drab. It was as if Will Meiser wasn't necessary anymore.

It was as if Will Meiser didn't even matter.

Jack Coal daydreamed of Meiser's death a thousand times. Sometimes it occurred on a French battlefield. Sometimes, in a Burmese jungle. Other times, at a USO review in Butte.

But it always ended the same:

A land-mine blast and Meiser's meerschaum thirty feet in the air.

When Meiser returned to New York unscratched in 1946, he resumed the helm of the Apparition and promptly took the book to previously-unchartered heights, fusing a re-invigorated, satanic inkstroke with a wild new cinematic approach to page layout. The stories were tauter, grimmer, and more uncompromising than before. If anyone had *ever* mistaken the Apparition for a children's series in the past, this would not happen again.

Even the highbrows begrudgingly had to admit it:

This was ART.

Jack Coal read Meiser's new work with gaping awe.

He'd been entirely wrong.

Will Meiser *did* matter.

When he'd inquired about the source of this new creative wellspring, the bald man had reached into the pocket of his vicuna topcoat and palmed Jack Coal a handful of small, linty Benzedrine tablets.

In 1949, Will Meiser signed a lucrative contract with the US Army. Illiteracy had become a serious problem within the rapidly expanding military. To combat this, the generals decided to issue instructional comic books alongside field manuals, and Will Meiser was to draw them himself. In turn, Meiser assigned the Apparition chores to an in-house team of writers, pencilers, inkers, and letterers.

This team did not include Jack Coal.

Despite the painful slight, Jack Coal kept mum about it. Complaining simply wasn't his style.

But still, it ate at him.

The following summer, at the studio's Fourth of July party, Jack Coal, a teetotaler, had swallowed three glasses of punch before noticing that it wasn't a virgin concoction. But, by then, it was far too late; he'd already cornered his boss and begun pouring his stoic heart out.

"Was it...was it because...my work wasn't good enough?"

Meiser's soft, brown eyes had welled with whisky tears as he embraced his old employee with both arms.

Jack Coal had never been held so tightly by another man in his entire life.

There was a mothball-scent to Meiser's fawn Palm Beach suit. It was only a faint trace, but he knew that Dot would detect it later, and he knew that she would not be pleased. The only things Dot disliked more than the smell of mothballs were the Communist Party and its sympathizers (the Democratic Party.)

Will Meiser pulled back and wiped at his face with a silk orange pocket square.

"Jack, is that really what you thought? Really? Good GOD, man! How many times must I tell you this? Second to me, you're the most important man in the shop! I couldn't afford to spare you for a dying feature like the Apparition. Only a shmeggege would do a thing like that!"

Jack Coal was taken aback.

The man seemed sincere, but he simply couldn't fathom how Meiser found him so damn important. He just wasn't an important person. Nor could he understand why he'd refer to the Apparition as a dying feature. As far as he could tell, it was as good as it'd ever been.

Meiser recognized the confusion on Jack Coal's sagging, drunken face.

"Jack, listen ... Elastic Man is a very, very special thing. You're doing something unique here. Something unprecedented. Something...maybe historic."

Jack Coal shook his head.

"Will, don't try and josh me. What YOU do is great. I know it. You know it. Everybody knows it. It is what it is. But MY work, and pretty much everyone else's ... it's... it's GARBAGE. Elastic Man is garbage. Superman is garbage. Batman is garbage. Wonder Woman is garbage. Comic books are garbage! It's ALL garbage. WE are garbage! We draw stick-men on rag-paper for snot-nosed brats and drooling morons. I'm sorry to babble...I'm very embarrassed. But...I just really enjoyed working on the Apparition. It just ... made me feel...less ... like garbage."

Will Meiser tilted his head and looked at Jack Coal sadly.

"Jack, I'm very, very sorry to hear that's how you feel. I really hope that's just the punch talking, and these aren't your genuine opinions."

Meiser shook his head as he withdrew an amber pipe from his pocket and stuffed it with rusty tobacco from a worn leather pouch. He stoked the bowl, drew on it, and let the sweetish smoke fill the air as he spoke again.

"No, siree, I hope not! Jack, when you hand me a pile of fresh pages, they sure don't look like they were drawn by someone who feels that way. No, sir indeed. Not at all. They strike me as the work of someone who packs a HELL of a lot of energy, imagination, and love into their work. They look like they were drawn by someone who cares very deeply about their craft. 'Garbage' would be just about the furthest thing away from what I see on my desk!"

Jack Coal sighed and hung his head in shame. He was sorry he'd said anything. A MAN should be able to keep his feelings to himself.

Meiser gave him a playful rap on the chin.

"Jackie, don't listen to anyone else. Regardless of whether

they're too stupid to realize it or not, what you do is very, very important. You're just as important to society as a fireman, a policeman, a doctor, or a lawyer. Maybe more so. You make a million kids happy every month. Think about that! How many other people can say that? You make kids as happy as chazzers in dreck, and, guess what? It's ART, goddamnit! It's ART, Jack, despite what a million squares will try to tell you. You're a real artist, and someday...someday people will realize this."
The drunk man sighed.
"But what about the drooling morons?"

Jack Coal stood up with a shot and grabbed Will Meiser's right arm with both of his hands before catching himself and letting go.
Meiser, shocked by Jack Coal's strength, rubbed at his bicep. It'd been tenderized.
"Will, *Sir*...please! Let *me* handle the Apparition in outer space. If Elastic Man is getting the axe anyway, perhaps there's some kind of tie-in there. A noble end. Elastic Man is killed by a meteorite on a space walk! Or...maybe he jumps in the path of a Martian ray-beam aimed at the Apparition...and he's vaporized in the process! Something dignified like that!"
Meiser chuckled and shook his head.
"Oy. Getting vaporized is dignified?"
"Or something, Will. *Please*. Let me end this on a decent note."
Meiser shook his head again.
"Won't wash, Jack. I've hired a new boy to handle it anyway. You just make that last Elastic Man story a nice, gentle goodbye for the old fans. You can cut all the tits and blood out of this one. Something sweet, and maybe a little sad. Give me the old Jack Coal. Just do your thing. Do what makes you *you*."
Jack Coal's face remained perfectly blank, but inside; things were different. He was not feeling sweet and maybe a little sad.

He was feeling murderous.
Will Meiser winked as he walked away, puffing smoke.
Jack Coal wanted to knock him down and crack
his ribcage open with a t-square. He wanted to
eat his heart.
It probably tastes like old greenbacks.
"*Who*, Will? Who is this new guy?"
Meiser, still shaking the circulation back into his arm,
smiled as he stepped through his office door.
"Young boychick. Nice-looking fellow. Ex-
paratrooper. *Good*."
Jack Coal nodded solemnly
"He's good, huh?"
"Well, yes...he is! He's *very* good. But that's not what I
meant. That's his name: *Wallace Good*!"
And then, Jack Coal was staring at a closed door.
A glass door he could see right through.

AND HE IS SHACKLED TO HIS HENCHMAN.

JACK Coal and Bert Meskin had lunch at the Third Avenue Horn & Hardart. Bert, who wore bow-ties exclusively, was an inker at the Meiser shop. Most of the other boys took their lunches at local bars, where corned beef sandwiches were free with beer, but Bert followed Jack Coal everywhere, like a faithful dog.

The automat was a brightly-lit, large room lined with walls of small glass-fronted, token-operated lockers. Each square locker contained a single lump of pale food upon a bone-colored dish. The long tables were flanked with benches, much like a prison mess-hall. It was filled to capacity as usual, mostly with senior citizens, disheveled vagrants, and negroes of various ages and sizes. Everyone seemed to be screaming at each other for no apparent reason; Jack Coal and Bert Meskin had to speak very loudly in order to be heard, though their faces were less than three feet apart. Bert, who'd just been released from a six-week stint in Bellevue's psychiatric ward, had selected a tuna on pumpernickel and a cup of tomato soup; while Jack Coal had opted for a fat cheeseburger and a plate of french fries.

It broke Jack Coal's heart to watch his friend struggle with his nervous condition. He'd been to the sanitarium no less than nine times in the ten years they'd worked together.

He imagined the sheer hell it must've been on Mrs. Meskin and her children.

Those poor, poor kids.

When one of Bert's hospital visits had strayed particularly long, Jack Coal had even considered offering to foster the Meskin boys sight-unseen (he'd never met Bert's family), but Dot had stopped him, suggesting the idea might upset his wife.

Now he'd returned home with a pronounced stutter. He'd never stuttered before.

Jack Coal wondered just what those doctors were doing to poor Bert. He seemed to get progressively worse with each visit.

He smiled at his friend, who looked like a ghost in a sweater vest.

"Bert, what *is* it? Is the tuna bad? You've barely touched it."

Bert picked up the soggy, limp, steamed sandwich, removed another small bite from it, and forced a pathetic smile.

"N-n-n-n-no. It's good. I l-l-l-like it. R-r-r-r-really. Ce-ce-ce-celery!"

Jack Coal shrugged and remained focused on his cheeseburger until it was gone. When he looked across the table again, Bert's sandwich was still resting on its small plate, barely touched.

"Bert, do you mind if I ...?"

"N-n-n-n-n-n-no, Jack. T-t-t-t-take it. I-I-I-I-I'm just...n-n-n-n-not hungry, I g-guess."

Jack Coal consumed Bert's entire sandwich in four mouthfuls, but still he hungered.

He felt like he could eat an entire wedding banquet, including the table, the guests, and the parson. He'd felt that way for years now. His waistline and double-chin reflected these feelings.

He'd been reed-thin in his youth. Everyone on both sides of his family had been reed-thin well into their dotage. Jack Coal simply couldn't understand where this emptiness was coming from, and he didn't like it.

Nor did Dot.

While he was dressing for work the month prior, she'd asked him if he'd realized that he'd developed a few grey hairs on his pubic mound.

Jack Coal was genuinely surprised, and slightly amused. He chuckled feebly.

"Ha. Really? No, Dot, I hadn't noticed. Hmmnnn...'Age, with his stealing steps, hath clawed me in his clutch!'"

Dot stared back at Jack Coal with a pity-tinged disgust.

"If your goddamned stomach wasn't so bloated, you might've noticed. I have a few too. Not that you would've noticed those either."

Jack Coal smiled at his wife and draped his flabby arms around her still-supple, wasp-like waist.

"Hon, I'm sorry if I haven't been as attentive as I'd like to. It's just that...it's just that I've just been working so darn hard lately. I just ... want things for you. I want you to have everything that you deserve, and I'm going to make sure you get it too. You're going to have that house in Connecticut if it kills me!"

Dot smirked and rolled her green eyes.

"You mean 'us'."

The joke was lost on Jack Coal, who opted to view his wife exclusively through a filter of positivity.

"Yes, that's EXACTLY what I mean. Us! Gazebo in the back. Weekends at the club. The works! I want all of that for you. For US!"

Dot pressed the tip of her right index finger into the flesh around Jack Coal's midsection and let it sink down to the second knuckle.

"Speaking of clubs...why don't you dust off your set and take them up to Van Cortlandt on Sunday? It's been ages,

and you could really use the sun. I don't like you being indoors so much. It's not healthy"
Jack Coal smiled at Dot sadly. She'd given him the sack of Wright & Ditsons for his thirty fifth birthday, proudly explaining they were the same brand that Charles Lindbergh used. He'd left the house with his golf-bag, a tartan cap, and a smile on several occasions; but he'd never actually set foot on a green. He hated golf, though he'd never dare admit it.

Bert smiled as Jack Coal drank the cup of discarded tomato soup like a glass of water.
"J-J-J-J-J-Jack. I-I-I-I-I'm sorry. B-b-b-but...I have a qu-qu-qu-question."
Jack Coal set the cup down and wiped his mouth with a paper napkin, forgetting that his lips were were chapped. He cringed and stared at the flecks of blood on the napkin before hurriedly dropping it back onto his lap.
He put on his bravest smile.
"Ask me no questions and I'll tell you no lies!"
Bert averted his eyes.
"I-I-I-I-I...I--I-I'm sorry, Jack."
"Bert, *for crying out loud.* I'm just kidding! What *is* it? Are you okay? Problems at home? Anything that I can help you with, I'm here for you, Bert. *Always.* I hope you know that."
"I-I-I-I-I do, Jack. I d-d-d-d-do know that. A-a-a-a-a-and I a-a-appreciate it. A l-l-l-l-l-l-lot."
Jack Coal's eyes narrowed.
"Was it...something in the institution? Did they *do* something...unethical...to you, Bert? I know a good lawyer. Issur Danielovitch. Brutal man, a real bulldog. Real Jew *asshole.* No offense, but that's what you want in a lawyer."
"N-n-n-n-no, Jack. N-n-n-not exactly. B-b-b-b-b-but y-y-yes, k-k-kind of. J-J-J-J-Jack...h-h-have you ever h-h-heard of D-D-D-D-Doctor W-W-W-W-

Wertham?"

"*Wertham?* Can't say that I have. That's an odd name,
I think I would've remembered it. Did this Wertham
fellow do something bad to you?"

"N-n-n-n-n-no, not ex-exactly. H-h-h-h-he's a psy-
psy-psychiatrist from G-G-G-G-Germany, I-I-I-I
think. He v-v-v-visited us in the h-h-h-hospital.
H-h-h-h-he was m-m-m--mainly w-w-working in
the j-j-j-j-juvenile w-w-w-ward, b-b-but w-when he
f-f-f-found out I was in the c-c-c-c-comic b-b-b-b-
books, he w-w-w-wanted to sp-speak with m-m-me
t-t-t-t-too."

Jack Coal silently cursed whichever devil invented
stuttering, for it was certainly not the work of God.

"Well? And *what* did he want to know?"

"J-J-J-Jack...it was b-b-bad. Very b-b-b-bad.
H-h-h-h-he w-w-wanted to kn-kn-know what I-I-I
th-thought...m-m-m-my op-p-p-p-p-pinions.
H-h-h-h-he wanted to kn-kn-kn-know if I-I-I th-th-
th-thought I was h-h-h-h-hurting k-k-k-k-kids."

Jack Coal's testicles began to knot-up and throb again.

"*Heck.* Hurting kids? What does *that* mean? Why did
he think you're hurting kids? *How?* I'm confused,
Bert."

"He...h-h-h-h-h-he...he runs a cl-cl-clinic in H-H-H-
H-Harlem, and he's b-b-been d-d-d-doing a st-st-
study on th-th-th-the influence of c-c-c-c-comics on
j-j-j-j-juvenile d-d-d-d-delinquency. I-I-I'm s-s-s-s-
sorry, J-J-J-J-Jack."

The pain in Jack Coal's testicles worsened. He shifted
his rear-end on the bench to remove some of the
pressure, but the monkey's fist was callous and
persistent.

"It's okay, Bert, calm down. Don't be sorry, you've
done nothing wrong. I *knew* something like this would
happen eventually...it was only a matter of time. This
is a crummy, garbage industry we're stuck in. Strictly
for the birds. *Garbage!* I should have never lost sight

of a syndicated strip. Once I had a few bucks socked
away, I should've begged off Meiser's and given it
a real stab. Like Bushmiller! Bushmiller has *class*.
Bushmiller drives a Packard."

"M-m-m-m-m-me t-t-t-t-too! I-I-I-I sh-sh-sh-should
h-have t-t-t-t-too, J-J-Jack!"

Jack Coal shook his head sadly.

"Yeah…we both got lazy. It happens, man. Settle into
a comfortable gig, get a regular cheque rolling in,
before you know it…you've lost sight of what *really
matters*."

Jack Coal stared at the old Greek woman sleeping
next to him in front of her macaroni salad. He wanted
to yank her beard, which was at least two inches long.
Her oily green skin reminded him of the catfish he
used to net in the creek. His mother would refuse to
cook catfish on general principle:
It was strictly food for negroes.

"Well…what exactly is this Wertham character
planning to do with this study? Or did he even say?"

"A-a-a-a-a b-b-b-book. An article, or a b-b-b-b-b-
book, I th-th-think."

"Cripes. *Great …*"

"J-J-J-Jack. I'm…I-I-I-I'm s-s-s-s-sorry to say this,
b-b-b-b-but he had some c-c-c-c-comics with him.
S-s-s-s-some he asked me a-a-about. A-a-a-a-a- f-f-
f-few of th-them… a f-f-f-few of th-th-them…w-w-w-
w-w-were *y-y-y-y-yours*."

"*Judas Priest*, Bert. This is not good. Not good. Not
good at *all!* Did have any Elastic Mans with him?"

"Y-y-y-y-yes, o-o-one or t-t-t-two…but th-th-there
was a c-c-c-c-c-crime b-b-b-b-book too. A-a-a-a-a-
about a g-g-girl and a d-d-d-d-dope ring. F-f-f-from
a f-few y-years b-b-b-back. I-i-i-i-i-it w-w-w-wasn't
s-s-signed, b-b-b-but I knew it was y-y-y-yours
b-because I in-in-in-inked the b-b-b-backgrounds."

Jack Coal covered his face with his large palms and
sighed through them.

"Don't even tell me. It was *'Murderous Morphine and I'*, right?"

"Y-y-y-y-yeah. Yes..."

"Jesus. I *knew* that one was a mistake. Fucking Meiser. He *really* pushed me on that one too. Even then, I knew it was too much. *'The kids want more crime! The kids want more sex! Dope, rape, kill!'* I should have told him to get stuffed a long time ago. Do you know what he did today, Bert? Do you know what that moth-bally, penny-pinching *heeb* did today? Well...let me tell you what he did..."

"W-w-w-w-what d-d-d-did he d-d-d-do, J-J-Jack?"

"HE CANCELLED ELASTIC MAN."

"Oh. Oh *g-g-g-gosh!* Th-th-th-th-that's *b-b-b-b-baaaad* news, Jack. I-I-I-I-I'm awful s-s-sorry."

Jack Coal propped his elbows on the table and let his plump chin fall into his waiting palms for support.

"Tell me about it. What on Earth am I going to say to Dot? She's gonna have a conniption. That book pays our rent!"

Bert perked up and raised a finger.

"G-g-g-g-g-g-g-g-g-g..."

Jack Coal sighed.

"Bert, don't think so hard. Just let it come out..."

"G-g-g-g-goldfish!"

"Goldfish?"

"Y-y-y-y-y-y-y-yes! *G-g-g-g-g-goldfish!"*

Jack Coal noticed a small red-haired child at the next table, sucking baked beans through a plastic straw. He stared at the boy – hungry and transfixed – and shook his head.

"Bert, that's the stupidest thing I've ever heard."

"I like all the crime comic books. I like all kinds of comic books really. Science ones, *Andy Panda, Buster Crabbe;* everything really. I buy quite a few. I get 'em from my friends. Some of 'em give 'em to me and some of them, loan 'em to me. I like crime comics such as *Clue*. It's all about when this man, he and three other men, they robbed jewelry and broke windows and they took the rings and ran away and a cop's car comes and shoots 'em. Sometimes they get killed, the gangsters, the cops kill 'em. Sometimes they hit each other when one of 'em does something wrong. Sometimes they use knives..."

The old doctor sat behind his desk and looked at the greasy-haired boy, who'd stated that he was thirteen though he was more than six feet tall and wore the lanky musculature and wispy mustache of a seventeen-year-old.

He spoke with a wheeze-tinged Brooklynese and was known to be tough. He'd once bullied another boy to such an extent that the boy's mother had gone to the authorities to seek protection for her son. Three truant officers were later found unconscious, beaten and stabbed. There was not enough evidence to make an arrest.

His attitude, a mixture of bravado and evasiveness, included nothing to indicate that he had any feelings of guilt regarding his assorted crimes and sins.

"My mother don't like me to read crime comic books no more, but I sees 'em anyhow. I like *Superman, Penalty, Jumbo*. I like the Jumbo books. They have lots of girls in 'em. There's a lot of fighting in 'em. There's men and women fighting. Sometimes they kills the girls, they strangle 'em. Shoot 'em. Sometimes they poison 'em. In that magazine, Jumbo, they stab 'em a lot too. The girl doesn't do the stabbing usually, she gets stabbed mostly. Sometimes, the girls stab the men, sometimes they shoot 'em. I read one comic book where they ties people to the trees, ties 'em in front of stampedin' herds. They ties 'em to the trees, then cut the trees the sap runs over 'em, and the bugs goes to work on the sap. Then, the bugs eats the peoples. Sometimes they torture girls the same way, by stabbing and beating 'em. They throw 'em in rivers and make 'em swim where alligators come. Sometimes they hit 'em with weapons on the back. They don't have much clothes on when they hit 'em with weapons. It excites me a little bit!"

Dr. Wertham stared at the boy through the cracks between his thin, gnarled, steeple-folded fingers and nodded slightly.

"Floyd...this excites you *how*, precisely?"

"Excuse me?"

"In what way do the comics *stimulate* you? Do they stir up your emotions or imagination? Do they provoke a *penile erection?*"

The boy shrugged.

"Eh, I dunno...They just...make me...*happy*. Y'know? Sometimes, I got a lot on my mind and they just... make me forget."

"So, they provide a form of *escapism?*"

The youth lifted his palms.

"Uh-uh! No sir, no how! When they sent me up to Warwick, I ain't never tried no escape! I *did* my bit, fair and square!"

The doctor sighed, removed his spectacles, and rubbed at his eyes.

"You mean, '*To escape.*'"

"Yeah. That's what I said! *Never.* But in some comics, they show you how."

"Showed you how to what?"

"*To escape!*"

Dr. Wertham scribbled something into his policeman's notebook.

"And...what else do these *Jumbo* comic books show you how to do?"

"Eh. A lot of things. All sorts of stuff. Stealing. Killing. I like jungle books. But I read the others, too. My sister buys romance books. I like them things too. *Diary of Real Life, True Romance, Sheena, Jo-Jo, Jungle Jim*...boy, those are excitin'! I like to see the way they jump up and kick men down and kill 'em! It makes me laugh! I like *Penalty* and *Criminals Never Win* too. I don't like how the crooks always gets caught. I'd like him to get away with it too sometimes, like in *real* life! But at least they show how you steal. Yeah...so in one book, a woman walked in a store and took a dress and walked right out and a woman caught her. I like to see women catch 'em. I like women cops. I want 'em to frisk me too...you know, work me over! Sheena, she's got a big jungle she lives in and people down there like her and would do anything for her. And her headlights... *oh brother!* Wowie wow wow! *Va-va-voom!* When I get ready to go to bed I read the Sheenas. About four of 'em usually. It helps 'cause I'm hungry a lot at night and it takes my mind off the gut. We don't all the time have enough to eat, because my mother ain't got enough money to buy food. I learned to steal food from comic books too."

Dr. Wertham peered at the greasy-haired boy skeptically.

"Your mother doesn't have enough money to feed you and your sister? Does she know about government relief? And where is your father?"

"Oh...he bought it in the war."

"He bought *what* in the war?"

The lanky youth chuckled.

"Eh, a nip hand grenade. It was on sale because the pin was missin'!"

Dr. Wertham jotted down something else in his notebook.

WHEN Jack Coal presented Dot with the small, circular bowl, she smiled politely, but within her eyes lingered a deep suspicion.

There were two fish in the bowl. One a solid orange, the other white with orange and black spots.

She shook her head.

"I don't understand. Couldn't you have just gotten *two* yellow ones?"

"But, then...then we wouldn't be able to tell them apart. The spotted one is you. Spots...'*Dot*'. Get it?"

Dot looked at her husband sadly.

"Yes. I get it, Jack. And you're the yellow one. Of course."

Dot gently removed the bowl from his hands, set it down upon the center of the dining room table, and kissed Jack Coal's left cheek.

"Thank you, dear. They're *lovely*."

Dot returned to the kitchen and began chopping

carrots loudly.
Jack Coal stared at the goldfish.
They were very cute.
Why didn't she like them?

He waited until after dinner to tell Dot about the
cancellation. She'd made Yankee pot roast with
browned carrots and fingerling potatoes; he didn't
want to spoil the mood. Instead, they talked about
early American furniture and colonial saltbox houses,
which were Dot's current obsessions. Afterwards, they
sat in front of the television set and ignored Arthur
Godfrey while Dot knitted and Jack Coal read
the paper.
Finally, during a commercial break, Dot asked
Jack Coal how work had been.
After twenty four years spent together between dating
and marriage, he knew better than to beat around the
bush with his wife.
He spoke frankly about his day.
Dot stared at Jack Coal as if he were a complete
stranger. An unwelcome one.
"And...that's *it?*"
Jack Coal avoided Dot's eyes and kept to his paper. He
was ashamed and he feared stoking her anger further.
Instead, he stared at an advertisement for vacuum
cleaners and shrugged.
"Well, Hon...what could I do? Meiser is the boss.
Oh hon, look here! Electroluxes are half-off...
let's get one!"
Dot stared at her husband incredulously.
"*The boss?* This man...this stingy little *kike*...nixes your
livelihood...thirteen years of blood, sweat, and tears...
and all you have to say is, '*Well, he's the boss?*' That's
really *all* you have to say? Jack, we've worked too
hard. You simply can't stand for this. No. You will not,
because I will not let you! No. *N-O. No!*"
"But, Hon."

"*No*, Jack. *No!* You're to tell him tomorrow that under *no* circumstances will you accept this. You're to tell him that you will take Elastic Man to a different publisher if need be. He simply cannot do this to us. You're forty one years-old, Jack. *I am forty one years-old.* There's no starting over from here. There is no *second* chance. This man is *ruining* us!"

"But, Hon, I just *can't.* Meiser *owns* the character. I explained this to you years ago...Meiser owns the rights to any and all the material the shop produces."

"So? So *what?* Then we'll *buy* the goddamn rights from him, and take it to another shop, though it seems silly to me that we'd even have to do that. After all, *you* created Elastic Man. It's yours by *moral* rights! But – if need be – we'll just buy it back. He might even just *give* it to you. That would be the *right* thing to do. You *do* call him your 'friend', do you not?"

"Yes, Hon. But it's just not that simple..."

Dot turned away from her husband and placed her hands over her face. She simply couldn't stand the sight of him. She took deep, labored breaths in an effort to regain her composure.

Then, she sighed mournfully.

A full minute passed. Jack Coal spent it watching Julius LaRosa's young, gypsyish face contort with agony as he rhapsodized over his lowdown, dirty blues.

When Dot resumed speaking, it was with her eyes still covered.

"What about that *Kirby* fellow? The one with that big horrible cigar? He runs a shop, doesn't he?"

"Kirby...yes. He does, Dot. But I haven't really spoken with the man in years, and I can't just spring something like that out of the blue. That's not how a business relationship works. First, I'd need to-"

Dot stamped a foot.

"*Jack!* Shut up. Just shut up, you stupid *fool!* Don't say anything. You're a piece of *garbage* working in

a *garbage* industry. I don't really know why I ever
expected anything *more* from you than *garbage* itself.
Maybe I'm the *real* fool here. Maybe mother was right
about you all along and I just should've listened.
Maybe this is all *my* fault!"
Dot threw her needles and yarn down to the carpet
and left the room.
Jack Coal heard the shower tap go on as he picked
up the mess. He hadn't had a chance to mention
his conversation with Bert Meskin yet, but perhaps
that was for the best.
He told himself that he'd tell her later.

SURE, I'M *CURIOUS*... ABOUT THE *BANDAGES*, I MEAN! BUT THERE'S *MORE* TO A *HUMAN BEING*...TO YOU... THAN A *FACE!*

WALLY Good squinted and laughed at Tatiana's shimmying flesh as she scampered about the one-room apartment, buck-naked, screaming in German. Finally, she turned towards him and addressed him with a thickly-accented English. The white of her left eye was a burning, bright pink.

"You swine! I told you not to get it in my eyes! Do you have any idea how much this hurts? I should shoot you! I should put a hole in the side of your head right now!"
Wally Good, also naked, squinted, smirked, and stuck a Camel in his mouth. He lit it, inhaled deeply, and savored the tingle in his lungs. He blew the smoke towards Tatiana's almost-pretty, round face as she approached him and reached for the cigarette. She took a long drag and blew smoke back in his

direction.

Wally squinted at his wife's large, pendulous breasts and lifted his palms above his head, as if her nipples were tiny pink gun barrels trained upon him.

"Sorry, Killer. You know I didn't mean it."

He picked up a corner of the loose eggshell top-sheet and handed it to Tatiana; an olive branch.

"You got some on your chin too."

Tatiana smiled softly and wiped at the semen as she sat down next to him at the edge of the bed.

He studied her dark-eyed Semitic face.

He hadn't known any Jews growing up in Minnesota. She was still exotic to him.

They'd met at a dancehall in Germany, where Wally had been stationed post-war. It'd been an awful place, but a huge improvement over Hokkaido and its strange, lumpish aborigines.

He knew that his wife had been through a meat-grinder, but never prodded her about it. Some things were meant to be kept secret.

(He had a few himself.)

Tatiana rubbed at Wally's lean, pointed shoulders and kissed his neck gently. Her lips were soft and warm.

She smiled at her husband.

"So, you start a new job tomorrow?"

Wally Good squinted as he nodded. He squinted most of the time, even when he was looking at nothing.

"*Please*, Liebling. Don't make no trouble this time. We need the money bad."

Wally smiled, and his abnormally-high forehead fractured with creases. He was only twenty seven, but could have easily passed for forty one.

"Babe, we got any of that whisky left?"

Tatiana nodded, stood up, and shuffled across the room to the kitchenette. She returned with a nearly-empty pint of Four Roses. He inhaled the remainder and tossed the bottle into the laundry basket.

He clapped once loudly and rubbed his small

palms together.

"Babe, don't worry. I'm *not* gonna blow this one. This is the big time. This is *'the Apparition'*. This is the Meiser Studio. Dignity, class...all that horseshit. More importantly, this means some real money. *Finally!*"

He stood up and put his shorts on.

"Wally, where you going *now?* It's *late*."

Wally walked across the room and rotated the switch of the brass gooseneck lamp next to his drawing board. He selected a thin brush from the jelly-jar he kept his utensils in – licked it once – and squinted at the tip carefully, gently smoothing its point with his thin, tapered fingertips as he spoke.

"*Calm down.* Jesus. Not going anywhere. Got work to do. I gotta finish this seven-pager for Avon by tomorrow morning and drop it off on the way to Meiser's."

Tatiana frowned.

"But *Wally*, you should sleep! Tomorrow..."

"Babe, *you're the one* always complaining about the money. It's gotta come from somewhere. Just relax. If I start to fizz, I'll pop a bennie. No big deal."

Tatiana frowned again, but kept her mouth shut.

"There's a fin in my wallet. Run down to the corner and get us a couple more packs of smokes. Pick up another bottle."

"But *Wally*. I'm not dressed."

"Just put your robe on under your coat. It's Jerkwater Central, not Gramercy Park. You think anyone out there is gonna give a flying fuck whether your hair is done or not?"

Tatiana frowned once more for show, and then smiled warmly.

Wally carefully set down the brush and spanked at her large bare rump as she donned her robe. He noted the dozens of tiny crater-shadows the cellulite formed as it jiggled and shivered. It reminded him of a lunar surface. He froze the image in his memory-bank.

"*Chop-chop*, babe! This machine runs on *whisky!*"
Tatiana slammed the front door behind her and Wally
leaned over to turn on the small bakelite radio. He
spun the dial around until he found a station playing
'*Slowly*' by Webb Pierce. He leaned back and squinted.
He really liked that song.
Wally placed the brush back in the jar, lifted his
chipped old Kay, and strummed along as best he
could, nodding his head in time to the music.
Hillbilly songs reminded him of his youth.
He thought about laying across that calico rag-rug in
front of the fireplace they'd burn the old Collier's in,
listening to Jimmie Rodgers yodel through the large
wooden Airline his father had swindled from a gullible
Slav. He'd listen carefully and illustrate the lyrics
on greasy, used butcher-paper. First with crayons,
and then later with pencils. When he'd accumulate a
full stack of drawings, his mother would bind them
together with her Singer.
He remembered his father coming home drunk one
night and ripping the butcher-paper books to shreds
for no good reason at all.
Wally Good squinted at the pages he'd been working
on over the past three days as he strummed his guitar.
It was a soap-opera on a rocket-ship, full of Raymond
swipes and Jane Russell bosoms. It was a boring,
forgettable story, but Wally had done his best, as
usual. Everything was beautifully shaded with a
mixture of heavy blacks, hair-fine cross-hatching, and
Craftint grays. The figures were heroic and the women
were shapely and seductive.
But it was Wally Good's backgrounds that really
separated him from the pack. They were obsessively
detailed, far beyond the call of duty. Every inch of
each page was crammed with wires, spokes, stars,
shadows, gears, and gleams.
Wally Good often wondered to himself why he took
a throwaway element like backgrounds to such

extremes. Nearly every other artist subsisted on dots
and dashes. He wondered if anyone ever even noticed.
He wondered what a psychiatrist would make of it.
Then he wondered if psychiatrists read comic books.
He hoped not.
He lit another Camel, and blew smoke at the pages.
He looked at the damp fancy knickers and brassieres
that Tatiana had hung to dry over the lip of the kitchen
sink. For a woman who claimed to care nothing
about clothes, she was very particular about her
underthings.
A cockroach was standing on a yellow girdle, its
antennae slowly groping around, like a blind man
reaching for a toilet chain.
Wally squinted at the cockroach and shut his eyes.
He fell asleep with the guitar on his lap.

WILL Meiser arrived at the studio at seven thirty AM. It was empty except for one large buzzing horse-fly that'd seemed to appear from nowhere.

The fly's existence irritated him greatly.

He wondered how on Earth a horse-fly had made it all the way to November. Perhaps it was some form of mutant strain, a direct result of the Atom Bomb.

Or perhaps it was a message from God.

Both thoughts were equally distasteful.

He swatted the insect out of his office and slammed the glass door, creating a large web of hairline fractures.

He stared at the door and shook his bald head.

Perfect.

Though he was amongst the youngest members of his own staff, Will Meiser was already a Methuselah within his industry. He hadn't invented the comic

book, but he was unquestionably one of its fathers.
He'd grown up in the Bronx.

In Vienna, Papa Meiser had been a professor at the
Akademie der bildenden Künste Wien; Mama, a tutor
of concert pianists. In New York, the most lucrative
position his father could obtain was that of sign-
painter; his mother sewed men's vests in a sweatshop
owned by a Chinaman.

Young Will showed an early propensity for
draftsmanship on the sidewalks of Highbridge,
specializing in chalk-scrawled nudes in
compromising positions. By the time he'd reached
DeWitt Clinton, he'd won over a dozen regional art
contests – still focusing on nudes – but now in oils.
He was going to be a famous painter, the painter his
father *should* have been.

When a new special high school for the arts opened
on Midtown's east side, young Will transferred
immediately. There, his talents continued to blossom.
One day, Harold Gray visited the School of Music
and Art and gave a lecture to the entire assembled
student body. It wasn't Gray's invigorating speech that
inspired Will Meiser to become a cartoonist, it was the
chauffeured silver Duesenberg he'd arrived in.

Papa Meiser warned young Will that cartooning was
a less-than-respectable industry, and that he should
stick tightly to nudes; but when his son brought
home his first ten-dollar cheque and a sliced cow's
tongue for supper, Papa Meiser quickly revised these
opinions. Soon afterwards, Will discovered that there
was even more money in selling the work of other, less
business-minded young cartoonists than in merely
peddling his own efforts.

Within five years, Will Meiser was the chief of the
largest shop in the entire fledgling comic book
industry with a staff of twenty five men beneath him;
churning out dozens of comic books per month, both
for his own line and that of other publishers.

1938 brought Superman, and comic books exploded
in popularity. By twenty two, Meiser had purchased
his parents a comfortable house in Westchester
County, right next door to his own. He'd married
his high school sweetheart at Tavern on the Green,
and had traveled to London, Paris, and Rome. In his
closet hung a rackful of bespoke suits and Borsalinos
in twenty shades of grey. He golfed regularly at
an unrestricted country club and had even once
entertained Mayor O'Dwyer at a Passover seder.
From virtually any angle, it was hard to argue that Will
Meiser was a true American success story.

Then came his recent woes.

They'd begun with soft, almost-undetectable
whimpers...
Piddling little diatribes regarding the evil influence of
comic books on America's virginal youth had begun
appearing several years earlier; the efforts largely
relegated to magazines that few took seriously, like
Redbook and *Ladies Home Journal*. But the writing
on the wall soon became much larger, and much
clearer. Serious periodicals for educated men were
now running similar tomes; *Time, Newsweek,* and *The
American Mercury* amongst them. *The Kansas City
Star* ran an interview with the Lipstick Killer in which
he stated that, besides Albert Camus, his reading
material was exclusively comic book-oriented.
That hadn't helped.
And now, a strange man had phoned Will Meiser
at his home the evening prior.
A government man.
The man said he represented something called *the
Senate Subcommittee on Juvenile Delinquency*. Will
Meiser had not liked the sound of that. He had not
liked it at all.
He'd quietly requested that the man call him again at

the office the next morning. The last thing he needed to do was cause poor Ann any more worry than he'd already had.

He'd gone next-door to visit his father, but Papa Meiser wasn't much help.

"So, Mister Bigshot needs his father after all? Imagine that! Huh. Well, it doesn't take Herr Einstein to figure out this one. You wanna get blacklisted and go broke? You want no more fancy cars? No more gold watches? No more golfy-golfy with the little stick? No more pheasant under the glass? Maybe some jail even? And... for what? Progress, Wilhelm! Progress is the path of the true American! Sentimentality is the path of the true schmendrick. Which are you? You must decide. And that – that is my advice for you, my son – the big-shot. Now, you will kindly excuse me. 'Boxing from Eastern Parkway' is on. I want to see this Maxim bum get flattened."

Will Meiser spent the entire night listening to Ann snore peacefully while he stared at patterns in the slap-brush plaster on the bedroom ceiling.

In the dark, it resembled cake frosting.

He glanced resentfully at the electric clock on his office wall. It made an annoying buzz, much like the horse-fly.

He thought about standing up, walking out of the office, and never coming back. He wondered what that'd be like. He thought about it long and hard. Perhaps Mexico. He could be another Sidney Franklin. (He already had the heroic jaw.) Or Morocco. He'd wanted to visit Tangier ever since he'd read *The Sheltering Sky*.

Morocco...

Maybe it'd be a nice place to live.

He wondered if the Lipstick Killer would like Paul Bowles too; and decided that he probably would.

The phone rang at precisely eight AM.

It was the government man.

Will Meiser let the man say his peace, paying only scant attention. He'd already composed his response on the trainride in.

"Sir, I share your concerns on this matter. While I've always strived to keep my comics wholesome and free of corrupt morality, there are some financially-motivated, less-scrupulous publishers who, unfortunately, do not share my stance."

When the investigator asked Will Meiser specifically to whom he was referring, to whom he could point the finger at with the strongest conviction, it took him about an eighth of a second to respond.

"Millard G. Gaines, for one."

THE overweight, bow-tied young man in tortoise-
shell glasses sat behind his desk and rolled the small
amber bottle around with soft fingers.
He squinted through the bifocal lenses to read the
tiny lettering on the bottle's yellow and white paper
label. He held it up to his right ear, shook it like a
maraca, then lobbed it onto the naugahyde couch
across the room, where it bounced once and rattled a
bit before settling.
He pressed the red intercom button on his telephone,
which was the color of store-bought key lime pie.

"Vera?"

A nasally female voice answered.

"Yes, Mister Gaines?"

"Vera, you ever hear of *'Dexedrine'*?"

"No, sir. It sounds like a drug or something? Is it some kind of drug, or a medicine?"

"Never mind."

Millard Gaines lit a cigarette with a gold-plated lighter, rolled his chair back, then lifted his legs and crossed his creased, brown Weejuns along the ridge of his desk, which teemed with four piles of finished bristol comic book pages.

Each pile was at least a foot high.

The rest of the office was equally cluttered and messy. The carpeted floors were covered in more ephemera, liquor bottles, orphaned nuts, ash, and discarded food wrappings. The wood-paneled walls were largely obscured by overstuffed barrister bookshelves, mustardy aluminum file cabinets, and mass clusters of framed photographs, lithographs, and paintings.

Even the ceiling was crowded, the room's lone hanging lamp surrounded by an entire fleet of model Fokkers, Messerschmitts, and assorted dirigibles. Millard Gaines ran his soft fingers through his stiff black flattop and held a drag in for five long seconds.

He slowly exhaled and set his feet down.

He picked up his telephone again and pressed the first in the row of four yellow buttons that followed the red one.

A man's voice answered. It was also nasally.

"Feldman?"

"Yeah?"

"Feldman?"

"I said, 'Yeah'?"

"The doc gave me something called 'Dexedrine'. Know anything about it."

"Yeah."

"Well...what is it?"

"Diet pills. It's like bennies, but for rich Jew housewives. What'd he give you that for? Because you're so fucking fat?"

"So, it's a happy pill? Is that what you mean?"

"Yeah, that's what they say. But I'm the wrong guy to ask. You know I don't touch that crap. I know some of the boys use it when they got a tight deadline."

"Well, maybe you should try it. I just read your last scripts."

"Yeah?"

"They're from hunger!"

Gaines heard a *click* at the other end and chuckled to himself as he stood up, clumsily navigated around the carpet debris, and lifted the small pill-bottle up from the couch.

He unscrewed the cap, shook three of the tiny white tablets onto his florid palm, and slapped them past his lips. He looked towards his water-cooler and cursed.

It was empty.

He vaguely remembered depositing a fifth of Old Overholt in the elephant's foot umbrella-stand a few nights earlier, and his recall proved correct. He took a deep slug from the bottle and said *'Wow'* involuntarily as he dropped it back in.

He read the hand-written label again, this time more carefully.

'Take one tablet <u>with food</u> every six hours.'

Gaines scanned his office with some grunting concern and lifted a gallon-sized, brass colored can of Utz potato chips that he found in a dark corner on the floor. He removed the lid and crunched down a handful of stale chips.

He looked at the umbrella-stand again. Its skin had once been almost pinkish, but was now mottled with yellow stains after years of neglect and abuse.

His father had shot the elephant himself, on an African safari in 1938; an albino bull. Millard had attended the safari as well, but spent the bulk of the vacation in a British-owned hospital with symptoms of malaria.

Gaines slowly made his way back to his desk and buzzed Feldman again.

The rye was acting quickly, and the pain in his knees and elbows was suddenly less unbearable.

"*Yeah, what?*"

"Ok, so I got an idea. For 'Vault of Evil.'"

"*Yeah?*"

"Take this down: So, there's this rich guy. Mean as fuck. A real cocksucker. Always telling his son *he's not good enough.* At anything! So, one day, the old man forces the boy to go on a safari..."

WALLY Good showed up at the Meiser Studio at eleven AM with a warped black pasteboard folder in the crook of his left arm and his Kay slung over the right shoulder of his scuffed A-2 jacket. The guitar's strap was made from a length of the same fuzzy twine that kept the folder bound.

Jack Coal, standing next to the water-cooler by the front door, cringed at the sight of the disheveled interloper. He tapped at Bert Meskin's shoulder and whispered to him.

"You wanna tell this buffoon to get lost, or should I?"

"Y-y-y-y-you b-b-b-better d-do it, J-J-J-Jack. N-n-n-n-nobody l-l-l-l-listens t-t-to m-m-m-m-me anymore."

Jack Coal looked at Bert Meskin, hurt.

"That's not true, Bert. *I* listen to you. *I'm* not a nobody, right?"

Bert Meskin winked and grinned playfully.

"N-n-no, J-J-J-Jack. Th-th-that's n-n-not w-what I

m-m-meant. Y-y-y-you're a *s-s-s-somebody!*"
Jack Coal straightened up his posture as best as he could. He enjoyed telling callow youths that there was no work for them to be had.
It was all in good fun. Part of the hazing ritual.
Paying one's dues.
He'd been through it himself, and he'd ended up just fine.
Jack Coal stepped in the young man's path and raised his right index finger to speak in his best Fonda-as-Lincoln impression when Will Meiser came bounding out of his office – blazing past the drawing tables – puffing away at his meerschaum like a steam locomotive. His right arm was already outstretched to shake the young man's hand.
"Wally, Wally, Wally! Good to see ya, lad! C'mon, c'mon, c'mon. Follow me! Let's just shoot the breeze for a while... and then get you all settled-in."
Meiser stopped and turned to Jack Coal almost as an afterthought. He patted his shoulder.
"How's that wrap-up story coming along, Jack?"
The bald man wagged an index finger at eye-level.
"Again, nothing *too* gruesome. Just sweet...and kind of sad. You know, just do your thing."
Jack Coal watched in dumbfounded silence as Wally Good slowly followed Will Meiser back into his office.
The young man hadn't even noticed him.
Bert Meskin tapped lightly at Jack Coal's left shoulder.
"Th-th-th-th-that's the n-n-new g-g-g-g-guy? H-h-h-h-h-he looks l-like a-a-a *de-de-de-de-de-delinquent! A r-r-real j-j-jay d-d-d-dee!"*
Jack Coal ignored Bert Meskin. He was too disgusted to talk. Too disgusted and too angry. And now, he was hungry again. He dug into his pockets and came up with a depleted roll of Lifesavers.
He slapped three into his mouth and offered the stub to Bert out of automaticism more than generosity.
"N-n-n-n-none for m-m-me, th-th-th-thanks. *Hah!*

I-I-I-I-I'm b-b-b-beyond s-s-s-s-saving."
Jack Coal shook his head without laughing and
walked back to his table. He looked at the sheet of
bristol taped to it, the first page of the final Elastic
Man assignment. He'd tentatively titled the story, in
which Elastic Man gives up crime-fighting to open a
saloon, *'The Buckets of Tears Cried Over Spilt Beers'*.
Jack Coal stared at the caption long and hard.
Then he picked up an eraser and rubbed it out.
After another minute of staring at the blank space, he
refilled it with *'The Beastly Bad Bitch and her Bloody
Bucket of Bohemian Barf'* in an elaborately jagged,
drop-shadowed font.
He looked up from his table and peered grimly
through the glass door to Meiser's office. There were
cracks in it that hadn't been there yesterday, but Jack
Coal's mind was on other things.
Like the conversation inside.
Meiser would begin with fondling Wally's testicles
over his military record, quizzing him for all of the
smallest details. He was an abject homo for the
soldier-boy stuff.
*"So, Wally, my boy...tell me about the paratroops. What
was it REALLY like? Did you ever jerk off mid-jump? How
hard would your penis actually GET in that one-piece? If
you don't want to explain verbally, just whip it out and
demonstrate physically."*
*"WELL, Mister Meiser, SIR! Being a paratrooper was
fabulously wonderful. Just wonderful! But instead of
telling you, why don't I just PLAY you a ballad I've
written about it? Here...I'll accompany myself on this
hobo guitar I've inexplicably brought to a place of
business."*
Jack Coal's line of vision was suddenly severed by Bert
Meskin's long-suffering smile.
"J-J-J-J-Jack. D-d-did y-y-y-y-you w-w-w-watch
G-G-G-G-G-Godfrey last n-n-night? Th-th-th-th-th-
that f-f-f-fellow o-on it l-l-l-l-looked j-j-j-j-just l-l-like

y-y-y-y-ou! Br-br-br-br-br-br-br-br…"
Jack Coal turned away from his old friend disgustedly.
He wasn't in the mood to listen to his stupid stutter.
He stared at the drawing board.
He wished he could dive right into the page, Beastly
Bad Bitch or not.
"BRUBECK!"
Jack Coal shook his head.
He wanted to cry.

SEE! I-I TOLD YOU...
L-LOOK!! THE CRYPT
IS OPENING!

DOT Coal maintained only the iciest civility with
her husband.

They both knew what she was waiting for:
His announcement that he'd successfully cemented a
deal to obtain the rights to Elastic Man.

And, he'd honestly intended to get to it a few times
already; but the moments hadn't seemed just right.
This was a touchy subject that needed to be handled
with care and precision.

Meiser had been uncharacteristically jumpy lately.
Jack Coal had twice seen him cough a sticky ball of
congealed blood into a handkerchief – stare at it sadly
– then toss it into a garbage-basket.

Of *course* the man had ulcers. Wally Good's work
probably wasn't as magnificent as he'd expected or
hoped. A little angst was understandable.

He'd broach the subject with Meiser when conditions
improved. Ol' Jack Coal wouldn't let his Dottie down.

Never. Simply wouldn't do.

That night, Jack Coal dreamt he was nineteen again,
back in Pennsylvania and working on the line at
American Can.
Dot's hair was still bobbed like Clara Bow, and her
cheeks were rosy-red.
The old, sweet Dorothy.
Then her belly swelled, and she gave birth to a litter
of black and white kittens, which Jack Coal happily
drowned in the Shenango River. He didn't have a sack,
so he just dunked them one at a time, while Dot sat along
the muddy bank and giggled as she baked in the sun.
A green-skinned catfish with a two-inch beard grabbed
one of the white kittens from Jack Coal's hands with its
fanged mouth and swam off with it.
Dot clapped, laughed and cooed.
"Jackie-dear...Elasticism is Americanism with its
sleeves rolled-up!"
Jack Coal expanded his arm to a length of sixteen feet in
pursuit of the catfish, but it was just too darned slippery.
Dot urged him to reel it back in, and continue drowning
their children.
"Don't be greedy, Hon. Even nigger-food has to eat
sometimes!"
He awakened at two AM and rolled over to face Dot,
who was wheezing musically through the same smile
she'd been wearing in the dream.
This made Jack Coal immeasurably happy. He loved
his wife's smile. It'd been absent for almost a week.
The smile-high made returning to sleep difficult. He
counted sheep unsuccessfully. At nine hundred, he
went to the bathroom to sit on the toilet and think
in the dark.
He thought about Dot's suggestion.
Perhaps there *was* something to her idea.
Maybe Meiser *would* just let him have Elastic Man
gratis after all. What would Meiser really need with

the property if he was scrapping it anyway?
And just what *had* he ever really done with it when
one really stopped to think about it?
Had he marketed Elastic Man?
Had he even tried?
Maybe things would have been different if he had.
There were Superman cartoons. Superman serials.
Superman cereals. Superman dolls. Superman
paddle-balls. Superman diapers. Superman aspirin.
Jack Coal had once even seen a man fondling a yellow
package of Superman cigarettes on the subway. There
was Bat-everything. Blammo-everything. Captain
Marvel-everything. Captain Marvel Junior-everything.
Even Spy Smasher – a character with virtually zero
sex-appeal – had been merchandised to the hilt.
But Elastic Man?
NOTHING.
Not even a giveaway sweatshirt transfer or a cheap
plastic whistle.
To be fair, Meiser had done nothing with the
Apparition either. But the Apparition, highbrow or
not, was just a nebbish in a cheap blue suit and a ten-
cent mask. He had no powers to exploit, besides those
to whine and complain.
But Elastic Man...*was special.* He deserved better.
There was an entire world of untapped
potential there.
Jack Coal fumed on the toilet as his mind raced.
Elastic Man remained unique even amongst a flood
of clichéd, flying super-asses. He had no bones, skin,
blood, or nails. He was made *entirely* of rubber. He
could stretch himself for miles and miles and miles
and never, ever break. He could alter his appearance
to resemble anything – or *anybody* – that he chose. He
could be a rocking chair, a tommy-gun, an Egyptian
sarcophagus, a Socialist, or a grand piano. He could
be either male or female. Tall or short. Adult or child.
He could be Grandma Moses, Adolf Hitler, Shirley

*and his best friend was his younger brother Dickie, a
confirmed rascal.
Dickie was named after their maternal uncle, who'd
turned to suicide the day after the railroad forcibly
retired him. He'd simply put on his best clothes and laid
across the tracks to die. As he'd expired in his only suit,
Uncle Dick was buried in long woolen underwear, which
had once been red, but by then had faded to a soft pink.
At the funeral parlor, Dickie snickered and whispered
to his brother, 'I wonder if the old git is in three pieces
beneath that get-up.' Jack Coal, who'd immediately
shushed Dickie with a cross look, had been asking himself
that question ever since.
Jack Coal told Zach Kirby about the summer-break he'd
ridden his bicycle solo all the way across the country to
California to see what Hollywood looked like for himself,
and to visit the tar-pits.
He'd seen many things on the trip – some deeply
inspirational – but mostly just sad and horrible.
Nine weeks later, he returned to Pennsylvania a
young man of the world, deeply-tanned and full
of stories and starvation.*
"I even wrote an article about it. I sold it to 'Boys Life'.
With illustrations. In fact, it was my first sale! Five whole
dollars. I framed the cheque…"
*Jack Coal looked up from his buttered grits and smiled
weakly. Zach Kirby's tiny pupils bore deeply into his.
Kirby was in a trance, overly-masticating a piece of
salted ham. Kirby's interest took Jack Coal off-guard and
he stopped talking.
He wasn't accustomed to people paying him serious
mind. Only Dot ever did, or Bert Meskin.*
"Well? And?"
"And what, Zach?"
"Well and what'd you'd think of California?"
"Why, it was the most beautiful place I'd ever seen.
Heaven on Earth! Have you ever been to San Diego, Zach?
Have you ever smelled an orange grove?"

The little man tore at a piece of pale toast and shook his head.

"Can't say I have. Ok, so you're back in Pee-Ay. And then what?"

Zach Kirby spun his right index finger to indicate a wheel in motion.

"And then...well, then...then I went back to school. I married Dot before graduation, although we didn't tell anybody."

"You didn't tell nobody? Not even your parents?"

"No. Especially not them. I didn't even tell Dickie. Heck, I didn't even tell Ralph! I figured he might growl something about it in his sleep."

Kirby chuckled kindly and spoke with his mouth full.

"Hah. That's good! I gotta remember that one..."

Jack Coal smiled back, but inside he seethed with embarrassment. He did not like to be patronized, especially by his inferiors. Despite the respect Kirby seemed to command from seemingly everybody he encountered, at the end of the day he was merely a squat, ugly Jew in an overpriced hat.

He lowered his voice to a serious whisper.

"Well. You see, Zach...Dorothy was with child."

Kirby grunted through the ham pulp on his tongue.

"Knocked-up, huh? I know how that is, brother!"

Jack Coal did not like being called 'brother'. He was neither a Freemason, a negro, nor a Kirby.

"So your kid...must be about twenty years old now, right? He in college? The service? Or wait...maybe y'have a girl. I got two of them myself. Hey...Doll! Can we get some Tabasco over here? Thanks, Doll."

The waitress handed Kirby a small red bottle. He slapped at the back of it and squirted pepper-sauce at his fried potatoes and onions in a manner that resembled target practice.

Jack Coal stared at the grits on his own plate. It looked like baby-food. He tried not to sigh.

"No. Dot lost the child. She...she hasn't been able to

conceive since."

Kirby frowned. Though it was a genuine frown, it struck Jack Coal as rather severe and dramatic. Overly-theatrical. He looked just like a baby crow.

"Aw geez...that's a real shame, Jack. Tough break. So, you got hitched, and then what? Got a place?"

"No. I stayed at my place, and she stayed at hers."

Kirby's eyes bugged.

"You mean, at your folks' place? After you'd gotten hitched?"

"Yes, Zach. Like I said...it was a secret."

"And then what?"

"Then, I went to work for American Can."

"What's that? Like a can factory or something?"

"Yes. A can factory."

Kirby said, 'Huh,' grunted, and shoveled a large forkful of blood-red potatoes and onions into his mouth.

Jack Coal watched the little man attack his food like a savage. It fascinated him. He was so ape-like. How could a primitive little monkey like this possess so much drive and talent?

"Where did YOU grow up, Zach?"

Kirby, occupied, did not even bother looking up. He spoke through his hash in guttural bursts.

"Me? Not too far from here. Lower East Side. Orchard and Delancey. It wasn't easy, Jack. No, sir. Not at all..."

Kirby belched loudly without excusing himself, took a large swig of water from a yellow glass tumbler, and continued to eat and talk simultaneously.

"No sir. I mean, you been down there. You know what it's like. And a shrimp like me ... It was sink-or-swim...all the time. Kill-or-be-killed. Every day a scrap. Every day a fight to survive, see?"

Jack Coal chuckled internally as he visualized a miniature, eight-year-old Zach Kirby battling a gang of neighborhood toughs in patched corduroy knickers. In his mind, the scene had all of the exaggerated dynamicism of a Kirby splash page.

At least he'd thought he was chuckling internally.
"Something funny, Jack?"
Jack Coal caught himself and tapped at the greasy
curved pane of the diner window. Across the street, an
immensely fat man in a lavender topcoat was leaning
over the curb, desperately trying to collect his toy
poodle's disproportionately large feces. The fat man
appeared frozen in his bent posture, shivering violently
as he struggled to right himself, teetering on the verge
of collapsing face-first into the turds. The immaculately
groomed dog sat by its work, its long pink tongue
bobbling. It appeared to be enjoying its master's pain.
Kirby chewed slower as he squinted at the fat man.
"Oh yeah. I see. That fat fuck! Well, anyway, yeah...then
the War happened. Held out as long as I could, but Uncle
Sam came a'knocking in the middle of Forty Three."
Jack Coal nodded and turned away from the poodle,
which he could've sworn had just winked at him and
blown a kiss. He turned back to Kirby.
"Oh, yes. You were in Will's outfit, right? He mentioned
that once. Working on 'Stars and Stripes'. He still
does a lot of contract work for the Army, you know?
Good money."
Kirby grunted.
"Yeah. I was with him, for a minute, until I slugged a
cracker lieutenant who got lippy with me."
"And then?"
"And then...infantry. Straight up grunt-work, see? You
heard of the Bulge, right?"
"Of course."
Kirby looked up, pursed his lips, and prodded his own
sternum with his right thumb.
"I was there!"
"And what was that like?"
Kirby stopped chewing for a few seconds and stared at his
potatoes as he gathered his thoughts.
"I gotta tell ya, Jack. What you said about seein' those
awful things on your bike ride...I can relate. I seen a lotta

things over there. Things no one should ever hafta see. Saw men burned to death right next to me. I watched the skin bubble up on a guy's forehead and his eyeballs swell up and pop right out. Just like a marble you'd shoot with your thumb, see? Or popcorn."

Jack Coal nodded.

"I seen a kraut with both his hands blown off, laying in the mud, screamin' like a little baby. Just like a little hungry baby in its crib! I killed him."

Jack Coal tried to visualize the scene at the Bulge, but all that came to him was an milky-pink infant in an oversized spiked helmet. It smiled at him sweetly. He wiped the thought away with some grits.

"Did you shoot him in the head?"

Kirby smiled.

"Nah, Jack. Like I said, he was a kraut. That woulda been too good for him!"

Kirby shoveled the last of his potatoes into his mouth, washed them down with black coffee, and belched again.

"I emptied a full magazine into his cock and balls."

Jack Coal nodded and forced a sympathetic smile.

"Well, it sounds like the fellow deserved it. He was a Nazi. After all they'd done to your people..."

Kirby shook his head and waved his stiff right fingers.

"No, no, that ain't right, Jack. I didn't say he was a Nazi. Most of them krauts wasn't Nazis. They was just soldiers, and sailors, and fly-boys...just like half of us who served wasn't Republicans."

Jack Coal nodded and rubbed his chin, trying to comprehend.

"But, if that's how you felt...then why didn't you just shoot him in the head?"

Kirby tugged at a hair on his left earlobe and thought about his reply for a moment.

"Y'know...I don't have an answer for that one, Jack. I don't know if I ever will really. Maybe I was just having a bad day. I'm not usually what you'd call a sadist. But sometimes...sometimes, we just do things. I just try not

to think about it too much, see?"

"I see."

"The things I seen in the whorehouses over there were worse. Far, far worse! Nightmarish worse! Pussies with sores as fat as cow's eyes. People so hungry, they ate snails..."

The waitress let a check float onto the linoleum tabletop. It landed on a puddle of Kirby's coffee splash. He waved Jack Coal off as he withdrew a long, flat eel-skin wallet from his jacket's interior pocket and nodded with authority.

"So...what was your war like, Jack?"

Jack Coal rubbed at the sudden cramp in his stomach and cursed the runny eggs.

"Oh. Not quite as glorious as yours."

Kirby grunted again as he pulled a paper napkin from the dispenser and rubbed briskly at his flabby, catfish lips. Jack Coal pictured them counting money.

"Oh, you was a P.O.W. or something? E.T.O. or Pacific? I hear them nips was none too friendly. I seen the picture of that Australian butterbar with the blindfold. Fuckin' animals, Japs!"

"No, no. None of that. I was declared unfit for service."

Jack Coal cringed at the boorish guffaw from across the table. He wanted to bash its source with the heavy, cut-glass sugar shaker his left hand rested upon.

He wondered if Kirby would bleed red, white, and blue.

"What? C'mon! A big, healthy guy like you? I don't buy it! What was it? A bum ticker? Mastoiditis? Incurable dandruff?"

With great effort, Jack Coal's face remained stone-calm.

"No. Nothing like that. There...there was a misunderstanding."

"HAHAHAHA! Did you tell 'em you was a fruit or something? Ah, Jack, old bean! You break me up!"

Jack Coal forced a smile and tilted his head. He hated having to tell this story time-after-time. He hated having to pretend that it amused him.

"Well, that's not far from what actually happened. When they asked what my occupation was, I simply told them I was an artist. But, that wasn't specific enough, and...they pressed me. So, I explained that I was in the comics."

"Yeah? And so what? When I told 'em I created Captain Blammo, they practically shat themselves with joy and made me general on the spot."

"Well perhaps, Zach, perhaps I should have lied and said I was your assistant. Instead, I told the truth. When I explained to them that I worked on Elastic Man, they all huddled-up at the back of the room. When they'd finished, the recruiting officer, that is, the one in charge, pulled me aside and asked me a few more questions."

"Questions like what?"

Jack Coal shrugged.

"Well, Zach, they were rather embarrassing, troublesome questions."

"Yeah? But, like what? What'd they ask you?"

"Well...first he asked me if I'd had a good relationship with my father. I said, 'Yes, of course,' but he just frowned. Then he waved one of the younger officers over and asked him to repeat something to me."

"Repeat what?"

"I'm getting to that. He asked the younger officer to tell me what he'd told him about Elastic Man. And he said, 'Well, sir, he's a convicted felon who's gained the power to become a man or a woman who traverses the world fighting criminals with his flamboyant male companion, also an ex-con.' Then the older officer looked at me, rather sternly, and asked if this was an accurate assessment."

"And you said what?"

"Well, I couldn't just lie. While that wouldn't be the way I'd describe the feature to a stranger, there's obviously far more to it than that – a heck of a lot more – none of what the young man had said was technically inaccurate."

"And then what'd they say?"

"Then...they asked me if Elastic Man was a deviant."

"Like a fruit?"

"That wasn't the word they used. They said 'deviant'."

"To which you say?"

"Zach, how could I deny that he was a deviant? He is, after all, an ex-criminal."

"And then what'd they say?"

"Then they asked me if I was a deviant too."

"And?"

"I said, no, I didn't think so, but that they're welcome to ask my wife."

"And then what'd they do?"

"I gave them my phone number, and they called Dot."

"And she said what?"

"Well, I don't know. I've never really asked her. But, after the older officer hung up the phone, he pulled out the red ink-pad and stamped a big 4-F on my form."

Kirby leaned back in his chair and studied Jack Coal's face. He smiled with amusement, and some pity, but there was a clear tinge of disapproval and mistrust not far beneath. He withdrew a fresh cigar from his breast pocket, severed the ass-end with his chipped front teeth, and spat it onto his empty greased plate. He lit the cigar with a wooden match, filled his cheeks with heavy blue smoke, then let it seep out on its own accord. The smoke hung over the table as if it'd been placed on a shelf.

He smiled in a friendly manner.

"Well, Jack...I guess someone had to stay home and deliver the milk. Right?"

A redhead at the next booth tapped Kirby on the shoulder. She was about twenty seven, wore her hair in a large netted bun, and had somehow reached pretty despite an unfortunate nose.

"Mister, that thing really stinks! Would you please take it outside if you're done so's we can eat our lunch in peace?"

Kirby seemed to ignore the woman, not even bothering to turn and face her. Instead, he slid a crisp five dollar bill out from his wallet, crumpled it into a tiny ball, and tossed it backwards over his right shoulder.

The ball landed in the redhead's split-pea soup and floated like a frosty paper crouton.

THE fat man leaned against the brick wall on Lafayette Street and gathered his wind as passing pedestrians glared at him with contemptuous, mocking eyes. He shivered. This Eastern air was just too cold for him. He thought about California.
He looked down to his tiny grey poodle, who returned his gaze through crusty eyes above a long, limp tongue.
Even *she* regarded him as a joke, having chewed up his best toupee the night before. As the pair began to move again, the fat man pulled his kitten-finished black homburg tighter onto his head.
He was afraid of catching a draft.
They turned west on Bleecker Street and walked towards Washington Square Park, the poodle moving faster than the fat man. He struggled to keep pace with the little dog, but she found herself repeatedly

choking against the tension of her red leather collar.
Despite this, she refused to slow down.
She did not like to be seen in public with the fat man;
if she was going to have to be, then she at least wanted
to project the illusion of being in charge.
The little poodle missed the other fat man dearly. The
one with the yellow hair that the strange dark men
had carried away a few months earlier. He'd brushed
her wire coat every night.
The fat man missed the other fat man too.
Life wasn't fair, and this had been doubly-so for his
beloved Butch. He'd been a beautiful, shining gem of
a man, gentle as a lamb. All he'd ever wanted to do
was make to children happy, strum his mandolin, and
write poetry. The hard, cruel world had beaten him to
death with a proverbial truncheon.
Who dies of a heart attack at age thirty three? Really?
The fat man and the poodle stopped in front of a old,
blind Italian violinist playing 'Blutrote Rosen' to an
audience of no-one. Butch had *loved* that song. The fat
man smiled sweetly at the musician, but the poodle
wasn't interested in standing still and tugged at her
lead fiercely.
She had rats to chase in the park.
As the fat man was dragged off, he dropped some
silver coins into the blue velvet lining of the open
violin-case.
The blind man sniffed at the fat man's cologne and
spoke with genuine gratitude.
"A thank you, a madame."

The fat man settled into a worn green bench on the
East side of the park and released the poodle into
the anemic lawn behind it. Unleashing one's dog in a
public park was against city ordinance and meant a
possible citation, but the fat man didn't see a viable
alternative. If Stella didn't get her afternoon scamper,
she'd be irritable for the rest of the day.

She'd even begun to snap at him recently.

At the worst, getting a ticket simply meant that he'd have someone new to talk to for a few minutes. That really wasn't so bad. Money wasn't a concern anymore. Butch had willed the fat man his share of his family's successful candy business in Saint Louis.

If only *he* had someone to share it all with.

He looked up at the sky. It was the color of faded chambray and full of moist, unmoving clouds. One resembled James K. Polk. Another, a wedding cake that'd been allowed to collapse in the rain. Still another was the unmistakable outline of a giant horse-fly.

The fat man chuckled to himself as he lowered his head.

Before him stood a small negro wearing an old tartan mackinaw and a wide checkerboard smile.

The fat man smiled back. As frightening as they were fully-grown, there was nothing cuter to him than a young negro child. Especially the boys.

They silently admired each other for about thirty seconds before the fat man finally spoke.

"Well, *hello* there! Aren't *you* something!"

The boy nodded.

"Hello."

The boy continued to stare at the fat man for a long time, just smiling.

"And what is *your* name, young man?"

"My name Lester."

"Lester? That's a very dignified name! I knew a Lester once. *Very* strong fellow. He was in the Marine Corps. He died in Belgium..."

The fat man waited for Lester to react, but he just continued to stare and smile.

"He was killed in the war. It was a real shame. He was very handsome, and very gallant."

Lester nodded and smiled.

"That's nice."

The fat man wiped a tear from his left eye and suppressed a sniffle.

"Yes. He *was* rather nice."

Lester pointed beyond the fat man's shoulder.

"Mister, is that be your dog?"

The fat man turned backwards and faced the direction of Lester's pink fingertip.

Stella was rolling around in the chalky, brown dust; snarling, with a large, bloodied rat in her mouth. The rat's screams – which sounded vaguely like that of a tiny human infant – ceased with a crisp popping sound.

The fat man turned back to the boy.

"Yes, that's my dog all right. I inherited her from a friend. *He's* dead too."

"What he doing?"

The fat man shrugged.

"Well, *she*...likes to hunt rats."

"Don't you have no money to buy him no dog food?"

The fat man chuckled.

"Oh yes. I have plenty of money! And *she*...she gets *plenty* of food. The expensive brands too. She'll only eat the best. Very refined taste, you see. She's French."

"Then...why he do that?"

The fat man shrugged.

"Some people, some *things*...are just...born to kill, I guess. Some things are lovers. Some are killers. And *some*, are both."

The boy smiled widely at the fat man, who couldn't help but smile back. Lester's smile was like an infectious disease.

"Mister?"

"Yes?"

"Can I have a quarter?"

The fat man reached into his hip-pocket and fished around before he realized that he'd given all his loose change to the blind Italian violinist.

He raised a finger.

"Lester, you're in luck today. Today – you get a *whole dollar* for being such a charming little boy!"

Lester beamed as the fat man withdrew from his pocket a folded sheath of money held together by a gold clip in the form of an uppercase 'B'. The fat man unfolded the money and fretted his eyebrows as he shuffled through it.

"Oh Lester, I'm very sorry. I don't have any singles today…"

The fat man kept his head down, but sneaked a quick peek beneath the brim of his homburg just to make sure that Lester was indeed frowning.

"*…So I'm going to have to give you a whole ten dollars instead!*"

Before the fat man could even lift his head, Lester had already snatched the ten dollar bill from his manicured fingertips and was galloping away towards the fountain in the center of the park.

The fat man leaned back on his bench and looked back up to the clouds above the Garibaldi statue. He imagined the fun Lester would have over the next few days.

Licorice twists and cowboy pictures!

The fat man turned towards Stella.

She was carefully disemboweling the rat while a flock of hungry pigeons circled her, keeping a vigilant watch for stray viscera.

.JJ ACK Coal stood behind Wally Good's drawing board and watched as the young man began to slowly sketch-out the opening page of *'The Apparition in Outer Space'* with a blue pencil.

He smirked when he noticed that beneath Wally's table was a worn scrapbook split open to a pageful of glue-stained Hal Foster panels.

Jack Coal had never swiped anything in his adult life. A real professional didn't need to steal. Nor did they use blue pencils.

He felt a profound sense of pity; not only for Wally Good – but also for poor, ulcerated Will Meiser and his crummy sense of judgement. This stupid kid was going to ruin his baby. He was going to drag it straight down from outer-space and into the mud to fester with the worms, corpses, maggots, and rats.

Jack Coal smiled and winked at Bert Meskin, who was

too busy studying Wally's technique to notice.
"So, son...I hear from the boys that you like using that
Zip-a-Tone bunk, eh? *Not me*. No, sir! Too nit-picky,
that stuff. All that tracing, that cutting..."
Wally's hand stopped in mid-sketch. He turned
around and squinted at Jack Coal.
"Saves time. Creates consistency."
Jack Coal shrugged and smiled.
"Well, I prefer to just *draw* the little lines myself.
That's how *Will* does it too."
Wally squinted again, nodded curtly, and turned
back to his work.
"My name's *Coal*, by the way. *Jack* Coal. I draw Elastic
Man. I occupy that table right over *there*."
Wally turned around again and squinted with more
severity.
"Oh yeah? I heard you worked here. Nice to meet you.
I like your stuff."
He turned back to his table.
"So...what's the old string-box for? Subway-busking?"
This time, Wally didn't bother turning around. He
shrugged and spoke as he continued to sketch.
"I bring it along pretty much everywhere. Just feels
better to have it around than not have it around. I play
with some fellows in the Village sometimes. Western
stuff mostly. That alright with you?"
Jack Coal made a funny face at Bert.
"Sure, sure...that's jake by me. Good to have some
color in here, finally. Things *were* getting rather dull."
Wally Good continued to draw silently.
"Well...*welcome aboard!*"
Wally Good grunted something between a cough and
a swear-word.
Jack Coal stood behind Wally Good for another thirty
seconds before he realized that the conversation had
withered, died, and blown away.
He returned to his stool and stared at his own work.
He still hadn't managed to get past the splash-panel.

Perhaps *'Bitch'* was too strong a word.
He rubbed out the **B** and replaced it with a **W**.

ZACH Kirby sat on an old wooden milk-crate and chewed at his cigar while he penciled. It was another boring romance story.

He was sick to death of love and romance.

The studio was located in the musty basement of his partner Joe Hyman's house in Forest Hills. Beside Kirby's feet on the moldy, cracked cement floor lay a pile of freshly-penciled pages waiting to be inked. While most pencilers completed one-to-three pages per day, Zach Kirby regularly completed seven-to-ten (and sometimes as many as twelve.) This was far too much work for Joe to ink himself, and the duo was forced to farm the surplus to hired hands.

Zach Kirby didn't have to think as he drew.

In fact, he never thought at the board, the work simply flowed from his right hand. It was as if the drawings were already fully-realized within his pencils and all he had to do was scrape them across the paper. There was no logical explanation for this phenomenon, but

Zach Kirby never questioned the source of his magic powers for fear of jinxing it. He secretly suspected that he was a conduit to another dimension.

Joe Hyman opened the basement door and descended the unpainted pine staircase with a pile of loose 16"x20" sheets of Strathmore board in his left arm.

Joe, handsome and a full foot taller than Zach, handled most of the pair's business matters.

Zach Kirby scowled through blue smoke and swatted at a buzzing horse-fly as he stared pensively at the pages in Joe's hands. They were inkless, unfinished. Kirby hurled his pencil at the cinderblock wall and frowned like a baby crow.

"What the fuck is that?"

Joe Hyman shrugged as he dropped the pages onto the extant pile by Kirby's milk-crate.

"Russo returned them. Said they stunk."

"What the fuck is that shit? Who the fuck is he? *Fucking Picasso?* You tell me, Joe, do those pages stink? I tried my best. I always try my best! Since when does it even matter what this crap looks like anyway? It's garbage for snot-nosed punks and drooling morons!"

Joe Hyman chuckled.

"Now, now Zach m'boy...compose thyself! The work is swell! He meant that the pages *literally stink*."

"Ah! Then it's your fault, see? You wrote that bowl of tripe!"

"No, no, no, bubala. 'Literally' means 'actually'. He means the paper *actually* stinks!"

"Wha? Stinks like what?"

"Like cigars. He's got a small place. Works in his kitchen. Says his wife can't take it anymore."

Kirby shrugged.

"Imagine that? That fat greaseball smells like an overturned garlic-cart and he can't stand a little cigar smoke. Can you *imagine* what his wife's *queefs* must smell like?"

Zach Kirby cringed and shuddered. He yanked the

wet, blackened stump from his lips just as the horse-fly landed on the cherry and collapsed against the unfinished page, singed and flightless. Kirby brushed the wounded insect to the floor. Joe finished the job with the right heel of a tasseled cordovan loafer.

Hyman and Kirby always worked as a team.

The shorter man continued to shake his head. It was hard for him to forgive easily. Grudges and gripes had been his stepladder to success.

"I mean, really...who ever *heard* of such a thing? That dumb guinea can't stand the smell of a little smoke? He says he was at Wake Island...and a little cigar smoke bothers him? It don't hold water."

Joe Hyman shrugged as he leaned over to inspect the page on Kirby's table.

"He said his wife can't stand the smoke. What do you want from me, baby? I'll find another inker. *Say*...Zach! That's *some dish* you're working on there! Yassuh, boss! I'm gonna ink this one myself..."

Joe Hyman smacked his lips with lust.

"I *do* love a dame in a tight sweater..."

Kirby looked down at the page and sighed.

"Joe, I gotta tell ya. I wanna *do* things...*different* kinda things, see? I wanna do things that ask for *answers*. Things that *DEMAND* answers! Like, *philosophical shit*, see? Ever since the war...I dunno. I just see things... *differently*. A *grander scheme* or somethin'. I mean... there's gotta be more to this than just kissy-poo bullshit. Right? See?"

The taller man stared at his partner, dumbfounded.

"God...not *this* again, please. Zach, I have absolutely *no* idea what you keep talking about! You want answers? Answers to *what?* Our sales are good! Great even! Not a lot of folks can say that right now. This television business is killing almost everyone else. Just be thankful! *That's* an answer!"

"Ah...well, yeah...I am. I *am* thankful. But...don't it ever eat at you? Not even a little? You know...*like life's questions?* The deep shit? Joe, don't you know what I mean? *Why are we here? What's it all mean? Where are we going?* And what will it *cost?* Didn't the war change you none *at all?"*

Joe Hyman smiled.

"I was in the Coast Guard, remember?"

"Yeah. But don't you ever sit up at night and wonder about things on a *Galactic* scale? Don't you ever wonder about things that *have been*...and things that *are to come?"*

Joe Hyman placed his fingertips to his temples and tapped at them as he spoke.

"Honestly, Zach, *bubala*...baby...hand to God, I love you like a brother! But, no...I *don't* understand! I simply have *no* idea what you're talking about. When I sit up at night and wonder, it's about how in the blazes am I going to pay for Seth to go to private school while Bessie runs up twelve hundred dollar tabs at Gimbel's every other month. *That's* what I worry about! You want the meaning of life...ask a freakin' rabbi or something!"

Kirby waved his right hand once.

"No thanks, Joe! I'm through with that rabbi hokum. Where have *they* been? What have *they* done? *I been through war, Joe! I really lived!* I been thinkin'. I been thinkin' a lot, see? I think we can really *do* something here."

"What? With the funny-books?"

Zach Kirby smiled and nodded.

"Yes! With the comics. Something with real *meaning!"*

A door creaked open at the top of the stairs, and the shrill voice of Mrs. Hyman shot down through the crack.

"Joe! Oh Joe!"

Joe Hyman winced in pain and Zach Kirby shook his thoughts aside to grin at his partner's performance.

"Yes, Bessie sweetheart? What *is* it, oh Dearest One?"

"JOE!!!"

"Oh, what *is* it, my bountiful bundle of bodacious beauty?"

"Joe! What are we gonna name the baby? It's almost time now, and I still don't know what to tell my mother!"

Joe Hyman winked at Zach Kirby.

"I *told* you, Honey! If it's a *girl*, then we name her *'Tinkerbell'*! If it's a *boy*, we name him *'Simon'*!"

"Simon?"

"Yes! *Simon Hyman!*"

The door slammed shut, but it was too thin to mask Bessie's anguished sobs.

Joe Hyman looked down at the voluptuous sweater-girl on Kirby's incomplete page and smiled. He slowly ran his right index finger along the graphite outline of her bosom, which bulged like netted melons.

"*Meaning*, huh? Ok, ok...I'm hep, Daddy-o. You mean something like Mailer, right?"

Zach Kirby withdrew another cigar from his shirt-pocket, severed the end, spat, and scratched at his thick, coarse curls.

"Nah. No. Not *quite* like that, see? But close. I'm thinking more like...*'The Fountainhead'*... meets...*'Frankenstein'*...meets...*the Old Testament*... meets *'Flash Gordon'*...meets *Sigmund Freud!*"

Joe Hyman whistled saliva through his large front teeth.

"Yeah, Zach. I'm sure the kids are really gonna *love* that. Especially the pickaninnies...they really go for that heady stuff!"

LESTER returned to 88 Perry Street and slowly climbed the worn wooden stairs, carrying a handful of comic books and a candy-filled paper sack that he'd purchased from an old hunchback's newsstand across from the Waverly Theater.

He'd been sent up North several months earlier when his family's shack in Beaufort had been burned to the ground by nightriders. His mother feared it was no longer safe in the Carolinas for little black boys, and that Lester had a better chance of survival under his brother's tutelage.

Cornell Humberto Jackson, Lester's older brother, was very refined, very smart, and his parents were very, very proud of him. He'd received an English diploma from New York University, being the first member of the Beaufort Jacksons to finish high school, much less attend college.

Lester's presence and living expenses had been very hard on Cornell, who, despite his constant diligence, had been unable to secure a teaching position.

He'd applied to nearly every school within the five boroughs with zero success. He'd even been shunned by his own kind in Harlem.

He was simply too dark for the whites, and too erudite for the blacks. (That he was an obvious homosexual only further complicated matters.)

Fortunately, Cornell was a tall, handsome, and well-spoken man, and was thus able to earn enough money as a male prostitute for both he and Lester to survive on with a fair degree of comfort.

He was ironing his best blue oxford in the kitchenette when Lester entered the apartment, and scurried past him without a hello.

Cornell scowled at his younger brother as he entered the bathroom.

"*Careful*, Lee-Lee! I just had that suit on the door pressed. If you muss it, there will be *consequences!*"

Lester ignored Cornell and slammed the bathroom door.

He stared at the pretty grey herringbone suit hanging from the brass hook. It smelled like artificial flowers, just like Cornell. Lester loved his brother, but sometimes he just wanted to jam an icepick through his eyes while he slept.

Lester removed the wet, wadded-up glob of Juicy Fruit from his mouth and gently pressed it between two folds of the crisp, polka-dotted silk square in the suit jacket's breast-pocket.

He stood on the toilet seat, slid the crusty narrow window above it open, and took hold of the labeless soup-can hanging from the dirty grey string outside.

After he'd gently yanked the can back and forth several times, he cupped it over his left ear and waited for a response. When none was forthcoming after a few seconds, Lester jangled the can again; this time violently. A yellow dragon-lady's head popped out from a window one floor above and yelled down towards him through an angry Japanese accent.

"You bad boy! You reave Bobby arone now. You go way, bad boy! Bobby no rike you no mole!"
Lester chuckled to himself as he shut the window, gathered up his booty, and headed towards the front door. As he passed Cornell on the way out, he handed the paper sack to him.
"And what's this?"
"Two Milky Way, Butterfinger, Goldberg Chew, Boston Bean, Mounds, Juicy Fruit, and a pack of Pall Mall."
Cornell furrowed his eyebrows.
"I thank you very kindly for this profound generosity. But *where* did you get the money for this, hmmnnn?"
"A fat white man give it to me."
Cornell placed his hands on his hips and leaned backwards slightly, a gesture he'd absorbed from their mother.
"Lee-Lee... A *white* man gave it to you? Did he happen to be sleeping on a subway car, hmmnnn?"
"No, *honest!* He just a fat man in the park. On a bench. Awake. I *told* you about him before. He a nice man. He know a dead Maureen too."
"And just *what* did this fat man on a bench ask you to do for this money, Lee-Lee?"
"Nothin'! *Honest.* He just a nice old man. He have a dog that eat rats too."
"Lester, I don't want you taking money from strange white men. It isn't right."
"But why not? You do it all a time!"
Cornell was about to interject, but Lester was out the door before he could think of anything to say.
He shrugged and picked up his iron. The boy had a point.
Bob Fujitani was already waiting on the stoop when Lester arrived. He was drenched in sweat. Bob Fujitani was *always* drenched in sweat. This struck Lester as very strange.
"How come you all sweaty? Chinese people don't sweat."

"Because I'm fat. And I'm *not* Chinese. I'm *Japanese!* Japan! Different country! How many times do I have to explain this to you?"

Lester shrugged indifferently. He neither knew nor cared.

Bob Fujitani and Lester pored over the new comic books with the zeal of tomb-raiders. Lester had carefully chosen the issues with the scariest, bloodiest covers. Magazines with titles like *'Crime SuspenseSpectacular'*, *'Cavern of Cadavers'*, *'African Witchcraft'*, *'This Magazine is Condemned'*, *'VooDoo Nightmares'*, *'Crimes by Women'*, *'Weird Tales of Disease and Death'*, and *'Web of Devils'*. As a special concession to Bob Fujitani's outdated tastes, Lester had purchased one lone superhero comic, *'Wonder Woman'*.

Lester simply couldn't understand why his neighbor enjoyed a girl's comic book so much, but Bob Fujitani was his only friend in New York City, so he chose to overlook this character flaw.

Bob Fujitani held open a page to Lester and tapped at a panel.

An evil man with Semitic features was hopelessly ensnared in Wonder Woman's golden lariat. However, the man didn't appear to be upset about his predicament. On the contrary, he was smiling.

Bob Fujitani's leer mirrored that of the cement gargoyle perched thirty feet above him.

"I like it when she ties people up!"

Lester noticed the tiny erection in Bob Fujitani's corduroys, and silently felt a deep and profound pity for him.

DOT showed up at half past four.
Jack Coal was alerted to her presence by the squeak of
every unoiled stool in the shop.
The goldfish were with her.
She held them out towards him. The fish stared back
at him helplessly, blowing kisses.
"Darling, you need to take these back."
Jack Coal looked at the fish, bewildered.
"But why?"
"They're just...*too loud*. I can't get anything done with
these things bumping around that bowl all day. I can't
even hear myself *think* anymore!"
Jack Coal removed the bowl from Dot's hands and
looked for a flat surface to set it upon. Every stool was
occupied, and the drawing-tables were set at forty five
degree angles. He walked to the corner of the room
and gently balanced the fishbowl upon the dusty,
white-washed radiator by the insect cemetery.

When Jack Coal turned around, Dot was staring over Wally Good's narrow shoulders. He scurried back across the room, placed his arm around his wife's waist, and pretended to admire the drawing too.

An image was finally beginning to take form, a large, full-page splash-panel. The Apparition's face was reflected within the observation window of his rocket ship as he surveyed a rich, gaseous, meteor-streaked background.

The masked man looked completely insignificant against the awesome vastness of space, and his depressed expression indicated that he was fully aware of this.

Jack Coal took a deep breath to compose himself. He hadn't thought it was possible for a background to be more interesting than a drawing's central figure. Nor did he think it was proper. It was pretentious and show-offy.

But somehow, it made him feel small too.

Very, very small.

Dot placed her hand against Jack Coal's ear and whispered to him. He didn't like the reverence in her voice.

"Jack, who is that man...and why is he working on the Apparition?"

Jack Coal whispered back.

"Ah, he's just some new kid."

"I see. He's pretty good..."

Jack Coal shrugged.

"He's alright."

Dot studied Wally's drawing again, then turned back to her husband.

"Dear, did you talk to Kirby?"

Jack Coal shook his head sorrowfully.

"Not yet...but I'm on it."

Dot nodded, kissed her husband on the cheek, and pivoted away before she lost her temper; her voice rose as he walked her to the door.

"Gosh, it's so filthy in here! Even the air. I don't know
how you stand all this smoke."
Jack Coal nodded.
"Sometimes I wonder myself..."
Dot stopped at the door and smiled at her husband.
"What do you want for dinner, Hon?"
"Pot roast?"
Dot nodded.
"Pot roast it is."
A hulking, redheaded acromegalic letterer named
Babe Kanegson guffawed loudly in the corner.
Jack and Dot Coal turned towards the laugh in robotic
unison.
The giant was pointing at the fishbowl, which was
bubbling over with steam.

I..I'LL DO SOMETHING **DESPERATE!** I SWEAR IT! YOU CAN'T LEAVE ME!

OH, STEVE..PLEASE! YOU SCARE ME WHEN YOU SAY SUCH THINGS!

IT'S NOT UNUSUAL FOR A GIRL TO FEAR BREAKING AN ENGAGEMENT BECAUSE THE MAN THREATENS TO DO SOMETHING OVERLY DRAMATIC. SUCH THREATS ARE RARELY CARRIED OUT, AND ONLY SERVE TO SHOW THE INSTABILITY OF THE PERSON MAKING THEM. THAT'S REASON ENOUGH TO CALL OFF THE MARRIAGE!

HE looked up at the clouds, which were black with soot. It was going to rain.

This was not Dick Steele's day.

He had a horrible headache and needed something to kill the pain.

He stopped at a Chinese druggist's and purchased a large bottle of Paregoric. Outside, he tossed the cap over his right shoulder for luck, then stood on the curb and downed the entire contents in a single swallow. He dropped the empty bottle into a wire rubbish-bin and continued southwards down the Bowery.

An olive-skinned wino crept out of a shadow and withdrew the bottle from the garbage. He held it upside-down above his head and slapped at the heel, desperately trying to coax the last few drops out onto his cankered white tongue.

Dick Steele – mellowing with the opium's high – stared at his hands as he stumbled along, walking through

anyone blocking his path.
His fingers were caked with blood.
He felt worlds better.
She asked for it, and I gave it to her. End of story.
Tomorrow – today will be yesterday.
He stopped at Chatham Square in front of a
combination barber shop-tattoo parlor. He peered
at the faded, sepia cabinet-cards in the window. All
of the photos featured a dashing young gent in top-
hat and tails tattooing a different nude in each. The
women all wore their hair curly; piled-high in Gibson
Girl fashion.
Dick Steele stared at the dead, yellowed roses that
surrounded the cabinet-cards, and at the dried
corpses of the horse-flies beneath them. One of the
flies appeared to have a thin streamer attached to its
body. There was some kind of writing on the streamer,
but it was too faded to decipher.
Dick Steele wondered to himself what kind of sick
fuck glues a streamer to an innocent fly.
He staggered into the barber shop and walked straight
past the thin bald man who asked him with a Genoese
accent if he'd like a shave. Dick knew what he wanted
and headed for the back, where a large Portuguese
sailor was having a snarling panther-head engraved
into his hairy beige shoulder.
The tattooist, Charlie Wagner, was a shirtless old man
with a nose like a veined lightbulb. His full head of
hair appeared to have been slicked back with black
shoe polish and he reeked of dried sweat, tobacco,
and Listerine.
Dick Steele stared at the old man for several moments
before recognizing him as the young fellow from
the cabinet-cards. The years had been unkind. Dick
wondered to himself if the years were ever *not* unkind.
Charlie Wagner had been vending scabs in the rear
of the same barber shop since 1895, and the wood-
paneled walls surrounding his cramped workspace

were hung with an impossible myriad of career mementos. There were many more cabinet-cards, a photo of Charlie next to a nearly-naked old man (donned only with a medal-covered sash and spired crown), various tarnished, illegible plaques, ribbons of merits, diplomas, and dozens of yellowed, bloodied, torn, and faded sheets of water-colored daggers, ships, skulls, roses, and hearts.

Charlie Wagner glanced at Dick from beneath his spotty green celluloid visor and spoke curtly as he resumed applying the panther-head.

"Have a seat, m'boy. I'll be done in a jiffy!"

Dick Steele grunted and stared at a wrought-iron stool upon which somebody had finger-painted a tic-tac-toe game on the plywood seat with what appeared to be dried blood.

(The Xs had been victorious.)

He lowered himself onto the game.

A stack of dog-eared periodicals sat atop a Japanned copper stand next to the stool. There were copies of *Time, Look, True Detective, The Ring,* and *Argosy.* Above the stack hung a pair of faded magazine pages; matted and gilt-framed behind a cracked sheet of wavy old glass.

Dick spat at the glass and wiped away the dust and flyspecks with the cuff of his shirtsleeve.

The pages contained an article from the Spring, 1927 issue of *EAST COAST MECHANIC'S QUARTERLY:*

FROM A MASTER TATTOOIST

By Professor Chas. Wagner Esq.

By way of introduction, I am Professor Charles Falstaff Wagner of New York City.

For some thirty years now, I have wielded the reputation of the world's leading practitioner of the ancient art of skin illustration. I am also the world's foremost historian and safe-keeper of the ancient art of skin illustration. In addition, I am the world's sole reputable producer and distributor of professional tattooing supplies and equipment.

*The practice of skin illustration is not a modern
phenomenon, but an ancient rite, and dates back in
recorded human history over three thousand years,
though it has been noted by some anthropologists that it
is quite possible men first began decorating their bodies
whilst still dwelling in caves. Many of the world's best
known historical figures wore tattoos proudly. It is a
known fact that the ancient Sumerians were quite adept
at tattooing, a skill they passed on to the Vikings, who
later passed on the secrets to the Hebrews. Portraits of
King Solomon, rendered while the monarch still reigned,
often depicted him covered head-to-toe in beautiful
tattooing of a floral motif. Alexander the Great was
known to wear a rose tattoo over his heart in honor of his
beloved mother Olympias. Jesus Christ himself had many
tattooings inscribed into his divine flesh, most of the
tattooings being recitations of sacred Judean scripture.
I myself have had the distinct honor of administering skin
illustrations upon the flesh of the cream of the Earth's
gentry, everyone from Presidents McKinley, Roosevelt,
and Wilson, to King Harold the great monarch of mighty
Sweden, to heavyweight boxing champion Jess Willard.
But I beg you not to think me a snob. I am just as home
tattooing a Times Square 'copper' as I was last year when
I was visited by none other than the great diva herself,
Isadora Duncan. Indeed, no other tattooist can factually
claim to have provided full-body skin illustrations for
nearly every major tattooed lady attraction in North
America and Europe.*

*In addition, I have been provided with a generous
retainer to remain the exclusive tattooist of the entire
St. Louis Cardinals pitching staff. Whenever the boys of
the 'gas house gang' are in town to play the McGraws
or Superbas, they stop by for a few new masterpieces. In
fact, one of the lads (whom shall remain nameless) has
on his throwing arm the names of every dancer in the
Ziegfeld Follies. What a lulu!*

In days passed by, skin illustrations were etched by hand, usually in a bluish carbon ink. After years of careful research, I have patented my own unique system of electric tattooing in four bright colors based on the principles of electro-magnetic dynamics. Though I must acknowledge the past contributions of the innovators Sailor Sam O'Reilly and Doctor Thomas Alva Edison (himself an amateur tattooist of some note), the machines I have developed are more than mere devices, nay, they should be more properly referred to as works of art. Henry Ford himself, a close personal friend, has told me on several occasions that if he set his top five engineers a'cracking to create a more effective tattoo applicator, they could toil for a hundred years and still fail yet to improve upon my universally recognized and admired design.

There are a few questions regarding skin illustrations that are commonly asked of me. Here, I will address these questions and hopefully provide the answers you will find satisfactory to them:

1. Is receiving a tattoo a painful procedure?

The short answer is: yes, the application of a skin illustration is an excruciating process when applied by the average tattooist. However, I alone have concocted a unique, patented system based upon thoroughly tested scientific principles that has rendered my technique absolutely painless. In fact, many of my valued customers have commented on how receiving one of my skin illustrations is not only painless, but downright pleasant. In addition, I offer for sale in my parlor a tonic made from the finest Oriental opiates that will not only ease pain, but also provide a pleasant night of sleep.

2. What is the most unusual skin illustration you have applied to a customer?

This question has always been a bit of a corker for me, as anyone familiar with my repertoire of motifs will tell you, I make a habit of specializing in the complex, the outlandish, and even the exotic. Offhand, I usually recall

the young pock-marked boy whose father had me provide
complete facial and body coverage with the spots of a
leopard in order to make his appearance less garish, the
lady of the night who requested a permanent placard
above her money-maker which read 'please tip your
vendor to insure proper service', or the dashing young
Austrian army officer with the windswept hair onto
whose upper lip I applied a small, box-shaped 'Charlie
Chaplin' mustache. But, as of this writing, the most
unusual engraving I can recall was done on an extremely
dignified Englishman who had sustained a grave genital
injury from a Boer's hand grenade. The poor devil's
testicles had been shorn in the blast. Above the scars of
each missing 'stone' I placed a cleverly crafted grave-
marker, each with it's own epitaph.

3. For whom will you not provide skin illustrations?
I am a natural-born American, and thusly I take great
pains to insure that the sacred Liberty the Lord has
blessed our Great Nation with remains intact. Therefore,
the list of those I will not provide service for is exceedingly
short. Women are welcome. However, children under the
age of ten will only be tattooed with a note of permission
from a parent or older sibling. I do not discriminate by
race. Both tame chinamen and redskins are welcome. I
have specially developed kosher pigments for sheenies.
Darkies are accepted after seven o'clock every last
Wednesday of the month. For them, I use a brilliant
white ink that contrasts simply marvelously against
their niggardly skin. The one group I do have a problem
with is the Irish, and not because of any personal gripes I
may hold against their often radical political beliefs, nor
their worship of Roman popery. Unfortunately, the Celtic
proclivity towards habitual drunkardry (which has gone
unchecked for thousands of years) has simply rendered
the Irish blood types far too thin to sustain pigments in
their skin for any reasonable length of time.
In conclusion, it is my sincere hope that this humble
article has provided you with a better understanding of

the world of skin illustration. Please consider yourself
forever a welcome guest to my parlor's hospitalities. Do
not be fooled by rival 'professors', 'masters', impostors,
amateurs, or would-be's, as there is only one,
Professor Chas. Wagner Esq.
208 Bowery
N.Y. City

As Dick Steele finished reading the article, he
detected the scent of Listerine directly behind him
and turned around.
Charlie Wagner stood alone. The sailor had vanished.
There was a proud smirk on the tattooist's mouth that
Dick Steele would have been tempted to wipe away
with a fist were he not so blissfully intoxicated.
He poked Charlie Wagner in the sternum. It felt as
thin as balsa wood.
"Pops, I had a row with my old lady today. She just
doesn't listen. All I wanted was a Pepsi, and she
wouldn't give it to me. And then, she called me a limp-
dick. I guess I got a little rough with her after. But you
tell me. *'Limp-dick'?* Is that wrong, or is that wrong?"
Charlie Wagner studied Dick Steele's expression
slowly, as if he were reading a newspaper. When he
finally spoke, he paused after each sentence. He truly
believed that he was constantly in the process of
making history, and he wanted to allow ample time for
each and every word he uttered to be jotted down for
posterity by some mysterious, invisible scribe.
"M'boy, if there's one thing I know, it's *people. People,*
and *troubles*. And *you* ...you, my friend, you are a
fellow with *troubles!*"
Dick Steele followed Charlie back to his work-station
and sat in its old white porcelain dental-chair. The
leather upholstery had been largely replaced with
cloth tape, which was still moist from the Portuguese
sailor's back and derriere sweat.
"Yeah, Pops. I got troubles. But, so what? The whole

world's got troubles."

Charlie Wagner clapped once, and smiled.

"Too right, m'boy. *Too right!* But we are not here to bicker over the meaning of life. We're here simply to *live*. And what I sell is the gosh-darndest affirment of life there is! So...what's it going to be then? What can I do for you to help alleviate these petty blues? There's a *magic* in what I do, y'know? Thousands worldwide will testify to this! My artwork contains a juju equal to that of any native witch-doctor. Your wish, dear sir, is my humble command."

Dick Steele rolled up his left sleeve and tapped the ball of his muscular left forearm with his right index finger.

"Eh...I gotta make things right by this broad. Just put a heart there, and make it say *'Violette'*. With an arrow through the whole shebang. Violette with two Ts and an E. She'll like that."

The old tattooist adjusted his visor.

"Certainly. I think that's possible. That's my motto here: *possible!* In fact, I've erased *IM*-possible from my lexicon. I simply have no use for it! One magic heart – *coming right up!* Guaranteed to bring you good luck for life, plus six months. Barring cremation that is."

The old man reached for a straight razor and Dick Steele tensed-up.

"*Say*...what's the big idea?"

Charlie Wagner bowed theatrically.

"Son, son...calm down. I simply need to shave your arm first. It's an essential component of the skin-illustration application procedure. No monkey-business, I assure you!"

Dick Steele sank back into the old dental-chair.

"Sorry, Pops. Just having a bad day."

The old man reached for a shapeless, murky sponge floating atop a slime-filled iron bucket and dragged it slowly across Dick Steele's forearm before shaving it. Then, he applied some Vaseline, a powdered-carbon stencil, and picked up a strange brass machine, which began buzzing like a horse-fly as soon as he touched it.

A minute later, Dick Steele smiled for the first time in days.

"You know, Pops, this doesn't hurt nearly as bad as I thought it would!"

Charlie Wagner nodded and winked.

"I should say *not*, my good sir. That's my special, secret patented technique. My admirers call it *'the velvet touch'*. First one, eh?"

Dick Steele shook his head.

"Nah. I got one in the Navy too. On my tuchus. But that was over twenty years back. To be honest, I don't even remember getting it. It just showed up one day!"

The old man chuckled knowingly.

"That's just fine, m'boy. Just fine. An oft-told tale. All praises to the mighty Bacchus. *Huzzah!* This business was *built* upon drunks!"

Charlie Wagner paused, set his ancient brass tool on the dirty glass counter, and picked up another, similar machine, which he dipped into a large red ink-pot. The second machine emitted a slightly deeper, slower pitch; more akin to a hum than a buzz.

Dick eyed this activity with suspicion.

"And what's *that* for?"

Charlie Wagner laughed.

"M'boy, that's *red!* Every good skin illustration has lots of *red* in it! Why, it's the color of *love!*"

"Yeah. And blood."

The old man laughed at Dick Steele's joke.

"Yes! That too! *And blood!*"

Charlie Wagner set down the machine, stood up, and spoke with his right hand on his heart. He had a beautiful, resonant voice.

"I was a queen, and you took away my crown; a wife, and you killed my husband; a mother, and you deprived me of my children! My blood alone remains: take it, but

do not make me suffer long!"
Dick Steele stared at the old man, baffled.
A queen?
The old man's left eye twitched once oddly as he
smiled downwards at Dick Steele.
Then, like a string had been severed, Charlie Wagner
collapsed into his chair, stone-dead. His hand
remained on his heart.
Dick Steele stared at the corpse in disbelief.
He shouted towards the barber, who was lounging in
the front, sitting in his gleaming chromed hydraulic,
reading a copy of *Il Progresso*.
The barber hurried over and held a small, round
hand-mirror beneath the corpse's nose for a few
seconds. After he was satisfied, he placed his
newspaper over the corpse's face, and spoke as he
began removing the contents of its pockets.
"Yes. I a knew this a day would come a sometime. He's
a dead. God a bless him. He a was as a sweet a man as
they a come."
"He said he was a *queen*. Funny, I would've never
figured him for one..."
A pair of long shadows glided across the corpse and
Dick Steele turned to face their source. Two large
men in dark suits and grey Stetsons stood near the
entrance of the barber shop. One approached Dick
while the other remained by the front door, blocking
it entirely.
Dick Steele knew who they were.
He knew he was sunk.
The smiling detective by the door withdrew a blood-
stained ivory brassiere from the hip-pocket of his
coat. It did a little jig as it dangled between his thumb
and index finger.
Dick Steele looked down at his new tattoo for the first
time and shook his head sadly.
It read: *'V-I-O-L-E-N-T-T-E'.*
The other detective stood in front of Dick and waved

his snub-nosed .38 at Charlie Wagner's lifeless body.
"You been busy today, huh?"
As he left the parlor in handcuffs, Dick Steele looked
deeply into the Italian barber's wet brown eyes and
shook his head.
"This just isn't my day, fella."

"IN the concluding segment of this evening's See it Now, I'll be speaking with Doctor Fredric Wertham, former chief psychiatrist of the Bellevue Hospital's Mental Hygiene Clinic in New York City, and current chairman of the Lafargue Psychiatric Clinic in Harlem. Since emigrating from Germany following World War One, Doctor Wertham has had a very long, distinguished career here in America, and we're quite pleased to have this opportunity to speak with him. Welcome, sir."

"Thank you, Mister Murrow. It is very good to be here."

"Doctor Wertham, correct me if I'm wrong, but this reporter seems to recall you being prominent in the news a while back. Perhaps as far as some twenty years ago. This was during the infamous 'Brooklyn Vampire' trial here in New York City. Is this correct?"

"Yes, Mister Murrow, that is correct. That was the Fish trial, a very sad case indeed. I testified on behalf of the defense that Albert Fish was insane."

"That's right. Refresh my memory, though. Were your efforts successful?"

"That all depends on your personal definition of success, Mister Murrow. While the jury and judge unanimously agreed that Mister Fish was indeed insane, he was executed regardless of this fact."

"I see. Rarely in life are things ever black and white, especially concerning issues of morality, and particularly when harm comes to children. The Vampire Trial being a prime example of this."

"Rarely black and white. That's quite clever, Mister Murrow, considering what I'm here to discuss today."

"Unintentional, I assure you. Ladies and gentleman, Doctor Wertham is here to discuss what he sees as a disturbing trend regarding the influence of four-color comic books on America's youth. Doctor Wertham believes that these comic books have been a primary contributing factor to the alarming increase of juvenile delinquency. Doctor Wertham, did I sum that up correctly?"

"Yes, I would say that is fair."

"Doctor Wertham, I've read your recent articles and found some of your arguments quite compelling. Talk to us about these crime and horror comic books, and try to explain some of these negative impacts."

"Certainly. My only question is where to begin, my complaints are so myriad. As you well know, the public has judged television much more harshly than it has comic books. That comes from the fact that adults actually see television, whereas, as a rule, they have no idea what comic books their children really read, or what is in them. There are all kinds of atrocities in these 'magazines'. One may pick up a comic book at random and find several stories in which the stories of murder go from the simple, to the gruesome, to the weird, all in the same book."

"I see."

"One man kills his wife with a poker, another shoots a

*wolf which is his wife, a third man becomes transformed
into a huge crab and eats his wife. An 'autopsy' is
performed on a man who is still alive and he screams on
the coroner's table. An artist ties the hands of his model to
the ceiling, stabs her, and uses her blood for paint. A very
sexy-looking girl tells her husband that she is pregnant.
He opens his jacket and the girl looks at him, horrified.
There are gears and pistons. He tells her, 'You couldn't
be expecting MY child, now, could you, my frau? Not
very well when your husband is a ROBOT!' You will find
this type of 'variety' in the average crime comic. I must
also say that I do not mean to imply that all television is
harmful. There are many excellent children's shows, like
Mr. I.Magination, Uncle Lumpy, Mr. Wizard, Kukla, Fran
and Ollie and Paul Whiteman's TV Club. And, of course,
See it Now."*

*"Ha! I thank you for the kind endorsement, sir, as do our
rival networks. But please, go on. I'd like to hear more
about these crime comic books."*

*"Well, in another comic book the criminal is a police
lieutenant. He kills his wife by deliberately running
over her with his car. At the end, he is undetected
and completely unsuspected, and presumably lives
happily ever after. Six pictures on one page show this
policeman-murderer lighting and smoking a cigar,
walking triumphantly, with the full knowledge that crime
DOES pay. He goes free because at the police station an
innocent man is tortured into making a confession. The
child reader is spared no details. The man is punched
in the stomach, hit in the face, his arm is twisted behind
his back. Mind you, I am only describing stories that are
written, drawn, and printed. I see the results of these
monstrosities in my clinic on an almost-daily basis, and
what happens in real life is often far worse."*

"Describe, if you will, one of your typical patients."

*"Well, I recently had to examine a young man facing jail-
time in order to give an expert opinion about his sanity
for the courts. He was in serious trouble, being accused*

of attempted rape. He had enticed a girl to walk with him past a vacant lot, and then suddenly pounced on her, and a struggle ensued. The girl had stated that there was no actual rape and that she got away from him, bruised, and with her clothes torn. I told the young man that I wanted to know more about his life, and he told me his story. Since childhood, he had had fantasies of tying a girl up, especially tying her hands behind her. It started when he was about eleven and saw pictures of that in Wonder Woman comic books. From then on, he looked for comic books where that, the act of bondage, was especially depicted. For example, those with girls tied in chairs with their hands fastened behind their backs. He cut out these comic book pictures, and also he drew them himself. They gave him sexual fulfillment. He had no intention of actually raping the girl, an act of which he would have been less ashamed. All he wanted to do was just to tie her up. The struggle to do it had given him full sexual satisfaction. This is a typical example of the cases that made me resolve to study the comic book question systematically."

"I can certainly see how that might compel you. Doctor Werthstein, some of your articles have described teenage dope-shooting and the role comic books have played in this epidemic as well."

"WerthHAM. And yes, this is true regarding the narcotic usage. A very sad dilemma indeed."

"Could you please elaborate on this?"

"Well, we have known about childhood drug addiction for some time. It was one of the Lafargue guidance counsellors who brought the first child drug addict to my official attention. This boy of fourteen had come and asked for help. 'I am a mainliner,' he said. 'I want to get rid of the habit. I have been popping myself. I have been hitting the mainline.' He rolled up his sleeves and showed me the sores on his arm. He had a needle with a plain eyedropper attached with which he had given himself injections. A regular hypodermic needle was *too expensive for him. He had been stealing to buy the narcotics. When I asked him where he had learned to make such an apparatus. he said, 'From the crime and murder comics. They show you everything.'"*

"I see, that is indeed disturbing. Now, Doctor Wertham, is it just the crime comic books and the horror comic books, or do you take umbrage with other types of forms and varieties?"

"Certainly, yes."

"Such as?"

"Jungle comics are, to me, also crime comics of a special branch."

"No pun intended, I assume."

"Certainly not. Jungle comics specialize in torture, bloodshed, and lust in an exotic setting. Daggers, claws, guns, wild animals, overdeveloped girls in brassieres and as little else as possible, dark 'natives', fires, stakes, posts, chains, ropes. Big-chested and heavily muscled Nordic he-men dominate the stage. These jungle comic books contain such details as one girl squirting fiery 'radium dust' on the protruding breasts of another girl; white men battering helpless, well-meaning, simple natives; close-up views of breasts being branded; a girl about to be blinded. All this type of stuff can be found in Sheena, Nyoka, and what have you. And while the white people in jungle books are blonde, athletic, and shapely; the idea conveyed about the natives is that there are fleeting transitions between apes and humans. I have repeatedly found in my studies that this characterization of colored peoples as subhuman, in conjunction with depictions of forceful heroes as blond Nordic supermen, has made a deep, and I believe, lasting, impression on young children. And amidst all the violence between slaves, apes, and humans in these books are big pictures of lush girls, as nude as the US Post Office permits. Even on an adult, the impression of sex plus violence is quite definite in jungle comics."

"Interesting."

"Yes, that is one way of putting it."
"And your thoughts on the romance comics that seemingly every teenage girl in America reads?"
"Ah. The 'headlight' comics…"
"Headlight?"
"Amongst boys, 'headlights' refers to the breasts. There was a boy from a well-to-do family who was referred to me for psychotherapy after he had become very inattentive in his studies. During treatment, he told me once that he and three other boys, ages fifteen and sixteen, used to go to a candy store in the neighborhood where they ate ice cream cones, bought comic books, and talked big like boys will do. One evening, in one boy's parents' cars, they drove from the suburbs, where they lived, to Times Square. There, they picked up a young prostitute and took her to the home of one of the other boys, whose parents were away in Europe. Two of them had intercourse with the prostitute and performed various sexual experiments, the girl being very co-operative. They paid her five dollars each. After that, all four went out with her in the car to drive her back to Manhattan, as they had promised. On the way, they had a bright idea. They stopped the car, pounced upon the girl, and while one held her forcibly around the neck, the others beat her unmercifully about the face and body. They went through her handbag and took out all her money. One boy, hitting her in the face, said to her, 'You are too darned independent!' The girl did not fight back. She just sat there and cried and said it was not fair. After all, she had been so nice to them. Then, they left her at a subway station with just enough money to pay her fare. This is what America's children learn in romance comic-books."
"I see. Rather salty stuff, even for ten thirty."
"I apologize, Mister Murrow. I am simply here to tell the truth."
"But, Doctor Wertham, what about 'classic' comics? You know, the variety that re-tell great stories and literature

of the past? Do these have no educational merit as well? Do these too, in your opinion, also inspire crime and degeneracy? My own ten-year-old son – an honor student – has seemed to derive a great deal of both pleasure and knowledge from this variety of comic book."

"I'm sorry to tell you that I do not approve of these either. There is a great misconception amongst the general population regarding 'classic' comic books. Comic books adapted from classical literature are reportedly used in twenty five thousand schools in the United States. If this is true, then I have not yet heard a more serious indictment of the low quality of American education. These 'classic' comics utterly emasculate the books they claim to adapt. They condense them and leave out everything that makes the books great. Additionally, they are just as badly-printed and inartistically-drawn as any other comic books. They do not reveal to children the world of good literature, which has at all times been the mainstay of liberal and humanistic education. Quite the contrary, they conceal it. After being processed in this way, no classic comic, no matter who wrote it, is in any way distinguishable from the floppity-rabbit and crime comics it is supposed to replace."

"But to be fair, Doctor Wertham, I've looked at some of these 'classic comics' myself and have found some to be marvelous adaptations of their source material. I wouldn't let my son read them otherwise."

"Ah. Perhaps so. But supposing your son gets used to eating sandwiches made with very strong seasonings, with onions and peppers and highly-spiced mustard. He will soon lose his taste for simple bread and butter, and for finer foods as well. The same is true of reading strong comic books."

"I'll bear that in mind at the drugstore. Doctor Wertham, in your articles, you've also expressed problems with the so-called 'super-hero' genre. You've taken particular pains to stress your issues with Batman, Superman, and Wonder Woman. Could you elaborate on this

for us please?"
"Certainly. I have naturally emphasized those particular characters as they appear to be the most widely-read of the 'super-heroes'. My attention to this dilemma was piqued several years ago when a fellow psychiatrist pointed out that the Batman stories are psychologically homosexual. Our research at the Clinic confirms this entirely. Only someone ignorant of the fundamentals of psychiatry and of the psychopathology of sex can fail to realize a subtle atmosphere of homoeroticism which pervades the adventures of the mature Batman and his young friend Robin. Just as ordinary crime comic books contribute to the fixation of violent and hostile patterns by suggesting definite forms for their expression, so the Batman stories help to fixate homoerotic tendencies by suggesting the form of a Ganymede-Zeus type of love-relationship."
"Doctor Wertham, I'm afraid you have me at a disadvantage. It's been many years since my college days. 'Ganymede' refers to whom exactly?"
"He was a mortal that the Greek god Zeus kidnapped, seduced, and enslaved as his homosexual lover."
"I see. Thank you for that clarification."
"As I was saying, Batman and Robin, the dynamic duo, go into action in their special uniforms. They constantly rescue each other from violent attacks by an unending number of enemies. The feeling is conveyed that we men must stick together because there are so many villainous creatures who have to be exterminated. They lurk not only under every bed, but also behind every star in the sky. Every day, Batman and his young boyfriend are captured, threatened with every imaginable weapon, almost crushed to death, or almost annihilated.
Sometimes Batman ends up in bed injured, and young Robin is shown sitting next to him fawning. At home, they lead an idyllic life, where they are Bruce Wayne and Dick Grayson. Bruce Wayne is described as a socialite and the official relationship is that Dick is Bruce's ward. They

live in sumptuous quarters, with beautiful flowers in large vases, and they have an effete butler named Alfred. Batman is sometimes even shown in a dressing gown. As they sit by the fireplace the young boy Dick worries about his partner. 'Something's wrong with Bruce. He hasn't been himself these past few days.' It's like a wish-dream of two homosexuals living together. Sometimes they are shown on a couch, Bruce reclining and Dick sitting next to him, jacket off, collar open, and his hand on his friend's arm. Like the girls in other stories."

"An interesting take."

"It is the obvious take. Robin is a handsome, ephebic boy, usually shown in his uniform with bare legs. He is buoyant with energy and devoted to nothing on Earth as much as to Bruce Wayne. He often stands with his legs spread, the genital region discreetly evident. And in these stories, there are practically no decent, attractive, successful women. A typical female character is the Catwoman, who is vicious and uses a whip. The atmosphere is homosexual and anti-feminine. If the girl is good-looking, she is undoubtedly the villainess. If she is after Bruce Wayne, she will have no chance against Dick. For instance, Bruce and Dick go out one evening in dinner clothes, dressed exactly alike. The attractive girl makes forward gestures toward Bruce, while in successive pictures young Dick looks on, smiling mockingly, certain of Bruce's devotion to him."

"I wonder how Robert Kane, the cartoonist who created and draws Batman, would respond to your analysis."

"Mister Murrow, I would be happy to speak with Mister Kane anytime, anywhere. Please note that I am not accusing him of deliberately creating and disseminating homosexual propaganda, sometimes these things occur unconsciously. But the hard facts remain true. I have personally examined many overt homosexuals being treated at our Readjustment Center to find out what they thought about the influence of these Batman stories was on children. A number of them knew these stories *very well, and spoke of them as their favorite reading material. One young homosexual brought me a copy of Detective Comics featuring a Batman story. He pointed out a picture of 'The Home of Bruce and Dick', a house beautifully-landscaped, warmly-lighted, and showing the devoted pair side-by-side, looking out a picture window. He told me that when he was just eight, he'd realized from fantasies about comic book pictures that he was aroused by men. He said, 'At the age of ten or eleven, I found my liking, my sexual desires, in comic books. I imagined myself in the position of Robin. I wanted to have relations with Batman. They seem to be so close to each other. I remember the first time I came across the page mentioning their secret Batcave. The thought of Batman and Robin living together and possibly having sex-relations came to my mind.'"*

"Ladies and gentleman, if you're just tuning in, I'm speaking with Doctor Fredric Wertham of Harlem's Lafargue Clinic. He's speaking with us about subversive elements found in 'super-hero' comic book magazines, amongst other varieties of comic books."

"Thank you, sir. Now, the lesbian counterpart of Batman may be found in the stories of Wonder Woman. The homosexual connotation of the Wonder Woman type of story is psychologically unmistakable. For boys, Wonder Woman is a frightening image. For girls she is a morbid ideal. Where Batman is anti-feminine, the attractive Wonder Woman and her counterparts are definitely anti-masculine. Wonder Woman has her own female following. They are all continuously being threatened, captured, almost killed. There is a great deal of mutual rescuing, the same type of rescue fantasies as in Batman. Her followers are called the 'Holliday Girls'. Wonder Woman often just refers to them as 'my gals'. Their attitude about death and murder is a mixture of the callousness of crime comics, with the coyness of sweet little girls. In a typical story, Wonder Woman is involved in adventures with another girl, a princess, who talks

repeatedly about 'those wicked men.'"
"If I'm not mistaken, this character also carries a lasso with some form of magic properties?"
"Certainly, yes. Each and every Wonder Woman story features at least one instance of this golden rope being utilized to enact some kind of overtly-sexual bondage."
"Doctor Wertham, is it true that the Wonder Woman character was itself created by a fellow psychiatrist?"
"No. The late Doctor Marston was a psychologist, not a psychiatrist. Much of his life's work has been largely since discredited."
"I'm told that he was also one of the inventors of the polygraph, which, I believe, is still in regular use by many branches of our military, intelligence agencies, and police forces."
"That may be so. Of this, I am uncertain."
"I'm afraid we're running short on time, but, at the risk of a lawsuit from ABC, let's wrap this up with your thoughts on Superman."
"Certainly. The Superman comic books present our world in a kind of fascistic setting of violence, and hate, and destruction. Not a very sound diet for children, do you think? Actually, Superman, with the big S on his uniform, which I suppose we should be thankful is not an SS, needs an endless stream of ever-new Submen, criminals, and 'foreign-looking' people not only to justify his existence but even to make it possible. This engenders in children either one or the other of two attitudes: either they fancy themselves as Supermen, with the attendant prejudices against the Submen, or it makes them submissive and receptive to the blandishments of strong men who will solve all their social problems for them, by force. Additionally, Superman not only defies the laws of gravity, which his great strength makes conceivable, he gives children a completely wrong idea of other basic physical laws. Not even Superman, for example, should be able to lift up a building while not standing on the ground, or to stop an airplane in mid-air while still flying

*himself. On even the most basic scientific level, this is
unmitigated poppycock."*

*"Doctor Wertham, as educational as your visit has been,
I'm afraid we've now run out of time. Would you care
to directly address the millions of Americans parents
watching this program before signing off?"*

*"Why, yes. I would. And I thank you, Mister Murrow, for
the opportunity to be heard."*

*"It's been my pleasure. Just look into that camera. Yes,
that's the one. And now...you may begin."*

*"Parents of America, set your children free! Give them
a chance! Let them develop according to their full
potentials! Don't expose them to your ugly passions when
they have hardly learned to read! Don't teach them all
the violence, the shrewdness, the hardness of your own
life! Don't spoil the spontaneity of their dreams! Don't
lead them halfway to delinquency, and when they get
there clap them into your reformatories!
Don't stimulate their minds with sex and perversity
and label the children 'abnormal' when they react to
such stimuli! Don't continue to desecrate death, graves,
and coffins with horror stories and degrade sex with
the sordid rituals of hitting, hanging, and torturing!
Don't sow in their young minds the sadistic details of
destruction! These children are our future, and we must
protect them accordingly."*

*"Doctor Wertham, I thank you, sir. Ladies and
gentleman, what you've heard tonight are one learned
man's opinions. It is important not to confuse these
opinions with facts. With all due respect to the doctor,
and despite cries to the contrary that certain others will
preach or project upon you; the field of psychiatry is
undeniably still one in its infancy, and we must temper
our own personal conclusions with that awareness. We
should not be driven by fear into an age of paranoia.
We are not descended from fearful men. Nor from men
who feared to allow their own children the right to form
opinions and ideas for themselves. Guidance of our youth*

is undeniably essential, but of equal value is the virtue of strong, individual character and opinion. Like Doctor Wertham, I too believe the children are our future. Teach them well and let them lead the way. Good night, and good luck."

JACK Coal skipped dessert at the automat so he'd
have a few minutes to finally call Zach Kirby.
As he scoured Third Avenue for a vacant phonebooth
he almost doubled-over with frantic, stabbing
pangs of hunger. Although he'd eaten two Denver
sandwiches and a cup of onion soup (not to mention
Bert Meskin's entire plate of sliced liver), he was
still utterly famished.
The sidewalks were cold and crowded. He watched
a dour brunette push her twins past him in a double-
seat, blue canvas stroller. The smiling little boys
were wearing matching sailor suits.
Just like Mister Salty.
He purchased a couple of pretzels from a House O'
Weenies cart and gnawed at them both at once.
Finally, he found an empty booth on Thirty Eighth
Street. He spat on the receiver and wiped it down with
his handkerchief before allowing it near his face. Dot
had once contracted syphilis from a public phone,

and the ensuing treatment had cost him a pretty penny.

"Yeah?"

"Yes, hello. Zach?"

"Yeah?"

"This is Jack."

"Jack who? I know a lotta Jacks."

"It's Jack Coal."

"Ah Jack...the deviant!"

"Hah! Yes, that's me!"

"How are ya, old bean? Whaddya know, whaddya say?"

"Well, Zach, I'm pretty good considering...but things have been better. Ups, downs. You know how it is."

"Yeah, I do."

"But let me be frank."

"I appreciate that, Jack. I'm a very busy man. I'm pencilling five books a month now, you know."

Jack Coal bit his lower lip and closed his eyes tightly.

"Zach, Will Meiser is canceling Elastic Man."

"Aw gee, Jack, I'm real sorry to hear that. I know you put a lot of work and a lot of heart into that book. I really admired it too."

"You...you did?"

"Are you kidding, man? Of course! We all did! Me, Joe, Kida, Burgos. Every month, we'd look at your book. You got a hell of a lot of talent, old bean!"

"Why...I had no idea. I'm sincerely, deeply flattered. I really wouldn't have envisioned you fellows caring at all. But I do appreciate it. Sincerely."

"Yeah, well...I mean it. You're a talented guy, Jack. And I'm real sorry about Elastic Man, see? That's a real tough break. But, you had a real good run on it. And, look at the bright side: it ain't a closed door – it's a new opportunity."

"Yes, well, actually – speaking of opportunities – that's why I'm phoning you "

"Oh yeah? Go on. I'm listening."

"Okay. Well...Zach...I'd like to bring Elastic Man into

the Hyman and Kirby fold!"

There was a prolonged silence.

"Zach? Are you still there?"

"Yeah...I'm here. What exactly did'ja mean by that?"

"Well, I meant exactly what I said. I'd like to come work for you fellows, and bring Elastic Man along with me. After all, he's rather flexible!"

"Hah, Jack. Always with the good ones! But...I don't get ya. How's that even possible? Elastic Man is a Meiser property, yeah?"

"Well, yes. Technically. But I'm trying to work out an... arrangement with him."

"Jack, now...listen...and don't worry, I'm gonna keep this just between us...but shoot it straight with me, see? Have you even talked to Will about this yet?"

"Well, no. Not exactly. But, as you know, he and I have worked together for many years – and have quite a good rapport – so I really don't expect-"

"Don't do it. Don't even bother."

"I'm sorry?"

"I said: don't do it."

"Well, why the heck not, Zach? You're sending me mixed signals here!"

"Jack, you don't really read a lotta comics outside of your own work, huh? Not a big fan?"

"Well, I'm more of a newspaper reader to be honest. And of course I enjoy the classics. But yes, I like comic books, *sure*. Of course I do....I...why I think they're terrific!"

"And you still hadn't noticed that Joe and I ain't put out a super-hero book in six years now?"

"I'm sorry?"

"Just what I said, Jack. Those characters went belly-up for us only a year or two after the War ended. We do mostly crime, romance, and the scary-monster crap now."

"Oh. I see. Well...obviously – I'm aware the industry has shifted a bit, but, certainly, trends tend to swing and-"

"We tried bringing back a pajama-boy about a year ago. Nothin' doin'! Didn't sell for shit. Didn't even cover the printing costs."

"-and I think in time that Elastic Man will-"

"Listen....Jack. You're a good fellow. I like you, see? Really do. Honest. And I'm gonna tell you something personal...I don't like that Willie Meiser. Not very much at all. I mean, I certainly respect him as an artist, but he pulled some real crud moves on me in the service, and I think he's a first-rate prick as a person. Believe you me, I'd fucking LOVE to get one over on him, see? But, I know that he thinks the world of you, Jack. There's not a doubt in my mind that he's kept Elastic Man going this long purely out of regard for you. Hyman keeps track of the sales figures. Everybody's sales figures. That's how we figure out what to do next. He mentions things sometimes. Your book is great, Jack, but it ain't turned a dime in years now."

"I...see..."

"Anything else I can help you with, Jack?"

There was a rapping against the phone-booth, Jack Coal looked towards it.

Bert Meskin was hopping up and down, waving a tabloid frantically.

"Oh...Bert Meskin says 'Hello'."

"Bert? Bert who?"

"Bert Meskin. Inker. Wears bow ties."

"Bert Meskin? Jesus Christ, man! Ok, Jack...good talkin' to ya. You just take care of yourself, see? And thanks for calling!"

There was a *click* and the line went dead. The phone booth suddenly felt like a dirty glass coffin. Even after he'd exited it, Jack Coal could still feel death all around him. He looked at his friend, who appeared to be on the verge of hyperventilation.

"That was odd, Bert. Did you and Zach Kirby have some kind of falling out?"

"J-J-J-Jack! *L-l-look!*"

Bert Meskin held out the newspaper.
'EDITOR OF <u>CRIMINALS NEVER WIN</u> COMIC MAGAZINE SLAYS DIVORCEE AFTER 11-DAY TRYST IN GRAMERCY PARK HOTEL'
Beneath the headline was a large photo of a sobbing Dick Steele in handcuffs.
Jack Coal turned back to Bert Meskin, gritting his teeth to restrain the grin that was desperately trying to break loose and flower.
This was nothing to smile at.
So why did he want to?
"Holy smoke, Bert! This is *Dick Steele* they're talking about. Good ol' sweet Dick!"
Bert nodded grimly.
"I kn-kn-kn-kn-kn-kn-know. He b-b-b-b-b-beat her t-t-to d-d-d-d-death w-w-w-w-with an i-i-iron."
Jack Coal processed the thought for a few seconds and continued to work on his soft pretzels.
He nodded as he chewed.
"I guess he needed to set something straight."

LESTER brought home more and more comic books.

Sometimes as many as ten a day.

Soon, there was a pile over two feet high beside his small aluminum-framed army surplus cot.

Every time Cornell asked him where the money for all of these funny-books was coming from, he'd receive the same answer:

"The fat white man in the park."

This didn't sit right in Cornell's stomach.

He'd been around the block a few times. He knew that strange white men on park benches did not give little colored boys money strictly out of the goodness of their hearts. Cornell also knew how to spot even the subtlest signs of sissies when he saw them, his livelihood depending on this talent. His little brother displayed none of these signs, neither inwardly nor outwardly.

"Lee-Lee, *Darling*, I'm really not cross with you. Really, I'm not. But, I *will be* if you do *not* begin telling me the *truth*. Admit it. You've been stealing again, haven't you? Hmmmn?"

Lester stared at the shellacked, wood-planked floor and shook his head dolefully.

"I ain't been though. I didn't stole nothin'..."

Cornell gently lifted Lester's round chin with the long, twig-like fingers of his right hand. Their eyes met, and Lester shifted his gaze over his brother's shoulder, focusing on the autographed 8"x10" photograph of John Derek that Cornell had thumbtacked to the stucco wall. It was a publicity still from *Rogues of Sherwood Forest*.

Lester was once very proud that his brother knew Robin Hood personally. Now, that meant nothing to him.

"*Lester Phineas Jackson*...You *do* remember what the truant officer said, do you not?"

"But I done *told* you already. I ain't stealed *nothin'!* The fat white man *give* me that money. Why you not believe that? You my brother, ain't you?"

"And *why* would this stranger...who doesn't know you from Adam...*give* away his hard-earned money to a poor little black boy?"

Lester shook his head and shrugged.

"Dunno. 'cause he like me...and 'cause he rich maybe..."

Cornell pulled his hand away from Lester's chin, leaned back against the wall, and folded his long, slender arms. He thought, pursed his lips, and nodded.

"Ok, little brother. Then I'd like to *meet* this mystery man for myself. I want you to take me to him.

Right now."

The fat man's park bench was empty. Lester pointed at the dead, bloodied rats behind it as evidence of his existence; but Cornell would hear none of it, arguing the park was full of dead rats.

Cornell was completely silent on the walk back to Perry Street, his face remaining outwardly calm. Only his vice-like grip around Lester's left hand betrayed his anger.

Once back home, Cornell carefully removed and hung his coat, tie, and shirt before addressing Lester – who moped before him – staring at his threadbare Keds as he kicked at the floor moulding.

"I suppose you know what this means?"

Lester nodded.

He pulled down his faded dungarees, and then his cotton drawers while Cornell sat erect on a kitchen chair. Lester bent himself at a right angle across his brother's lap and braced the muscles of his brown rear-end tightly. As Cornell raised his pink right palm to begin the punishment, Lester turned his head backwards and cooly addressed the stoic face above.

"You can whup me, Corny, but I *ain't* lyin'! You see later, and then you be sorry about it. And when I get big too...*then I will kill you!*"

Cornell flinched and froze. The complete deficit of fear or remorse in his brother's eyes chilled him to the core. He lowered his hand slowly.

"Ok, Lee-Lee. I'm going to grant you the benefit of the doubt, because I love you very much, and because everybody deserves at least a second chance, if not a third and a fourth. We'll go back to the park tomorrow. I *sincerely* hope that man will be there then."

Lester stood up and pulled his dungarees back around his waist.

"Well, I *don't* love you. *Uh-uh.* Not at all. I *hate* you. *I hate you!* And I hate Ma. And I hate Pa. And I hate that stupid fat man. I *hate* this whole stupid city. I don't even care if it burn up like Rome or Chicago!"

"That's fine, Lee-Lee. You're upset, and I understand. Is there anything or anybody that you *don't* hate right now?"

Lester thought for a moment.

"I don't hate Bobby from upstairs. *He* my friend."

Lester grabbed a comic book from his pile and opened the front door. Cornell placed his hand on his brother's shoulder.

"And *where* do you think you're going, hmmmnn?"

Lester pulled away from his brother and frowned.

"Leave me alone, Corny. I goin' up to the roof now. I need some private time."

Lester slammed the door behind him.

Cornell sighed and lifted a paperback that laid upon the formica top of the kitchen table. It was Beckett's *'Murphy'*, a book he hadn't taken off the shelf in months. He split it open and looked at the title-page. Written in purple crayon was a swastika and the words *'Korny I love you. From lester.'*

"IF you'll excuse me for saying so, Mister Senator, I am a *bit* disappointed."

"And why is that, sir?"

"There is no *'coonskin'* cap!"

The senator chuckled.

"Ah, well. I only wear it when *Time* takes my picture."

The senator insisted on sitting in Dr. Wertham's own chair, behind Dr. Wertham's own desk, in Dr. Wertham's own office. The doctor obliged him without hesitation, but made a mental note of the obvious grandiose delusions, indicating possible symptoms of secondary mania.

The senator folded his hands together and smiled.

"So, Doctor, that was *some* kind of show you put on CBS the other night. I didn't think it was *possible* to make that Murrow fellow so plumb-fidgety, but *you* sure did."

"Perhaps so, but this was *not* my intention. I simply wanted to tell the truth."

"And this man in the papers...this...*Dick Steele* fellow.

You say he works in the funny-books too?"

"Yes, Mister Senator, although I'd venture to say *his* particular brand of *'literature'* is not so funny indeed." Dr. Wertham lifted and unbuckled his calfskin briefcase, split it open, and withdrew a thin pile of brightly-colored comic books which he laid gently across the desk's cork blotter.

The senator, Estes Kefauver, a thin middle-aged Democrat from Tennessee, wore horn-rimmed glasses and a crisp blue suit. He found Dr. Wertham's thick German accent and haughty mannerisms distasteful and expressed his displeasure by ignoring the stack, even after Dr. Wertham began tapping at it with a gnarled right index finger.

Estes Kefauver allowed a full thirty seconds to elapse before speaking again in his soft drawl.

"And these, I presume, are the work of Mister Steele?"

"You would be correct, sir. These are the six most recent issues of his primary venture, *'Criminals Never Win'*, a murder comic book of the most sordid variety."

The senator looked down upon the pile and studied its peak. It was a glossy cover printed with lurid hues of orange, brown, purple, and red. The central illustration featured an ethnic-type in a garish pinstriped suit and wide-brimmed fedora wrestling with a buxom blonde above an oven-range. A jet of blue flame was shooting up from each burner. The gangster, whose left fingers gripped the blonde's soft bicep so tightly that they'd sunk knuckle-deep into her flesh, used his right hand to shove her head onto the fiery stove. Above him, a word-balloon declared, *'You cooked MY GOOSE with the bulls, baby! Now I'm gonna cook YOUR STUPID FACE!'*

Senator Kefauver laid the comic book back on its stack and nodded – his thin lips drawn in a tight, straight line.

"I will admit, Doctor Wertham that this *is* rather

disturbing material, and the circumstances behind its creator make it all the more discomforting. But remember, you're living in *America* now, not Germany, and we don't take kindly to censorship here. Surely this kind of stuff is at least *intended* for the adult reading market."

Dr. Wertham stood and paced across the dull red carpet of his office as he spoke. He did not feel comfortable sitting in front of his own desk, like some kind of supplicant.

"Ah! One would think so, yes? Or at least hope that to be the truth, But the reality, is NO. *'Criminals Never Win'*, with a circulation of roughly three million, more than that of even the great *Superman* mind you, is the most widely-read comic magazine in North America today...*by children*. The bulk of its readership are beneath twelve years old!"

The senator removed his spectacles and rubbed at his shiny nose with his right thumb and index finger as if he had a headache.

The doctor made another mental note. *Early stages of Parkinson's or Huntington's; of this I am sure.*

Dr. Wertham approached his desk and tapped at the pile as if he were trying to penetrate it.

"But the *content* of the crime comic book story alone is *not* the only problem. No, my dear sir. Not at all. The advertisements are just as harmful. Perhaps even *more* so. Please, I implore you. Take a look."

Senator Kefauver yawned, nodded, and selected a copy from the middle of the stack. He browsed through its pages; chuckling when he noticed the ink staining his fingertips.

Tired of all that extra padding? No date to the dance? Try Reduct-O, the miraculous new technique from Europe that will help you trim that flab away like a hot knife through butter. Proven scientific technique guarantees a loss of ten pounds in first week. No pills! No exercise! No annoying dieting! Start reducing in comfort today!

(ONLY $5.95-limited time!)
A skinny scarecrow figure is neither fashionable nor
glamorous. Skinny Girls are NOT Glamor Girls! Ashamed
of your skinny, scrawny figure? Don't let them snicker,
do something about it! Estro-Fem can help you to add
pounds and pounds of firm attractive flesh to your figure!
Checked by our medical director, a well-known New
York practicing physician. Remember, the girls with the
luscious seductive curves get the dates. ($2.00)

The senator stopped to chuckle again and point to the
photo of Mamie Van Doren.

"Some rather apparent contradiction at play here!"

I BROKE HIS HAND LIKE A MATCHSTICK!
It was easy! He was helpless. He howled with pain!
Method of Offensive Defense, based on natural,
instinctive impulse-action...Smashing, crashing,
bone-shattering, nerve-paralyzing method...70 BONE-
BREAKING SECRETS! ($1.00 – formerly sold at $5.00)

Senator Kefauver looked up at Dr. Wertham.

"Nothing wrong with that, as far as I can see.
From what I understand, Judo is a very healthy,
normal activity."

Doctor Wertham nodded.

"Perhaps so. But please – read on. Turn to page
eighteen."

The senator stopped on page eighteen as instructed
and tapped at it. The advertisement featured before-
and-after photographs of a scrawny, pimple-faced
teenager and a handsome, Herculean he-man.

From a SKINNY WEAKLING to a MIGHTY MAN! I
gained 53 lbs. of MIGHTY MUSCLE. 6 and a half inches
on my CHEST; 3 inches on each ARM. You can do it in
10 minutes a day! Make YOUR Body Bring You FAME
instead of SHAME! Are You Skinny? Weak? Flabby? I
know what it means to have the kind of body that people
pity! I don't care how old or young you are or how
ashamed of your present physical condition! I can shoot
new strength into your old backbone, help you cram your

body so full of pep, vigor and vitality that you won't feel there's even standing room left for weakness and that lazy feeling …

The senator reclined in the doctor's chair and rubbed at his nose again. He didn't have a headache, he just plain needed a drink.

"Ok, Doctor. Now let's talk turkey here for one darned minute. And what exactly is wrong with this one? Are you seriously about to try and convince me that a *Charles Atlas* ad is harmful to America's youth?"

Doctor Wertham nodded balefully.

"You are correct."

"And just *how* is that, Doctor? I've met the man myself, and I like him! He's built an entire *empire* from nothing, just based on teaching people how to be strong and healthy. I'm sorry, sir; while I agree that you've brought up *some* points worthy of real consideration, I'm simply not buying this one."

The doctor began to pace again.

"Sir, advertisements for boys cover different areas, but appeal to the same kind of susceptibility to juvenile hypochondriasis as those for girls. The concern of boys with growth and body-building has been shamefully exploited for years now. They make the smaller boys feel shame about their bodies, which were given to them by almighty God. And often in these advertisements, with photographs of super-muscular he-men, they take great pains to portray over-sized genitals, just like some of the comic book heroes. Look very closely at that Mister Charles Atlas photo, if you will. Boys with latent, and not so latent, *homosexual* tendencies collect these pictures. They clip them out and use them for sexual stimulation. One of my patients started to cut out these photos at the age of only eleven. He was treated at the Clinic because he had prostituted himself to men. Does this sound *'strong'* and *'healthy'* to you?"

The senator gawked at Dr. Wertham incredulously.

"So – let me be absolutely clear on this – what you're saying...what you're telling me now...is that Charles Atlas advertisements contribute to, and possibly *create*, homosexual behavior?"

Dr. Wertham shrugged.

"Frankly, yes. Amongst other things. That is what I am telling you."

Senator Kefauver lowered his head, shook it, and muttered to himself as he continued to peruse the advertisements.

10-PIECE KNIFE SET
8-inch blade roast slicer
8-inch blade ham slicer
7-inch blade butcher knife
5-inch blade sandwich knife
4-inch blade utility knife
3-inch blade paring knife
4-inch blade grapefruit knife
8-inch sharpening knife
PLUS! Special spring-loaded Italian defense knife
FLINGS OPEN FAST! Big size! Whole set only $7.65.

Senator Kefauver dropped the comic book onto the desk and slapped at it.

"Now, just wait one darned second here! Is this a *switchblade knife ad* concealed within a kitchen-set advertisement?"

Dr. Wertham smiled triumphantly and nodded.

"*Yes*, Mister Senator. *Yes, it is!*"

"But...switchblades were banned years ago! I drafted the darned legislation *myself!*"

"Now turn to page thirty eight. It features the type of advertisement I call the *'arsenal ad.'* It consists of a whole page of illustrations and text offering pistols, rifles, throwing-knives, leather whips, slingshots, fencing-sets, and other useful toys for children of the comic book-era. You'll find more switchblades and flick-knives there too. Police have found whole arsenals of weapons in many children's hiding-places.

Most of these weapons trace back to these ads."
Estes Kefauver shook his head with dismay.
"*Switchblades!* Jesus Lord Almighty. Mother-lover...I
just can't *believe* that. *Gold-durn!*"
The senator closed the comic book and pushed back
the doctor's chair as he stood.
"Doctor Wertham, are you familiar with a fellow
named William *Meiser?*"
"Not personally, but I am of course familiar with both
his '*creative*' output, as well as his other publishing
ventures. The famous '*Apparition*' etcetera. He is one
of the primary figures in the comic book world. One of
the industry's founders, in fact."
"Yep, that's him. Well, he's agreed to testify on behalf
of the Subcommittee."
The doctor resisted his urge to reclaim his chair and
remained standing. He stroked his chin.
"That *is* a surprise, Mister Senator. Would you
consider it prodding of me to inquire as to why Herr
Meiser would testify against his own livelihood?"
"To be frank, Doctor Wertham, I'm really not quite
sure. Perhaps it's guilt. Perhaps it's just a sense of civic
duty."
"Or perhaps it's to protect a lucrative contract with
the US Army?"
"Yes...or perhaps it's that. But nonetheless, he's doing
the Subcommittee a tremendous service, and I'm
going to need your assurance that should we call on
you to testify – which now seems imminent – that you
go...lightly...on Mister Meiser. We've promised him
that he'll still have a career after this."
Dr. Wertham lowered his head, stared at the dull, red
carpet, and noted its many faint stains. He would need
to have it replaced soon.
"I understand completely."
The senator nodded and crossed the room to
remove his topcoat and hat from the standing rack
they hung from.

"One moment, Mister Senator. I trust you like
to read?"
Dr. Wertham walked around his desk and withdrew a
manilla envelope from a locked side drawer.
The senator stared at the envelope pensively before
accepting it.
It was thickly-filled. He did *not* like to read.
"And what's this?"
Dr. Wertham shrugged.
"Ach, just some notes."

MILLARD Gaines stared at his chicken chow mein and watched with a beatific awe as the candle-flicker danced across the fat-glazed noodles.

"Mill, you should really eat that. It's gonna get cold. It's no good when it's cold."

Gaines gazed above his table-mate's black parted hair and drank in the soft, warm glow of the paper lanterns hanging from the ceiling. They seemed to be pulsating light with a rhythm in perfect synchronicity with his breaths. Slowly, he lowered his head, like a steam-powered crane, and finally leveled-off at Al Feldman's disgruntled, potato-like face.

Millard Gaines was in a great mood. He was feeling *so* great, that although he was not a homosexual, he briefly entertained the thought of leaning across the small round table and kissing Al Feldman right on his grease-slickened lips. He was just *that* happy.

"No thanks. You're not my type. Too Rubenesque."

Gaines laughed.

"You a mind-reader now? How'd you know what I

was thinking?"

"Because you didn't think it, Ay-hole. You said it."

Gaines smirked and sipped at his plum wine.

He needed more of it quickly. He held the empty thimble-sized glass above his head and beamed at a stooped, white-jacketed waiter.

"Bring me the whole bottle, Louie! A fresh one this time!"

Al Feldman shook his head as he chewed and swallowed.

"It's them pills, eh? I'm glad that they're giving you so much zip – but listen, chum...you really need to eat."

Gaines slapped at the tablecloth.

"I'm too damned happy to eat! I feel like *Superman!*"

He looked down at the chow mein again.

"It is pretty though..."

"You're goddamned right it is! Ruby's doesn't fuck around. Give me some of that if you're not gonna eat it."

Feldman reached across the table and slid the chow mein across the linen cloth with a hairy, ape-like hand.

He spoke between large forkfuls.

"So anyway, Mill...we got a big problem."

"Yeah, yeah. Problem, problem. Always a problem."

Gaines shrugged to himself.

"We'll handle it. *You'll* handle it! That's what I pay you for, right?"

Feldman nodded.

"Yeah. I guess so."

"So, what *is* it this time? Ingels in the tank again? Should we send him to the cure? Would his pride allow that? Is he too uppity to accept our help? Do Catholics even take the cure? Is that against their beliefs? There are so many things that I don't know. I feel lost. Do you ever feel lost, Al? Probably not. Too strong. Too silent."

Al Feldman belched as he shook his head.

"Nah, Mill. It's not that. I mean, yeah, he's a wreck,

but when isn't he? As long as he makes his deadlines, I don't care how drunk he gets. He can drink battery acid for all I care. His liver is none of my business. Or yours. But this Wertham character...*he* is."

"*Wertham?* What's that?"

"Kraut shrink. Runs a clinic up in Browntown. And he's gonna make us kaput soon if we don't do something about it. And I *do* mean soon!"

Gaines pulled his chow mein back across the table and picked up a fork.

"What do you mean though? Why would a shrink want to hurt us? I *love* shrinks. I'm pretty sure I bought mine a bungalow in Palm Springs last year."

"Because this *particular* shrink doesn't like us, and he's got a big fucking mouth. This cat's been banging a helluva lotta doors lately. Going on and on about the evil of comic books. Says they're turning kids into delinquents and homos. Says Batman uses Robin's schwanz as a pogo stick, '*Young Love*' made some prep-school kids roll a hooker, and god knows what else. You shoulda heard this nut. Un-fucking-believable. Don't you watch Murrow anymore? You used to *love* Murrow."

Millard Gaines cleaned his spectacles while he processed the thought. The lenses were coated with a film of clear grime.

"Hmmmnn. Murrow, eh? That why we've been getting so much hate-mail lately?"

Feldman nodded.

"Might have something to do with it."

Millard Gaines looked up to the paper lanterns again, but there was no solace. They'd lost all their magic. They weren't even breathing anymore.

"But *c'mon*, Al. We publish *quality* material! For Christ's sake, half of our readers are fucking adults."

"Hey, Mill! I know. You're preaching to the choir. But that *ain't* the half he's yammering about."

"Well...what're *we* supposed to do about it? Put a

fucking hit out on him? We're not tough guys."
Al Feldman bent forward and leaned across the table
so he could speak softly – almost in a whisper.
"Listen, Mill. There's talk about some kind of Senate
Subcommittee meeting up on this. And if that
happens, we're screwed. *Fucked.* Everything we built
up, straight down the toilet. All for nothin'."
Millard Gaines made a circular gesture with
his right index finger.
"Nothing goes straight down the toilet. It winds
and curves."
"This *isn't* funny, man! This is as serious as fucking
cancer. Cancer of the dick."
"Okay...relax. I get it. But where does your
information come from? As far as I know, that's
all just rumors."
Feldman shook his head.
"It *ain't* rumors. My Cousin Solly works in Gulotta's
office. He *hears* things. He *sees* things."
"Well, can Cousin Solly fix this?"
"No, he's just a clerk, Stupid."
"Ok, but Gulotta has nothing to do with Congress.
What would he know?"
"Ah, he's chummy with all them bigwigs. There was
a gaggle of 'em in there the other day. Solly heard
everything."
Millard Gaines shoveled three forkfuls of chow
mein into his mouth, then a thought struck him
and moaned through the noodles before he began
chewing.
"Oh no. Don't tell me. It's that golden boy, right?
Peckerwood. Mob-buster. What's his name...
Keyflower?"
"Kefauver. Yeah. And I'm very sorry to say this, but...
your name was brought up specifically. That's why
Solly called me..."
Gaines made a sour face and buried it in his palms.
"*What?* And you're just telling me about this *now?* Just

when I'm on the brink of fucking Nirvana?"

"Yeah, yeah. It's *all* a big joke. Seriously, Mill. We gotta *do* something."

"Al, I agree. This *is* bad. But if Frank Costello couldn't stop this guy, what the hell can we do?"

Al Feldman looked at Millard Gaines with a deep, pleading stare of concern. His voice rose an octave. The noodle hanging from his lower lip did nothing to diminish his seriousness.

"And that means what? You're gonna roll over and die like a good boy? But what about *me?* What about *all* the boys? You're rich. You got no worries! But I got *kids*, Mill. A *lot* of us do!"

"Okay, Jesus. *Ok*. But, what can *I* do? It's fucking Congress, for Christ's sake. Not traffic court."

"You could *testify*. You could tell 'em what's what and where to get off, but in a pretty way. You can talk real good when you got a mind to."

Millard Gaines withdrew the small, brown glass bottle from his inner coat-pocket, shook it, and smiled at it lovingly.

"You know, Al...if you'd made that *same* suggestion a few weeks ago, I would've said you're meshugganah. But now that I'm *Superman* ... OKAY! No problem. Anything for you, ol' pal. Just one minor condition..."

"*No* – you can't fuck my wife."

Millard Gaines made a fist and grimaced.

"*Dammit!* Ok...how about I get to hide in the closet and watch? Just once?"

Feldman raised the middle finger of his right fist and held it aloft.

Millard Gaines smiled sadly at his friend through a soft, chicken-fat focus.

"A little peek at one shtup for saving an old pal's entire career? Is that *really* too much to ask? *Really?*"

ESTES Kefauver sat on the edge of his hotel-room bed, unbuckled his briefcase, and stared at Dr. Wertham's package for a few minutes.

His stomach was not agreeing with him, and he silently promised himself that never again would he chase Lobster Thermidor with any drinks containing crème de menthe.

He lit a cigarette, lifted the thick envelope from the briefcase, and slowly unraveled the red string holding its lip in place:

Boy. Age ten. Lamont. Referred to the Lafargue Clinic after pushing a younger boy into the East River so that the small boy drowned. Another boy saw him do it. Case was dismissed as 'accidental death'. Clinic asked to give the suspected boy emotional guidance. He had previously thrown stones at windows and on one occasion had hit and seriously injured a small retarded child in this same manner. Uses foul language often. Voracious comic-book reader. His mother stated that he reads 'whatever comic books he can get hold of.' After several months of non-progress, lobotomized. Still refuses to give up comics.

<u>Boy</u>. Ten. Treated at Clinic for a behavior disorder. He daydreams about murder. Study of this boy did not reveal any special hostilities or resentments. Told me that he liked classics comics and Woodie the woodpecker. Told him I was very much interested in all kinds of comic books. He then confides to me that what he really likes and reads a lot of is crime comics.

'I got a whole pile of Criminals Never Win. I want to be just like Machine Gun Kelly. He was very handsome. I want to shoot fat people and wear flashy neckties.'

<u>Boy</u>. Seven. Suffers from asthma and shyness. Inattentive in school. Improved with play-therapy. Note that instead of playing, he likes to pore over comic books a lot of the time. I weaned him away from them by giving him material to draw and paint with. But the comic-book spirit is still very evident in his art productions. Draws Donald Duck with a gun. Drawings always show the duck robber shooting the duck cop. The opposite could also occur, but never seems apparent in any of his numerous drawings. In another drawing, the duck robber executes a duck named Doctor Quack.

<u>Boy</u>. Fourteen. Referred to clinic after a schoolyard assault. Jerome Freeman. Avid reader of comic books.

Q: Where did it happen?

A: In the schoolyard.

Q: How did you know he had money?

A: Because I asked him how much money has he got, he said a dollar.

Q: How old was the boy?

A: About thirteen.

Q: How did you know he couldn't beat you?

A: Because I took money from him two weeks before that. I got a wallet and fifteen cents then. Also a yo-yo. It was a green one too. They are hard to find. Green is the color of sex.

Q: Did you ever do anything worse than that?

A: Yes. I stabbed a boy.

Q: When was that?

A: That was last year. The boy was about twelve years old. I stabbed him with a knife, a pocket-knife. I stabbed him in the dick. They put me in the shelter for two weeks.

Q: What else have you done?

A: We were pitching pennies in school. This kid was cheating. One guy grabbed me and pushed me against a water faucet. He bent down to get the pennies. I took my foot and kicked him in the head. He got two or three stitches in the head after. I laughed at him.

Q: Why did you laugh?

A: Because he looked like Frankenstein with the stitches. You would have laughed too.

<u>Boy</u>. *Fifteen. Having trouble in school. 'I don't read the comic books. I just look at the pictures. I can read, but I just don't like to take the time to. Sometimes, when it is a good story, I read it. You would be surprised how much you can learn just by looking at the pictures. If you have a good mind, you can figure things out for yourself. You don't need to read. Reading is for sissies anyway. Books are stupid. I like to smoke reefers and look at the horror and science-fiction comics. I just get tight and look at the pictures. The pictures take me to places far better than this world.'*

<u>Girl</u>. *Repeatedly arrested for delinquency. Tall. Thirteen. Very boyish appearance.*

Q: Which comic books do you read mostly?

A: Girls read mostly Crimes by Women or Sheena.

Q: Which crimes do women commit?

A: Murder. They marry a man for his life insurance and then kill him, then marry another man and then just go on like that until they finally get caught. Or they will be a dancer and meet the wrong kind of a guy and get involved in a bank robbery.

Q: What's the fun for you in reading that?

A: It shows you other people's stupid mistakes. In some of the crime comic books kids pick up ideas. They give them

ideas of robbery and sex.
Q: Sex?
A: Yes, plenty of sex. They show you exposed women, men beating up girls and breaking their arms. The fellows see that and they want to try it. They try to wrestle with the girls and get ideas. I know of fellows who imitate comic books. When I was young I used to read comic books and I watched the fellows and how they imitated what they did in the books. They tried it with all the girls around my way. They tied them up. The boys were around ten or twelve, the girls were the same age. They used to always read the comic books. I asked them what made them do that. They said they saw it in the comic books. They read Crime, Murder Inc., Criminals Never Win, most of those crime books. But they would never tie me up. I am too tough for them. I like sex, but not when I am tied up.
<u>*Boy*</u>. *Fifteen. Three burglary arrests.*
'*I read the comic books to learn how you can get money. I read about thirty a week. I read Criminals Never Win, Crime and Punishment, Penalty, Wanted. That is all I can think of. There was this one case. It was in back of a factory with some pretty rich receipts and money. It showed how you get in through the back door. I didn't copy that. I thought the side door was the best way. I just switched to the skylight. I carried it out practically the same way as the comic book did it, only I had to open two drawers to do it. I didn't do every crime in the book, some of them were difficult. Some of them I just imitated. I had to think the rest out myself. I know other boys who learned how to do such jobs from comic books. A few of them are dead now. Sometimes I think I see them when I drink beer, but I know that ghosts are not real, so I do not get scared.*'
<u>*Boy*</u>. *Twelve. Arrested for shoplifting.*
'*I saw a comic book where they do shoplifting. This girl was shoplifting and she was caught. They took her down to the Police Department. It was a love story. When she got married she still shoplifted and she broke down and*

told her husband. I didn't like it. She should not have
said anything. You should never say nothing. Ratting
is a sucker's bet.'
<u>Boy</u>. Fifteen.
'They get the idea: if she gets away with it, why can't I get
away with it too? I saw a book where a man has a hanger
in his coat with hooks on it. He opens his coat and shoves
things in and it disappears. It was a crime comic book.
The kids see that these men get away with it. They say:
let's try it. They learn the method of putting it in a jacket.
They teach you how to do it in the comic book. They
didn't notice it until somebody jumped on this man and
the things fell out. Otherwise they would not have caught
him. But if you have a gat they will let you go. Nobody
wants to get plugged for just a few clams.'
<u>Boy</u>. Filipino. Thirteen. Father deceased.
'I learned from crime comic books when you want to hit a
man, don't get face to face. Hit him in the back of the neck
so it snaps. That is how Robin does it. He has killed lots of
bad guys and he is still only in eighth grade.'
<u>Boy</u>. Fifteen.
'Gals don't approve of guys going to poolrooms
in Brooklyn. They pay for protection. They take a
switchblade and if a fella don't pay them a dollar, they
will rip up the table. I have been in with them. You could
learn that from a comic book too. I read some of that in
Criminals Never Win. That's a real good book.'
<u>Boy</u>. Age seven. Bad in school and daydreams a lot.
Previous diagnosis: schizophrenic tendencies.
'Sometimes I read a comic book ten times a day. I look
at the pictures a long time. I just imagine it as if they are
real. They go around stabbing people. They have eight
knives, and they rob a liquor store. They stab a woman
with a knife. They stab two women with a knife. One man
started killing people: five cops, six women, and eighteen
others. If anybody ever crossed him, he didn't give them
no chance. This famous artist painted this picture and it
was smuggled. Then it said the picture was torn up but

then I found out it wasn't. Everybody got swindled. I like adventures. I also want to kill a nigger someday.'
Boy. Kenneth. Age twelve. Reading tests show him to be at kindergarten level. 'Reads' fourteen to twenty comic books a day.
'Oh, yes! I can read some words! I can read guns, police, Donald Duck, and the horse one too. That's all. When I'm on the subway, I can read Times Square. But when I had to go to Floral Park once I couldn't read it, so I missed the stop. I was very sad about that.'
Boy. Raymond. Nine. Fourth grade. Father serving life sentence for rape. Mother says, 'He does not learn well in school and cries at night.' Reading at the first grade level. Avid comic book reader.
'My favorites are all of them. I like the escape stuff. I looked at comic books that had all about escape, like Batman, a prisoner escaping from the prison. I used to wake up at night screaming. Since my mother left the light on in the living room, I haven't had that so much. In the dreams, when I scream, I can't remember anything in the morning. I read about five comic books a day. I keep looking at them. I want to stop, but I do not know how.'
Boy. Twelve. House where family lives is in a very deteriorated condition. Sleeps in same bed with brothers aged six and nine. He is considered very wise in the ways of the street.
'I like ghost stories and murder comics. They teach you how to curse somebody and swallow their souls. They teach you how to bring the devil to your house.'
Boy. 'Ralph'. Eleven. Six feet tall.
Took money from children in the lower grades. Family lives in basement apartment with large rat-holes, broken floorboards, horse-flies, and leaking overhead pipes; furniture worn past recognition. Father unemployed; mother in poor health. Sleeps in one bed with two brothers, aged four and thirteen.
'In Roy Rogers comics, they murder people with guns and shivs and strangle them. They stick up banks and

*the stagecoach. My sister looks at murder comics and at
night and screams that she sees a man over there. Some
men kill girls because the ladies be rich. Men see a lady
walking down street and push them in front of train,
sometimes they tie them up. Some boys try to do like
what's in the comic books. They take ladies' pocketbooks
and beat them up and run off. Women kill the men too.
Sometimes they take men to dance and while they're
dancing they jook them in the back with a big shiv.'*

<u>*Boy*</u>*. Harry. Nine.*

*Apparent good home conditions. Parents employed. But
spends a lot of time with television. Avid comic book fan.
'I like comic books. Gangbusters, Criminals Never Win,
Batman, and Superman. They do murders, like shooting.
The girls in underwear do things to the men.
Catch bad men and take them to the law. Bullets bounce
off girls in Super Girl. She can fly and swing on ropes.
I want to be like her. I want headlights too, so I can
squeeze them at midnight.'*

<u>*Boy*</u>*. George. Age ten. Morbidly obese.*

*Very tough little boy who will fight anyone of whatever
size or age. Sleeps in one bed with three brothers, aged
two, four, and eleven.*

*'I don't remember the names of the comic books. They
hold up coffee stores and when a girl reaches for the gun,
they shoot them. Men make girls hold up stores.
Other people learn about killing and taking ladies'
pocketbooks. They learn about murders, but not me.
I learn good stuff. Don't take nothing from no kid's house
when you go up there or their father will make you take
your clothes off again.'*

<u>*Boy*</u>*. Enrique. Age ten but still in second grade.
Lives with foster parents who do not speak English.
Basement apartment consists of kitchen and bathroom.
Family sleeps in bathtub..*

*'I like Superman. I forget the bad things. I forget all that's
in the crime books. I forget about how they robbed the
bank. The men want to kill the girls. Maybe because they*

have jewels. I don't know. I forget.'
Boy. John. Twelve. Held back in school twice.
Sleeps with sixteen year-old sister in same bed.
Parents separated.
'Captain Marvel was fighting ants and the ants grow
big. He had a lady and they was going to kill her and
he said shazam and escaped and fought ants and saved
the lady. A good ant helped him too. In mysteries and
crimes comics, they poison each other, dynamite caves,
and blow people up. Girls play men for fools and when
men rob banks they give money to the women and they
buy mink coats and when men don't like it they kill the
men. Superman ladies hardly do nothing. I don't know if
Superman even likes girls. I think maybe he is afraid he
will kill them if he hugs them too hard. I wish he would
hug Lois Lane. She deserves it because she is bad.'
Boy. Dick. Twelve. Fourth grade.
Father left family when boy was very young.
'I like the way they fight and when they kill people.
The books tells about murder, killing, and shooting.
And some love.'
Boy. Peter. Eleven. Third grade.
Mother is dead.
'In murder books, men steal and throw the cop off the roof
and kill about five men. Some make you scared at night.
You dream about it and think somebody's coming to kill
you. Some tells about stealing, killing peoples, some stick
with knives, shoot with guns, beat them over their heads
with sticks, and stick them in the eyes, hit 'em over the
head with a poker and string them up with ropes. I can
read them now because I know what's right and wrong.
My aunt teaches me not to do bad things. She is very fat
but I love her still.'
Boy. Mahatma. Twelve. Fourth grade.
Very neglected child. Has to get up early in the morning
and prepare his own meals. Sleeps in the same room with
grandmother, brother aged four, and sister aged three.
'Cowboys comic books is bad. They steal money out of the

express office. The boys beat the girls up and Superman comes to help the girls. The boys is bad because they do things they shouldn't. The girls set houses on fire. The comics also teach boys how to rob and join up in gangs. I do not like comics but the library will not let me in because I is too loud so I still read comics.'
Boy. Sammy. Twelve. Expelled for masturbating in classroom.
Frequent family assistance from Department of Welfare.
'I read all kinds of comics except lovey kissy comics. I don't like them. The only time I read them is when I've seen all the rest of the comics. I don't like girls. I do not want to kiss them. I want to kill them.'
Boy. Paul. Ten years old. Fourth grade.
Mother deserted family; father works nights.
Chronic truant.
'I like Roy Rogers comics. The Indians shot a man in the eye with an arrow. The soldier took his sword and stuck it in him. The Indian took the soldier's rifle, killed everyone in the fort and the boy was shot right in the back, and a baby was shot with a bullet and then the troopers came and they warred. I don't like mystery comics no more because then I devil dream about them sometimes and then I can't sleep.'
Boy. Marvin. Nine. Third grade.
'Cops and robbers fight. Robbers need hop but don't have no money. They buy a cheap gun or a little gun and go rob a bank. The cops shoot them and take the money and buy beer with it. My daddy is in jail. I want to be in there with him because I miss him so much.'
Boy. Jimmy. Nine. Expelled. Father in tuberculosis sanitarium.
'I have no comics. I read my sister's. I like cowboy stories. They kill too much in the mystery comics. I don't like it because I dream about it. I dream ghost stories. But I like the wolf-man best because he can change. I want to change too.'
Boy. Thirteen.

One of eleven siblings. The boys sleep in one room in bunk-beds, Four brothers in the upper bed, four in the lower bed. The sisters have a bunk-bed in another room. 'I like Superman. A man be laying down in bed and the door be locked and the lady run outside for help and hollers. The man comes through the window. Girls always be getting hurt in comic books. Every time the girl goes with a man there is murder and the girl be screaming. My sisters scream too when we plays Superman.'
<u>Boy</u>. Ernie. Fifteen. Disheveled.

'There was one fellow, he was a friend of mine. He got this bright idea on the protection racket. He got it from crime comic books. I know he read them a lot. He used to say: You know what would be a good business? Making protection out of shoeshine-boys! He put that scheme into working. There are about twenty five shoeshine-boys in that district. He figured this would be the perfect set-up. He used to make them pay a dollar a week, and if they did not pay, their boxes or other equipment would be smashed. He asked me to go in on it. I didn't because it was pretty cheap. Nickel and dime racket. He kept it up for several months. Two or three boys worked with him. One had a zip-gun, the other had a stiletto. He was the chief, so he had nothing. In other words, he was smart. If they caught him he would be empty-handed. He learned that from comic books, too. One of the boys who was paying protection told his mother. They went down to the station-house and told the police the set-up. He is in Sing Sing now because he thought he was only seventeen, but he was really eighteen. He forgot about his own birthday. He wasn't as bright as he thought he was.'
<u>Boy</u>. Milton. Eleven.

'Now listen to this. If you see a bathroom window lit up, you know someone is at home. If it's still lit the next day, no one is at home. They leave the key in the mailbox, under mats, or in corners. If you see a milk bottle and a note in it, the note gives you a pretty good idea of the house. If you keep up with the notes, you know

everything. Another thing, if you can steal a dog then people will pay a lot of bread to get the dog back. Even for the old and smelly ones. As smart as I am, I never thought of this. I got it all from the comics. Pretty neat, right?'

<u>*Boy*</u>. *Andrew. Eight years old. Truant.*

'*I got my bad ideas from the comics, stabbing, robbing, stealing guns, and all that stuff. In a comic book I read two kids rob a store and steal guns and get away and grow up to be bank robbers. So I did the same thing, only I didn't grow up to be a bank robber yet. I just rob girls. And some old ladies.'*

<u>*Boy*</u>. *Earl. Seven. Above-average intelligence. Lives with aunt.*

'*In the comics I saw a cat kicked by a man, so I kicked a cat too because I saw it happen that way. I learned a lot from comics. Especially in 'Criminals Never Win'. I saw how to carry a gun in a suitcase and a shopping bag. If I ever had to do it, that's the way I'd do it. I learned how to rob cars from the comics. They tell you, if the door's open, how to switch the wires. I learned how to break a seal off a freight car from the comics, and how to put on another so you don't get caught. Comics can help make you smart. They are better teachers than school. That is why I skip classes.'*

<u>*Boy*</u>. *Fifteen. Parents from Greece. Very tough.*

'*I got this from the comics. The patrolman would make his beat, then we timed it with a wristwatch. We'd find out what time he goes past and back. Another idea we got was taping the windows and cracking them. Then you take the tape off and pick the glass out. When a train goes past, like the Third Avenue El, we'd crack the window with our fist. We got all this from comics. I made a lot of money this way. I bought this watch with it. It's gold.'*

<u>*Boy*</u>. *Moses. Age twelve. Referred to Clinic by police after truancy problems.*

'*In the comic books, it shows how to snatch purses. You should read them if you got the time. It shows a boy*

*going to a woman and asking her where the church is.
She naturally drops her arm and goes waving. So you
just grab the purse and run. Usually they can't run after
you, they have hi-heels on. She has the bag in her hand,
waving to a certain place. You just grab her arm. It was
in different comic books. They all build that stuff up. You
pick desolate places, where nobody is around. Every
fellow in my gang learned things this way. You can learn
a lot from reading comic books.'*

Incidents from the Associated Press wire feed:
*Three boys, six to eight years old, took a boy of seven,
hanged him nude from a tree, his hands tied behind
him, then burned him with matches. Probation officers
investigating found that they were re-enacting a
comic-book plot.*
*A girl of eight, her six-year-old brother, and a boy of
thirteen threw a rock at the face of a three-year-old boy
and beat him with a stick. Among other injuries the boy
had 'cuts inside his mouth'. Comic books were found at
the boys' houses.*
*A boy of eleven killed a woman in a hold-up. When
arrested, he was found surrounded by comic books.
His twenty-year-old brother, a US Marine, said, 'If you
want the cause of all this, here it is: It's those rotten comic
books. Cut them out, and things like this
wouldn't happen!'*
*An adolescent tortured a four-year-old boy, kicking
him so severely in the eye so that hospital treatment
was necessary. Reason: 'I just felt like doing it.' Comic
books and other pornographic material were later found
beneath the adolescent's mattress.*
*A seven-year-old girl broke into four homes and stole
money, watches, jewelry, two parrots, and a dog. Avid
comic book reader.*
*A train was derailed by three boys, one of whom was
eight, another ten. 'Criminals Never Win' had run a story
about a train-derailing three months prior.*

A boy of thirteen committed a 'lust murder' of a girl of six. After his arrest, in jail, he asked for comic books and cigarettes and beer. 'I refused, of course,' said the sheriff. A boy, who had participated when a group attacked and seriously stabbed another boy, was found with a knife which had these words on the sheath: 'KILL FOR THE LOVE OF KILLING!' The slogan originated in a Batman comic book story.

A boy of twelve and his eight-year-old sister tried to kill a boy of six. They threatened to knock his teeth out, stabbed him through his hands with a pocket knife, choked him, kicked him, and jumped on him. The police captain said, 'It is the worst beating I've ever seen, child or adult.' Comic books were found in both of the attackers' bedrooms.

A ten-year-old boy hit a fourteen-month-old baby over the head with a brick, washed the blood off the brick, and then threw the baby into the river. He later claimed that he was inspired by a story he'd read in Captain Blammo.

A fourteen-year-old crime comics addict killed a fourteen-year-old girl by stabbing her thirteen times with a knife. He did not even know her.

Four boys, two of fourteen, one fifteen, and one sixteen, carried out a comic-book classic. They beat the sixty-eight-year-old proprietor of a little candy store with a hammer; and while he was lying on the floor, one of the fourteen-year-olds drove a knife into his head with such force that the hilt was snapped off. The man somehow survived, but is now a vegetable. The attackers will all be released from juvenile detention at the age of eighteen.

A well-to-do plastic surgeon received an extortion note demanding $50,000 and threatening harm to his young daughter. Experts deduced from the note that it was the work of an 'adult white male psychopath under severe emotional strain.' It turned out to be a fourteen-year-old Chinese girl with a large crime, horror, and romance comic book collection.

Children threw rocks and bolts and fired air rifles at

passing trains and automobiles. One eleven-year-old boy who informed the police about this got such severe comic-book style torture-by-fire from the group of boys that he had to have twenty three skin grafting operations and twenty six blood transfusions. As a result, his grades suffered and he was left back a year in school.

A boy of eight who led three other boys on nine safecracking expeditions had bought himself a new pair of sneakers after one job so the detectives could not trace his footprints. He learned this technique in (where else?) a comic book.

Typical story: a fourteen-year-old boy mortally wounded a policeman with a sawed-off shotgun. A 'Criminals Never Win' comic book was found in his back pocket after he was killed by police.

While their parents were away, two boys, nine and eleven, hit their little sister (two years and eight months old) with a hoe handle and trampled her to death. Both avid fans of crime comic books.

Two fourteen-year-old girls robbed a taxi-driver while he was stopped for a traffic light. One of them, who called herself 'Wonder Woman', pressed a knife into his back, while the other tied him up and made him 'tell the truth'. They kissed the taxi driver, who is happily-married, and then fondled his genitals. Afterwards, they demanded his money. Then they grabbed the ignition key from the dashboard and fled the scene, leaving the poor man tied-up with his pants down.

A boy of eleven poured kerosene over a boy of eight and a girl of twelve. He lighted the kerosene with a paper torch and burned the children to death. He was later found hanging from a rafter of his basement. A large pile of 'Witches Tales' comic books were discovered in his toy chest. His parents had no idea that their son was a comic book addict.

A nine-year-old boy killed a five-year-old girl by stabbing her more than one hundred times. His nickname at school was 'The Flash'.

A thirteen-year-old boy stabbed an attractive young female teacher eight times in the back, five times in the face and, when she had fallen to the floor, masturbated over her as she expired. Authorities were bewildered by the behavior of this boy, who came from a good home background. Over three hundred comic books were later found in his bedroom.
A fourteen-year-old girl pupil was found battered and raped during the lunch recess in one of the corridors on the third floor of an all-boy's school. The victim was an avid fan of 'Hi-School Romance' and other such comic books.

Note:
Children are like flowers.
If the soil is good and the weather is not too catastrophic, they will grow up well enough. You do not have to threaten them, you do not have to psychoanalyze them, and you do not have to punish them any more than wind and storm punish flowers.
But flowers do require nurture, poison will only sicken them."

Estes Kefauver carefully straightened out the sheath of notes against the top of the hotel dresser, placed it back into its envelope, and slowly re-wound the red string.
He shook his head, lit another Chesterfield, and rang the desk operator.
"Hello. Can I help you, sir?"
"Yes, I hope so. Do y'all have Bromo down there at the coffee shop? I feel awful..."
"No, sir. But we have Alka-Seltzer."
"That'll do. Send me up a couple packets if you would."
"Of course, sir. Will there be anything else?"
"As a matter of fact – yes. I need an outside line. Put me through to Senator Henning's suite at the Carlyle."

A minute later, the phone rang.

"Senator Kefauver?"

"Yes, ma'am."

"Please hold for your call."

There was a loud *click*, and then another.

"This is Henning."

"Tom, it's Keef."

"Jesus, man. It's two AM! If I'd known it was you, I would've never picked up!"

Estes Kefauver chuckled.

"Well, who'd you think it was? And don't tell me your wife!"

"I was hoping on Marilyn Monroe."

"Ah Tom, you know I have more curves than that old biddy. They're just all political. But listen, I've got something *serious* to discuss."

"I should hope so. What's up?"

"It's that Wertham fella. The old kraut. Had quite a chat with him today up in Harlem."

"Good grief, that quack again? It figures that's where he works."

"Ok...ok, now...just hear me out. I agree, the man is a little...eccentric."

"A little!"

"And I agree that his research is a tad...shoddy."

"Just a smidge!"

"But, and this is a big *'but'*..."

"Oh, brother..."

"...but I really think we ought to re-consider using him as a witness. He brought up some very valid, very interesting points today at our conference. For instance: did you know that switchblades were still available via comic book magazine advertisements? *Still?"*

"Yes, Keef. I'm aware of that."

"Well. *I* certainly wasn't. And did you know that Charles Atlas has excessively-large genitalia?"

"The muscle man?"

"Yes. That's the one."
"Keef...have you been drinking?"

CORNELL and Lester returned to Washington Square Park the next day and found the fat man waiting on his bench – staring at the clouds.

The smile on the fat man's face evaporated instantaneously when he realized his young friend was holding the hand of an adult negro. He called to his dog nervously as he rose to leave.

"Come, sweetie! Time to go walkies with Daddy! Come-come!"

The poodle – her snout buried eye-deep in dirt – heard the fat man but did not bother acknowledging him. She could smell newly-birthed rats within the hole. (The candy of the rodent world.)

She could even detect the sweet odor of placenta. (She wanted these things desperately.)

Lester looked up and smiled at his benefactor.

"Hello!"

The fat man ignored Lester.

Cornell looked at the fat man sternly.

"Sir, I mean you no disrespect, but my brother here claims that you've *given* him a great deal of money recently. Is there any truth to this?"

The fat man answered sadly without averting his eyes from the poodle.

"I'm sorry, but I've never seen this boy before in my life."
Lester scowled with outrage and struggled to break
free from Cornell's hand, which now gripped him
tightly.

"Mister, you lyin'! You lie!"

As the fat man called to the poodle again, Cornell
forced Lester's shoulders around to face West and
attempted to drag him away, but the boy kept his feet
planted firmly. Cornell was shocked at the little boy's
strength, but also felt an immense sense of pride. His
little brother was going to grow up to be a *real man*
someday. A man who could take care of himself.

The boy yelled to the fat man.

*"Mister, why you be lyin'? He gonna whup me now! Tell
the truth or he gonna whup me good!"*

Cornell tugged again at Lester's arm and succeeded in
knocking him down to his knees.

"Ow! Stop it, Corny! Goddamn you!"

"Lester Phineas Jackson, will you kindly get up this
instant and begin walking...or am I going to carry you
home like a pathetic little baby?"

Lester looked towards the poodle and screamed to
her desperately.

"Stella! Stella! C'mere, boy!"

The dog immediately yanked her dust-covered nose
out from the rat-hole and bounded towards Lester
happily. Cornell released his grip and turned back
towards the fat man, who raised his palms defensively
as he lisped.

"Yes, I *did* give him some money. Just a little. But
there was *no* funny business, I promise you that! He's
just a sweet, adorable child, your son, *that's all*. And I
have more money than I know what to do with these
days. *Plenty!* Please don't hit me, you can have it all!"

The fat man reached into his pocket and withdrew
a clipped wad of green bills, thin but of high
denomination. He held out a fifty to Cornell, who
smiled and waved it away.

"As I said, he's my *brother*, not my son..."
Cornell slid down onto the fat man's bench, gently
patted the space beside him, and flashed the most
alluring smile in his repertoire.
"*Please.* A thousand pardons for any confusion or
misunderstanding. I really meant *no* disrespect. None
at all. Just looking out for Lester's best interests, you
understand. This city is full of...*unsavory* types."
The fat man nodded, smiled, and took a seat beside
Cornell.
Lester, holding Stella in his arms, scowled at Cornell
angrily.
"*What about me, Corny? You owe me a million pardon!*"
"Lee-Lee, you run along and play with the nice doggy
now, hmmmnn? I'm just going to speak with your
friend for a while, okay?"

Lester followed Stella back to the rat-hole while the
grown-ups talked.
Beneath the clouds overhead, a low-flying bi-plane
slowly trailed a banner emblazoned with the legend
'Drink Pepsi Cola!'

WHEN Dot finally drifted off on the couch, Jack
Coal stood up and smoothed out his trousers with his
wide, flat palms.

He had plans, and wanted to work in private.

He left the television-set on to mask any accidental
noises and tiptoed away in his socks.

In the corner of the dining room that Jack Coal
jokingly referred to as *'my den'* stood his favorite
possession, his trusty, old drawing table. His Uncle
Zeke had built it for his thirteenth birthday. It was
now comically small, but still, he loved it; it made him
feel like a little boy again. Dot tolerated its presence
only because it'd grown so battered and scratched
that it almost resembled a genuine piece of antique

American Primitive furniture, a valuable commodity.
Jack Coal slowly unzipped his steerhide portfolio and
carefully removed the blank sheet of bristol-board
he'd sneaked out of the shop supply closet.
Handling the bristol elicited a twinge of guilt.
Jack Coal didn't approve of thievery.
In fact, the slice of paper was the first thing he'd
actually stolen in his entire life. Dickie had always
been getting in trouble for stealing. He could never
quite understand why. They'd come from a warm,
comfortable home. Once, after Dickie had been
delivered back to the house in a Black Maria, Jack
Coal asked his little brother what drove him to such
lengths. Dickie had smiled and said, *'Because
being a yegg is the only way I know to make the
old man feel shame.'*
As he cut the stolen bristol into five long, thin,
rectangular strips, Jack Coal made a mental note to
repay Meiser at a later date.
He taped one of the blank strips onto the tabletop,
taking care to make sure it sat perfectly level across
the board, and began to rule-out five rectangular
panels with his t-square and an HB pencil. As
the panels took shape, a great wave of cool, clear,
cleansing relief slowly washed over his tortured
skin, nerves, and spirit.
A daily strip!
This was what he'd *dreamed* of doing as a young
boy, this is what he should've been doing all along,
and – *by golly* – this was what he was *going* to do
from now on.
Jack Coal ran his fingertips over the bristol, savoring
its tooth, and thought back to the correspondence
course he'd taken from the Landon School of
Cartooning.
Despite dropping to his patched knees and begging
with clasped hands, his father had refused to pay for
the lessons. He'd made sandwiches in the kitchen by

moonlight, and sneaked them to school in a hollowed-
out English primer until he'd squirreled away enough
lunch-money to cover the costs. It'd taken him
three months.
He wondered to himself if that qualified as stealing.
(He hoped not.)
Charles Landon himself had once personally noted
in the margin of a graded lesson that he saw a little
George McManus in Jack Coal's efforts. That'd meant a
lot. That had meant a *hell* of a lot.
And he'd dropped the ball.
It'd all been a waste.
Years later, Jack Coal heard at Meiser's shop that Milt
Caniff, Roy Crane, and Chic Young had all taken the
Landon lessons too. *And look where they were now.*
He wondered what'd happened to *him*. He told himself
that he just didn't know, but this was a bald-faced lie.
He knew.
The Depression had happened to him.
Jack Coal stared at the five blank panels for a full
hour before he finally realized that he had absolutely
no idea what in the world to draw. He got up to make
himself a cup of Nescafé.
As he stirred in the creamer, he picked up the paper
on the kitchen table. It was the World-Telegram.
Odd...Dot usually buys the News.
Jack Coal shrugged, and opened the paper to the
funnies. It'd be interesting to see a different selection.
The World-Telegram had a larger-than-average
funnies section. Many of the features were old
standards that'd been around for decades; but there
were some strips present that he'd never seen before.
Most were appallingly bad, all drawn in a similar
sketchy style that resembled the cheap animation of
made-for-television cartoons and dime-store novelty
greeting cards. The 'artists' hadn't even bothered to
use brushes, the hallmark of a legitimate, professional
cartoonist. This stuff was all scrawled with pens.

Jack Coal shook his head balefully.

The world was going to pot.

Six columns down was something called *'Peanuts'*. It was another miserable, poorly-drawn affair – about a self-pitying little boy and his small sociopathic dog. Jack Coal chuckled at its lack of both finesse and quality.

It'll never last. People want to feel good when they think about childhood.

The coffee went through Jack Coal very quickly, and he set down the paper to go the bathroom. He urinated very carefully, angling the stream to ricochet off the side of the basin, so as not to awaken Dot. He splashed some water on his face after he'd rinsed his hands. His jaw was getting awfully jowly. He was getting old. *Used-up.* He pulled the medicine-cabinet's mirrored door open and checked the left corner of the middle shelf. Will Meiser's benzedrine was still there. Jack Coal rubbed at his jowls with his right thumb and index finger. He cringed as they swung and shivered.

I am scrotum-cheeked.

The coffee had done nothing for him.

He needed some energy.

He didn't want to be a used-up, fat, loathsome turd of a man. He picked up one of the tablets and stared at it in his palm. It looked harmless enough. Just an innocent, little, yellow tablet really. He slapped it onto his tongue and washed it down with cold water that he drank directly from the tap.

On the way back to his table, Jack Coal stopped by the living room to check on Dot – thinking he might carry her back to the bed and tuck her in – but when he saw her laying peacefully on her side, wearing her serene little sleep-smile, he erased this notion.

He quietly fetched a soft, woven blanket from the linen closet, gathered up the knitting needles and wool yarn that lay by Dot's side, and draped the blanket over her, tucking in the sides beneath her, like a Cornish pasty.

Jack Coal stood over his wife and smiled happily
as she burrowed into the couch, wrapping the
blanket tighter.

My Dottie...snug as a bug in a rug!

As he placed the knitting utensils back into their
basket beneath the television-stand, he noticed an
odd shape attached to the needles.

It almost looked like a tiny sock.

He held the needles and yarn up against the warm
blue glow of the television-screen. The silhouette of
the tiny hanging bootie completely obscured Steve
Allen's wise, disapproving frown.

Jack Coal's heart suddenly began to beat
very, very fast.

He looked backed towards Dot and studied her
smiling, tranquil face carefully.

Can this be?

God in Heaven...have my prayers been answered?

He focused on Dot like he'd never focused on anything
before.

She was glowing...

She was GLOWING!

Jack Coal's blood began to pulse rapidly.

Thoughts raced through his mind like an F-86 Sabre.
He'd never changed a diaper in his life. *I'll have
to learn!* Names. Middle names. Schools. Picnics.
Slingshots. Circuses. Baseball. Vacations. *Sheepdogs!*
Jack Coal looked back towards Dot again. Should he
wake her? Nah...bad idea...

She needs all the rest she can get.

Sleeping for two now.

This was big. This was *really* big. This was everything.

Nothing else mattered!

Jack Coal was suddenly the happiest man in the
world.

He shot upright like a pinball, clicked the television
off, and trotted out of the room back to his

drawing table.
He felt terrific. Like a bat out of Hell.
Had he remained a second longer – he would have
witnessed Dot's glow fade and disappear with the
cooling of the television-tube.

Seven hours later, dawn was peeking through the
blinds when Jack Coal, drenched in sweat, finished
the last panel of the fifth and final strip.
The bursts of creativity had surged through his veins
so violently that he hadn't even had the time to wet a
brush; he'd sketched-in the entire job with one fine-
pointed quill-pen. *Like that Schulz fellow.*
He looked down, surveyed his work, and smiled
ecstatically. The idea had bludgeoned him like
a bag of wet sand.
And it'd been right there...under his nose...
the whole time.
In fact, it'd been there for years.
He'd just been too dumb to see it.
'*Dotty and Me*'
The misadventures of aging ex-teenage sweethearts
and their newborn son, trying to climb the ladder of
success in the big, cruel city.
But Jack Coal had *flipped* the roles. Junior was the
brains of the operation. The parents thought and
behaved like *children.*
Jack Coal smiled again, trembling in awe of his
own genius.
It had pathos, nerve, ingenuity, and laughs galore.
He *knew* this was a winner.
This meant money. *Bushmiller money.* A Packard of
his own. Dot would finally have that saltbox in New
Milford. A gigantic Jacobean dinner table to serve he
and Li'l Jackie pot roast on. A new mink.
Ten new minks, and some foxes to keep 'em company!
A big, fat, colored mammy for Junior.
He'd even throw in a cute little red Nash-Healy so Dot

could zip around, antiquing on weekends.
Jack Coal packaged the strips for mailing and danced
out the door for the post office. He hadn't slept a wink
– but he wasn't tired at all.
In fact, he'd never felt more awake.
Or less hungry.

THE apartment was filled with flavored steam. Tatiana was almost done preparing dinner when her husband arrived home with a strange young man in tow.

The stranger was tall and lean, in a broad-shouldered athletic fashion; but his bright red flattop, heavily freckled features, and green plaid sports coat all served to endow him with a menacing – almost freakish – appearance.

Wally, visibly inebriated, squinted, slapped the stranger on the back, and flicked a taut, translucent palm out towards his wife.

"Tats...this is Archie Andrews! Arch...this is Tatiana! Get used to each other. From now on...you two are gonna be great pals! Tats, Arch is staying for supper!"

Tatiana frowned involuntarily but recovered with a quick smirk. She untied her yellow apron and touched her hair.

"Ok, Wally...that's so nice of you! A little notice would have been-"
The red-headed stranger raised both palms above his head in the surrender-gesture.
"Hey Wally...I think I'll just go have a sandwich at the Blarney. I don't wanna put you out or nothing."
Wally threw a fake one-two at Archie's jaw and then actually slapped him with three – albeit lightly and with a smile.
"Are you fucking kidding me? You're staying right the fuck here if you know what's good for you!"
The stranger sighed and shook his head.
"I just...I just don't wanna intrude..."
Tatiana spoke up.
"Mister Archie, you sit down right now and make it snappy! I have a broil in the oven that will be more than enough for all of us. Rembrandt here usually eats like the little baby sparrow anyway!"
Wally Good laughed and kissed his wife's cheek sloppily.
"Who needs solids when there's whisky?"
The Good's second-hand television-set picked up nothing but snow, so the boys listened to rhythm and blues on a negro station while they primed themselves for dinner with whisky and cigarettes. They tossed nickels at pedestrians through the open window while Tatiana prepared the settings on the kidney-shaped coffee table with pink paper napkins left over from New Year's and a tallow-colored safety candle stuck in the mouth of an empty, wicker-wrapped Chianti bottle. They ate with the large chipped plates balanced on their laps.
Archie Andrews spoke through a mouthful of beef.
"Gee. This is swell, Mrs. Good. *Really swell!* I haven't had a real home-cooked London broil since I left for the service. Didn't realize how much I missed it!"
Tatiana shook her head.
"It's not enough salt, is it? Ever since the war ended,

I'm still not using enough salt. In anything..."

"No, no! It's *great,* Mrs. Good. *Really swell!*"

Archie piled on three extra forkfuls in rapid succession to support his claim.

Wally chortled and slivers of food spewed forth in a small cloud, like the shrapnel of a miniature grenade.

"Misses Good, MY ASS. That's TATS to you, buddy!"

Tatiana smiled and wiped at her thin, closed lips with the point of a napkin corner.

"Yes, please. Tatiana...or Tats..."

Wally leaned across the table and poured more Four Roses over the shrunken ice in Archie's tumbler before tending to his own and then his wife's.

"Yes, sir. Tats here is my only souvenir of good old Deutschland, and I couldn't have brought back a better one!"

Archie Andrews smiled warmly.

"I thought I heard a slight accent."

Tatiana laughed and waved a finger.

"You are making fun. Not nice!"

Archie rolled his eyes around in their sockets like a loop-the-loop and stuck his fat red tongue out.

"Me? Kid you? Never!"

"Yes, I am from Germany. This man in a uniform was irresistible to me...so *handsome!*"

"This was during the war?"

"No, no. '48, when I was with the Paratroops, stationed outside Berlin. I was in Japan too, before that. The War, I spent with the Merchant Marine."

"Aha. Wise choice. But why join the Army after it's all over?"

Wally Good squinted and shrugged.

"Eh, I didn't know what fuck all to do with myself. I'd seen the world. What was I gonna do, go back to Minnesota? Pump gas? Deliver mail? No, thank you..."

"Minnesota? Duluth? Saint Paul?"

"Nah. Not even close. That wouldn't have been so bad. No. Way, way up there. Coal country."

"Your family were miners?"

"Nah, my pop's a lumberjack. Runs a big camp."

Tatiana frowned at her husband.

"Wally, you told me your father is dead."

"To me he is."

Wally gave Tatiana a stern look and then smiled at Archie.

"What was your war like, Arch?"

Archie grinned and shrugged.

"It was rough. *Real rough.* Spent the whole stint in San Diego!"

Wally plucked a thin slab of broil from the serving-plate and flung it at Archie's forehead. It landed flush against its freckled target, and stayed glued in place. Everybody laughed.

As Archie lifted a broad right hand to peel the meat off, Tatiana noticed an oversized brass ring on its third finger. The ring was crudely cast, with coarsely ridged edges. In the center was a skull and crossbones. The skull's eyes were dots of bright crimson enamel. Tatiana pointed.

"That *ring*...where did you get that, Mister Andrews? What does it mean?"

Wally squinted at the ring as Archie held it out towards him with a balled-up fist.

"Ah, *Tats.* That's just some stupid jarhead shit. All these dumb meatballs have 'em!"

Archie Andrews scoffed at Wally Good and stuck his finger into his wide mouth for lubrication. With some difficulty, he wriggled the ring loose over his knuckles and lobbed it onto the coffee table. It landed with a sharp crack next to a wooden salad bowl filled with ridged potato chips. Tatiana picked up the ring and studied it at different angles by the candle-flame. Archie smiled.

"Nah, Goody. It's nothing leathernecky like that. I broke my ankle when my jeep rolled over in a ditch. After a couple weeks in the hospital, I got a week's

liberty to visit my folks in Riverdale. At the bus station, I said *fuck it* and went down to TJ instead. I bought that thing from an old Injun broad on a sidewalk with a couple pesos I won at a cockfight. Talked her down from five. Romantic story, eh?"
Wally yanked Tatiana's thin wrist towards him and examined the ring again.
"Hmmmn. You know...it kinda looks like the crap they hawk in the back of comic books? Johnson-Smith?"
Wally released Tatiana's wrist, refilled Archie's tumbler, and then his own. Tatiana continued to stare at the skull on the ring – transfixed; losing herself to the void.
Archie held up the back of his right hand and pointed to the verdigris halo on his ring finger.
"*Bingo!* Same fucking thing! 100% guaranteed to turn your mitts green!"
Wally squinted, chuckled, and shook out two Camels.
Tatiana hadn't seen a ring like that for many, many years.
Her mind drifted back to the old country.
Back to her childhood home.
Back to *Peter.*
He was a bookkeeper in her father's accounting firm.
Peter and his handsome, almost-imperceptible leer.
Every day at noon, Tatiana's mother brought her along to deliver her father's bagged lunch. Peter was always there, working in his dark corner, wearing a visor and sleeve-protectors. He'd stare at Tatiana from the corners of his eyes. Every time she'd glance in his direction – there he'd be – staring. Always staring. It was not a friendly stare. It was a hungry stare.
After a moment or two of eye-contact, the left side of Peter's taut mouth would bend upwards, ever-so-slightly. He'd maintain his secret grin until Tatiana would turn away with fright.
She used to loathe those trips to her father's office.
After a series of abnormally-intense, tear-drenched

*tantrums, her mother finally ceased insisting that
Tatiana accompany her to the office. Several months
passed, and she began to forget all about Peter, his dark
corner, and his leer.*

Then, one evening, the doorbell rang.

It was him.

*He had some documents that required Herr Weinberg's
urgent attention. He smiled at Tatiana hungrily.*

A week later, he was back.

*Soon, Peter realized that answering the door was
Tatiana's exclusive chore, and his evening arrivals
became a regular occurrence. There was always some
matter that needed immediate attention. Sometimes,
he wouldn't even bother bringing any papers at all –
delivering only the thinnest excuses.*

*When Tatiana finally complained directly to her father,
he p'shawed her discomfort as the product of a little girl's
romanticism gone wild.*

*"I cannot blame you, my daughter. Herr Jäger is a very
handsome man. But please do not concern me with such
womanly foolishness...these are matters to discuss with
your sister and your mother."*

He never touched her; nor said an impolite word.

Peter simply smiled.

Eventually, Tatiana began to smile back.

*Two years later, some grave accounting errors were
uncovered, and Herr Weinberg was forced to terminate
Peter's employment. Tatiana remembered her father
robotically describing the acrid language Peter had
spewed upon his exit – the words tainting a very nice
roast chicken dinner their maid Frida had spent three
hours preparing.*

*"He knocked his desk over. The papers went flying
everywhere, like a bomb had detonated! Then, he pointed
at me from across the room and called me a 'Diseased,
blood-sucking Jewish vampire'. He told me that he had
been nothing but the most devoted employee that a man
could ask for, despite the slave-wages I provided which*

*forced him to live in squalor. It was most unfortunate.
Most unfortunate! And very undignified. It was very sad
to see him so upset. I thought of him...almost as a son.
I don't think he truly meant those words. He couldn't
have. I believe that Herr Jäger will return and apologize
eventually..."*

*Tatiana's mother waited for Frida to clear the plates from
the table before speaking.*

*"Hans, do you truly believe Peter embezzled this money
that is unaccounted for?"*

*Herr Weinberg stroked at his neatly-trimmed grey beard
as he thought, coaxing the tip into a blunt, bullet-
like point.*

*"My dear, I do not know. I'd like to think that he didn't.
I want to believe that within the breast of every man
beats a good heart. But the fact of the matter is that I am
running a business. Whether the money was stolen – or
whether it was just an honest mistake – does not concern
me. The bottom line is that one cannot afford to let these
things occur without taking measures. You will note that I
did not call the police, as was my right."*

"I did note that. That was kind of you, Hans."

"Well, as I said, he was like a son to me."

That night – Tatiana cried herself to sleep.

*One evening, in 1938, Peter did return. He was more
handsome than ever, donned in the black uniform of
an SS captain, and behind him stood a charge of five
underlings. Herr Weinberg invited the men inside while
Tatiana's mother went to the kitchen to prepare coffee
(their darling Frida had been released years earlier, it
having been declared illegal for Jews to employ Gentiles.)
Tatiana and Shoshana were sent to their bedroom while
Peter and his men talked business at the dining room
table with Herr and Frau Weinberg.*

*She left the night-table lamp on as she laid across her
feather-bed, watching her younger sister busy herself
with a tea party for dolls.*

When a gentle knocking at the door awakened her an hour later, she noticed that Shoshana had fallen asleep on the floor, her toy duckling clutched tightly against her throat. Shoshana and the duckling wore identical half-smiles.

Peter held a black-leather finger up to his pursed lips as he entered the room, and dimmed the lamp. He removed his hat, gauntlets, and tunic, tossing them onto the featherbed. Then, he unbuttoned his blouson.

Tatiana stared at the coarse black hair that bristled across the hardened muscles of Peter's chest, and looked up into his cold blue eyes. There were tiny drops of blood suspended on his brows and lashes, as if they'd been sprayed there. Tatiana's vagina immediately warmed and moistened, and she felt an unusual, tingling stir in her nipples. As Peter loosened the straps of her silk nightgown with flicks of his index fingers, Tatiana noticed a ring on his right hand. There was a Death's Head on it. She gently touched the ring with a fingertip, and then kissed it.

"You like that, do you?"

Tatiana nodded. Peter smiled.

"I am the Angel of Death now."

As Peter unhitched the eagle-emblazoned, silver buckle of his belt, Tatiana looked down to Shoshana, sleeping on the floor.

"Kill her first, Peter."

Peter glanced at Shoshana and shrugged indifferently.

"But why? That is your sister...don't you love her?"

Tatiana shook her head and sighed.

"Does that matter?"

Peter smiled as he unlatched the Luger from his holster and handed it to her. It was heavy.

"Then you must do it."

Wally shook Tatiana's arm again.

"Babe! Are you listening? *Yes or no?*"

"I'm sorry, Wally...what was it?"

"I said: I forgot to tell you, the Coals invited us over

for dinner Tuesday. That alright with you?"
Tatiana stared at Wally Good blankly.
"*'The Colds'*? Who are the Colds?"
"Eh. Some old goon I work with and his creepy wife. I
didn't wanna be rude, so I said 'Yeah'."
Tatiana nodded.
"Sure, Wally...sure. It will be nice to be social."
Tatiana glanced around the room.
"Wally – where is your friend?"
Wally Good squinted and shrugged as he drunkenly
fumbled with the cellophane on a new pack of Camels.
"Dunno. I gave him five bucks to pick up some reefers
around the corner. That was over an hour ago."

LESTER had been very happy to see Cornell and the fat man quickly become such great friends, and soon, the trio had formed something of a family unit.

The fat man, so pleased to have companions again – even if they *were* colored – had been very generous with the brothers. He'd paid off their delinquent utility-bills; purchased them a brand new Westinghouse television set; outfitted both with three tailored suits apiece (each suit complete with an extra pair of trousers); and treated them to a plethora of nights on the town.

He'd even taken them to Jack Dempsey's famous Broadway restaurant, where Lester had shaken hands with the old champion as he cheerfully greeted customers by the front door.

"Why, you're quite the dapper little chap, aren't you now?"

"Yes, sir."

"And what're you gonna have tonight? We got a swell Porterhouse here! You like steaks, boy?"

"No, sir. I like catfish."
Jack Dempsey grinned widely and winked at Cornell
and the fat man.
"Well, I'm sorry, son. We don't serve no catfish here!"
Lester frowned and looked down at his gleaming new
patent-leather shoes.
He didn't like being patronized by this stupid, smiling,
white fool; no matter how big he was.
*"How about I let you sock me one instead to make up
for it?"*
Jack Dempsey put his hands on his hips like
Superman, smiled, and stuck out his pot-belly as a
target.
He nodded.
"Ok, boy. Do your worst!"
Lester furrowed his brow, planted his feet, and – with
all of his might – walloped Jack Dempsey squarely in
the testicles with his right fist.
The great champion dropped to his knees and stared
at Lester with dismay for longer than a ten-count.

IT took every ounce of reserve that Jack Coal could muster to keep mum about 'Dotty and Me' around his wife.

Only the fear of the Great Mystic Jinx prevented him from breaking down. That, and the consideration that any shocks – even happy ones – might be detrimental to a woman in her condition. Internally though, to say that Jack Coal was floating on Cloud Nine would have been an accurate statement.

The doorbell rang.

"JACK! Can you get that? I'm still doing my face!"

Jack Coal opened the front door to find Wally Good standing by himself, squinting as he sucked at a bent cigarette.

He was wearing the same plaid flannel shirt beneath the same greasy leather jacket above the same ink-stained dungarees over the same scuffed cowboy boots that he seemed to wear every day. His guitar hung by its frayed twine strap over his right shoulder. *At least he combed his hair,* thought Jack Coal to himself. *And at least he shaved.* The idea of Dot's imminent dismay both displeased and amused him. There was a large paper sack in Wally Good's hands. He thrust it forward and squinted at Jack Coal blankly. Jack Coal accepted the sack. It was heavy.

"Why, *hello,* Wally ol' chap! What's *this?*"

Still blocking the doorway, Jack Coal leaned over into the hallway and peered down both sides of the corridor. They were empty.

Wally Good shrugged.

"Just me. Tats isn't coming. That's kugel. She made it."

Jack Coal nodded and frowned.

"Oh, that's a darn *shame.* Dot was really looking forward to some good, old-fashioned girl-talk. You know how these hens *love* to squawk!"

He winked at Wally, who squinted and dropped his cigarette onto the doormat.

Jack Coal still blocked the threshold.

He smiled.

"So, what's 'kugel'?"

Wally Good shrugged.

"I dunno."

Wally Good put his head down and walked through Jack Coal into the apartment.

Jack Coal stepped on the smoldering cigarette, sniffed at it, and discreetly pocketed it before following Wally in.

He recognized the scent immediately.

Dickie had smoked Camels too.

Dot stood waiting in the living room, wearing a strapless, black satin dress that Jack Coal had never noticed before.

Must be new.

It was extremely tight-fitting for a woman in her condition.

He thought about whispering something to her, but

she was still keeping the big news a secret from him.
He smiled to himself as he thought about all the fun
she must be having with that.

They both had secrets.

She must be bursting at the seams!

He rubbed his palms together as if he were trying to
warm them.

"So...I believe you two may've met in passing at
the studio the other day, but let's make this *official*.
Dorothy, this is *Wallace Good*, the young man I've told
you so much about recently."

Dot nodded once towards her guest.

"It's *very* nice to meet you, Wallace. I've heard
nothing but good things from Jack about your work,
which is very high praise indeed. When it comes
to compliments, his lips are usually tighter than a
Scotchman's purse-strings."

Jack Coal fidgeted and shot Dot a hurt glance.

"Now that's just *not so*, Hon! I compliment you all the
time. In fact, I was just thinking to myself that you've
never looked lovelier in your life. You look radiant.
Almost *glowing!*"

Dot laid a hand on her husband's shoulder and
pecked him on the cheek.

"Relax, Dear...I'm just teasing."

Dot turned towards Wally Good.

"I take it all back, Wallace. This dreamboat here is the
best hunk of husband in the history of all-mankind."

Wally methodically chipped away at his Yankee pot
roast, whipped potatoes, and parsnips as Jack Coal
and Dot watched him.

Like vultures, he thought.

He squinted at the couple, and forced a small, close-
mouthed smile.

"This is very good chow, Mrs. Coal. Swell. First-rate
stuff."

"Thank you, Wallace."

"Please. It's Wally. Or Goody."

Dot smiled.

"Thank you, *Wally*. Ol' Jack here *loves* my pot roast..."

Jack Coal held up his fork and waved it like a flag.

"Guilty!"

"Which one look at his waistline should make *plainly* obvious."

Wally nodded uncomfortably and dropped his eyes to his plate before he could accidentally catch Jack Coal's reaction.

As he chewed the beef, he wondered to himself if twenty years of marriage would turn his sweet, loving Tatiana into a heartless bitch too. *I hope not,* he thought, *but it's probably inevitable.*

"So...Jack says you're married. Where's your wife tonight? I was *so* looking forward to meeting her. She's German, if I understand correctly?"

Wally Good cleared his throat and answered without looking up.

"German, yeah. She teaches a dance class Tuesday nights. Couldn't miss it. She sends her regrets."

Dot clapped once loudly.

"Oh! I simply *adore* dancing! Ol' Jack here and I used to cut the rug at least two nights a week when we were kids. We were a couple of regular jitterbuggers..."

"Ah...well...this is nothing like that. Not really. It's folk-dancing."

Dot tilted her head.

"I'm sorry? *'Folk-dancing'?*"

Wally wiped at his mouth with a linen napkin and carefully placed it back onto his lap.

"Yeah. Yes. Like...ethnic dancing. Y'know, like dances from all around the world. But mostly from Europe. And some Western-style stuff."

"*Western*-style? Do you mean like square dancing?"

"Yeah, pretty much. That's actually how we met. At a square dance at in Germany. We had 'em on base Saturday nights. Lots of yahoos in the Army."

"Oh! How lovely!"
Dot turned towards her husband.
"Can you *imagine* that? *A square dance in Germany?"*
Jack Coal pondered the thought for a moment, and
shook his head.
"Nope, I never would've thunk it. Did they use
accordions instead of banjos?"
Wally Good squinted.
"Yeah. Y'know...I guess they *did*. Funny...never
thought about that."
"Well, my father played the spoons at a heck of a lot of
square dances! Had his own jug outfit and everything.
'The Olde King Coal Band.' I wonder if that kind of
talent runs in families?"
Jack Coal picked up his soup and dessert spoons,
thwacked them together against his left palm, then
frowned comically.
"Aw *nuts*...must skip a generation!"
Jack Coal winked at Dot, who turned away, mortified.
Wally Good forced another smile.
"I dunno. Maybe. I guess so. Mind if I smoke?"
Jack Coal glanced towards Dot, who strongly
disapproved of smoking. He died a little as she smiled
and nodded. She pushed her chair back and stood up.
"Of *course*, Wally! Go ahead. Here. Let me just grab
something for your ashes, ok?"
Dot returned with a small blue teacup for Wally; but
also an opened bottle of red wine and two of their best
crystal glasses.
Jack Coal stared at the bottle in disbelief. *Didn't she
know better?* Maybe she'd forgotten? A little drop
wouldn't hurt, but he'd have to talk to her about this
later – when things were finally out in the open. Some
cutting-back was in due order. The last thing they
needed was a pinhead for a child.
As Dot filled the glasses and handed one to Wally, he
looked towards Jack Coal and squinted.
"What about you?"

Dot cackled.

"Aw, don't worry about him...ol' Jack here doesn't *indulge*."

Jack Coal lifted his right index finger.

"Just this *once*...I think I will. After all it's a special occasion. *We* are in the presence of a great artist."

Jack Coal pushed his chair back and stood.

"Dot, you stay put. I'll get my own glass."

Dot Coal sighed, shook her head, and gestured feebly at her husband.

"Sit down, Jack. I'll get it."

As Dot lumbered back to the kitchen, Jack Coal made eye-contact with Wally Good and winked.

"Wally, would you play a little something for Dotty and me after dessert? It's been so long since we've been serenaded."

Wally Good squinted at the ceiling and thought about Dot's breasts.

He was certain she'd been making eyes at him throughout dinner.

They were nice tits. Big. He wondered how low they'd hang unstrapped. He wondered if she liked to get her hair pulled.

Wally lowered his squint to Jack Coal and smiled sympathetically. He studied the rolling map of lines and creases that covered the long, tired, jowly face.

He lit a Camel and filled his lungs with smoke.

"Yeah...I guess I could."

SENATOR Kefauver stood and surveyed the room for a long moment. He cleared his throat, rapped his small wooden gavel, and began to speak.

"This meeting of the Senate Subcommittee Investigating Juvenile Delinquency will now be in order. Today and tomorrow, the United States Senate Subcommittee Investigating Juvenile Delinquency, of which I am the chairman, is going into the problem of horror and crime comic books. By comic books, we mean pamphlets illustrating stories depicting crimes or dealing with horror and sadism. We shall *not* be talking about the predominantly-wholesome comic *strips* that appear daily in most of our newspapers.

And we shall be limiting our investigation to those comic books dealing with *crime* and *horror*. Thus, while there are more than a billion comic books sold in the United States each year, our Subcommittee's focus is within only a fraction of this publishing field."

Millard Gaines sat on a bench in the back of the room, sucking black coffee from a paper carton while the speaker rattled on in his slow, deliberate, boring Southern drawl.

He'd run out of Dexedrine two afternoons earlier and he was nearing a state of complete emotional, intellectual, and physical ruin.

He felt like a putrefied, walking corpse.

He'd been horrified to see the two large, boxy orthicon-cameras present in the courtroom, and silently prayed to himself that these were solely for documentation purposes.

"Authorities agree that the majority of comic books are as harmless as soda-pop. But hundreds of thousands of horror and crime comic books are peddled to our young ones of impressionable age. Some of the types of crime and horror comic books with which we are concerned have been brought into the hearing room for your attention. I wish to state emphatically that freedom of the press is *not* an issue in this investigation. The members of this Senate Subcommittee, Senator Hannoch, Senator Hennings, and myself as chairman, are fully aware of the long, hard, bitter fight that has been waged to achieve and preserve the freedom of the press, as well as the other freedoms in our Bill of Rights which we so cherish here in America. We are *not* a Subcommittee of blue-nosed censors. We have no preconceived notions as to the possible need for new legislation. We simply want to find out what damage, *if any*, is being done to our children's minds by certain types of publications which contain a substantial degree of sadism, crime, and horror. This, and *only* this, is the task at hand."

A photographer's flashbulb exploded prematurely, setting his tweed suit ablaze. A ten-minute recess was called while paramedics arrived and removed the prostrate man, whose face and hands were blistered and blackened. Afterwards, Senator Kefauver resumed his introductory speech with a crooked tie and soiled collar, stopping occasionally to slap at the buzzing horse-fly that had somehow found its way into the windowless room.

"Since last November, the Subcommittee has been holding many public hearings into the various facets of the whole problem of juvenile delinquency. The volume of delinquency among our young has been quite correctly called the *shame* of America. If the rising tide of juvenile delinquency continues – by 1960 – more than one and a half million American youngsters from ten through seventeen years of age will be in trouble with the law each year. Our Subcommittee is seeking honestly and earnestly to determine *why* so many young Americans are unable to adjust themselves into the lawful pattern of American Society. We are examining the *reason why* more and more of our youngsters steal automobiles, turn to vandalism, commit hold-ups, or become narcotic addicts. The increase in craven crime committed by young Americans is rising at a frightening pace. We know that the great mass of our American children are *not* lawbreakers. Even the majority of those who get into trouble with our laws are not criminal by nature. Nevertheless – more and more of our children are committing serious crimes. Our Subcommittee is working diligently to seek out ways and means to check the trend and reverse the youth crime pattern. We are perfectly aware that there is no simple solution to the complex problem of juvenile delinquency. We know, too, that what makes the problem so complex is its great variety of causes and contributing factors. Our work is to

study all these causes and contributing factors and
to determine what actions might be taken. It would
be wrong to *assume* that crime and horror comic
books are the major cause of juvenile delinquency.
It would be *just* as erroneous to state categorically
that they have *no* effect whatsoever in aggravating
the problem. We are here to determine what effect
on the whole problem of causation crime and horror
comic books *do* have. From the mail that we received,
we are aware that thousands of American parents
are greatly concerned about the possible detrimental
influence certain types of crime and horror comic
books have upon their children. We firmly believe
that the public has a *right* to the best knowledge
regarding this matter. The public has the *right* to know
who is producing this material and to know *how* the
industry functions. This phase of our investigation is
but the first of several into questionable, or, should
I say, *disturbing* phases of the mass-media fields. At
a later date, the Subcommittee will be attempting
to determine what negative effects – *if any* – upon
children, are exerted by other types of publications,
by the radio, the television, and the movies. This
is not to say that juvenile delinquency is wholly or
even substantially the result of certain programs
and subject matters presented by the mass-media.
But there can be *no* question that the media plays a
significant role in the total problem. I will now ask the
assistant counsel to call the first witness."
Millard Gaines inhaled the courtroom air deeply.
It tasted tinny. Like stale, weak tea cooked in a
scorched copper kettle.
He shook his head.
This fucking sucks.

Jᴏʜɴ ᴊᴜsᴛ sᴛᴏᴏᴅ ᴛʜᴇʀᴇ, ᴡᴀᴛᴄʜɪɴɢ ᴛʜᴇ ᴘʟᴀʏɢʀᴏᴜɴᴅ ᴇᴍᴘᴛʏ ᴏᴜᴛ ᴀʙᴏᴜᴛ ʜɪᴍ! ʜᴇ sᴛᴏᴏᴅ ᴛʜᴇʀᴇ - ꜰᴇᴇʟɪɴɢ sᴏᴍᴇ- ᴛʜɪɴɢ ɪɴ ʜɪs ᴘᴀsᴛ ʀᴇᴛᴜʀɴɪɴɢ - ʀᴇᴛᴜʀɴɪɴɢ ɪɴ ᴀʟʟ ɪᴛs ᴍɪsᴇʀʏ! ʜᴇ sᴛᴏᴏᴅ ᴛʜᴇʀᴇ - ᴀʟᴏɴᴇ - ᴀɴᴅ ʙᴇɢᴀɴ ᴛᴏ ᴡʜɪᴍᴘᴇʀ...

A pimply-faced Western Union boy rapped against the textured, opaque glass door of the Meiser Studio and asked for Mr. John Coal.

Jack Coal tipped the youth a dime and stared at the unopened envelope dolefully.

He'd received only two telegrams since leaving Pennsylvania. One had informed him of the death of Ralph the Sheepdog – the other heralded the passing of his father. If Western Union was not the Angel of Death, it was certainly the Messenger of Doom.

Jack Coal exited the studio and carried the telegram to the tiny water-closet the entire floor shared at the end of the hallway. He didn't want to cry about his mother in front of all the boys.

He locked the door behind him and decided to stare at the graffiti on the walls until he'd worked up the nerve to face the bad news. There was certainly a lot of it.

'Leonore Silvian puts out for coke call MU8-3634.' 'I LIKE KIKE!' 'Dull jack coal mulled the pole of a foal.'

'Helen Gahagan Douglas just LOVES the negro people!'
Jack Coal shook his head.
Above the toilet was a large drawing of Christine
Jorgensen and the Apparition – both naked – laughing
– and deep within the act of fornication. On a shelf
in the background, a penis and testicles floated in a
mason jar. Although the obscenity was clearly signed
'Will Meiser', Jack Coal had little doubt that it was
actually drawn by one of the boys from the shop. He
shook his head again. It was a crude joke at best, but
it made him smile.
He looked at the envelope and sighed.
Using the dinged, old pewter penknife he'd purchased
in Los Angeles all those years ago, he carefully slit the
thin, waxy envelope open and held it beneath the bare
hanging yellow bulb with quivering fingers.
-DEAR-MR.COAL-stop-DOTTY-AND-ME-ACCEPTED-
stop-READY-TO-MOVE-FORWARD-stop-PLEASE-
DELIVER-SIX-WEEKS-OF-DAILIES-AT-EARLIEST-
CONVENIENCE-stop-EXPECT-STANDARD-CONTRACT-
IN-MAIL-SOON-stop-WARD-GREENE-stop-KING-
FEATURES-SYNDICATE-stop-

Jack Coal spent the next twenty minutes in the tiny
bathroom;
re-reading the telegram over five hundred times.
He'd doused his face with cold water from the grime-
encrusted porcelain sink, and then re-read the
telegram another five hundred times.
Then, he'd slapped himself.
Then, he'd slapped himself again.
Jack Coal looked down at the black and white tiled
floor.
It was thickly-slathered with dried urine that
hundreds of insects had floundered, perished, and
crystallized in.
He looked at the brown, split-creased old Florsheims
on his feet and smiled.

Soon, those would be shell cordovan J.M. Westons.
As one final reality check, he bumped his forehead
against the cracked plaster wall. While he'd meant
to do this very lightly, he'd miscalculated his own
nervous strength and splintered the glass in both of
his spectacle-lenses.
He laughed at his reflection in the rubbed little mirror
above the sink.
Jack Coal looked like a mad genius.
As he danced back down the hallway, he summoned
his best somber face, and readied himself to pull what
would certainly be a major coup of a gag.
All those busybodies would surely be aching to know
what that telegram business was all about.
Well, he'd give them a good show.
He'd tell them his mother *had* died; raped and
murdered by a drunken Polack; he'd make a real, long
sob-story out of it – then wait for their faces to drop.
Only then would he spring the good news on them.
He could hear their laughs and well-wishes already.
He could feel their hard, jealousy-tinged slaps on his
shoulder-blades. He could see the proud, fatherly
tears well-up in Will Meiser's eyes.
He was the man of the hour.
He stopped and briefly pondered buying a box of
Cuban cigars in the lobby first, then dismissed the
notion. The joint was smoky enough.
He opened the door.
To Jack Coal's astonishment and horror, the shop was
nearly empty. All of the tables were unmanned, aside
from Bert Meskin's.
Bert smiled dopily as Jack Coal handed him the
telegram.
"I-I-I-I-I'm j-just g-g-g-glad your m-m-m-mother's
n-n-n-not d-d-d-dead, J-J-Jack."
The ding of a typewriter bell clanged from Will
Meiser's office and Jack Coal went to investigate.
A fat, gum-chewing brunette looked up from her

station at his confused face.

"Edna, where the heck IS everybody?"

She shrugged, cracked her gum, and began pounding the keys again.

"Aw, they all went down to a bar to watch Mister Meiser testify in court. Or somethin' like that. It's on the teevee. You can go join 'em too. I won't say nothin'..."

"Court? *TV?* What's that all about?"

The secretary shrugged and continued pounding.

"I dunno. Nobody tells *me* nothin' around here..."

Jack Coal stood over Edna for a while, deflated.

The bell rang nine more times.

Finally, he nodded and turned to leave.

Edna stopped typing.

"Mister Coal, you sure you can see through them broken specs? Maybe you should go home and get your spares first, huh?"

Jack Coal looked at Edna. There were ninety six of her.

He nodded.

"Good idea."

THE WOLFHOUND SENSING HIS MASTER'S DANGER BE-CAME AS MURDEROUS AS DINKY! WITH SCREAMS AND HOWLS THE TWO BEASTS ROLLED ALL OVER THE CANVAS.. BITING, TEARING...

WOOOLFFF! GROOOWW! ARRR! GRRRR!

AS much as the fat man now belonged to Cornell - Stella now belonged to Lester.

Every day, he would feed her, rub her, brush her, walk her, and take her to the park to kill the rats.

Lester would clap with glee as Stella snarled, snapped, sheared, and savaged in the billowing clouds of rolling brown dust.

On several occasions, the fat man had even let Stella stay overnight at Perry Street; where she'd slept curled-up and nuzzled against Lester in his army surplus cot.

Eventually, the fat man made the obvious decision and allowed Stella to stay over every night – telling himself that Butch too would've agreed it was for the best.

Now, Lester and Stella were tired.

They'd spent the entire morning scouring the newsstands of Lower Manhattan in a futile search for the new issue of *Weird Tales of the Future,* and they turned onto Perry Street weary, cold, and defeated.

Beneath Lester's right arm was a sackful of pale substitutes – mostly with titles that he'd never even heard of before.

Worlds of Fear, Asphyxiation, Ghostly Weird, Terrors of the Jungle, Tormention, March of Crime, Secrets of the Demented, and *Thrilling Death.*

There was *one* promising contender in the lot – a new comic called *Lawbreakers Suspense Stories.* Its cover featured a buxom redhead in only a thin lace nightgown cowering from a bearded hobo in a dark, cob-webbed attic. The tramp brandished a large hunting-knife in one hand and a pile of severed tongues in the other. He leered at the redhead as he whispered to her.

"I know you're a mute, Miss Kimberly, but even if you could yell, the people downstairs couldn't call the police. You see … I already cut their tongues out!"

Lester rolled up the comic book and hid it in the back pocket of his dungarees. Cornell had seen a television news-program about the evil of comic books and had begun to scrutinize his reading material. The other books were expendable, but he couldn't risk losing this one good find.

Halfway up the staircase, Stella began growling and tugging at her lead. She surged forward, choking herself as Lester tried to keep pace.

"Dang, what's wrong, boy? Why you in such a rush? Ain't no rats up there!"

The pair ran up the stairs as fast as their six legs would carry them.

When they reached the third floor, Stella scratched frantically at the door to Cornell's apartment, leaving deep claw marks in the thick green paint. Lester, who wore his key on a ball-chain around his neck, unlocked the door as quickly as he could, and Stella burst forward, forcing the door open with her tiny head with the key still in the lock, choking Lester until he finally relinquished her lead.

Lester was still re-latching the lock behind him when he heard the fat man's screams.

"Get her off! Get her OFF! Oh no, no, NO!"

He rushed into the other room.

Cornell, naked except for a gleaming white singlet, stood upright in wide-eyed shock. On his knees before him was the fat man, wearing a wine-colored suit. Stella had latched onto his floral necktie with her fangs, and was shaking at it violently.

"Please! Get her off! Get her off! She's killing me!"

It was when Lester bent over to grab Stella that his forehead slapped against Cornell's turgid penis. The shockingly-large erection was purplish, veiny, and slick with saliva.

Lester lifted Stella's hard little body and wrenched backwards with all of his might – yanking the fat man off of his knees – his face making a loud **SPLAT** as it kissed the hardwood floor.

Lester pulled at Stella again, lifting her above his head. The fat man's rayon tie finally gave with a loud shredding noise.

The fat man gasped for air as Stella shook the scrap triumphantly.

Cornell barked at Lester, his penis bobbing as he yelled.

"You just go for a walk right now, young man! Can't you see I have company here? You know damn well what the red shoelace on the doorknob means!"

Lester left without bothering to answer, wiping at his forehead, taking Stella along with him. He could hear the fat man's sobs through the front door as he looked for the shoelace, which was nowhere to be found.

Good, he SHOULD cry.

I hope he choke on that big ugly thing too.

Halfway up the stairs to the roof, Lester cursed at himself. He'd left the sack of new comics on the floor of the apartment.

Now, Cornell would *surely* throw them all away.

SENATOR Hennings – a grim man of fifty four with wide-set eyes and heavy shoulders – stared down from the long oak committee table at Millard Gaines with unmasked disgust.

He pointed at a screen onto which a comic page had been slide-projected.

"Mister Gaines, what do you have to say about *that?*"

Millard Gaines peered at the screen through his bifocals, and rubbed at his eyes behind them. Without the Dexedrine, everything seemed to be diffused with schmaltz, no matter how much he polished his lenses.

"Well…I'd say they got what they deserved."

Senator Hennings clucked his tongue.

"Is that one of *your* series, the pictures of the two in

the electric chair, the little girl down in the corner?"
Millard Gaines smiled weakly.
He was beginning to sweat.
"Yes."
"As we understood from Doctor Wertham's testimony,
the little girl is not being *put upon* there, is she? She's
triumphant. apparently…"
"Sir, if I may explain, the readers don't know that until
the last panel – which is one of the things we try to do
in our stories…to have an O.Henry ending for each
story. We take great *pride* in our writing."
The senator bounced his pencil against his lower lip a
few times before speaking.
Millard Gaines suspected that he was probably
thinking about how much he needed a cigarette. He
thought to himself that he could use one too.
"That's very *nice*, Mister Gaines, your *pride!* It's a very
noble thing to take *pride* in one's work. But back to the
slide…what would be your judgment, or conclusion,
as to the identification of the reader with that little
girl who has – to use the phrase – *'framed'* her mother
and shot her father?"
"Well, if you actually *read* the story…you'll see in
the first six or seven pages that the child leads a
miserable life. It's only on the last page she emerges
triumphant."
"So, what you're telling me is that a *result* of the
murder and perjury, she emerges as triumphant?"
Millard Gaines sucked in at his saliva.
It was mostly dry foam.
"That's right."
"And this is the *'O. Henry'* finish from which your *pride*
emanates?"
"Yes."
"So, in *other* words, everybody reading that would
think this girl would go to jail. So the 'O. Henry' finish
changes all that. Makes her a wonderful-looking girl?
Is *that* right?"

"But, no one knows she did it until the last panel..."
The senator tapped his pencil against his lip again.
"And...you think it does the readers a lot of *good* to
read these things?"
Millard Gaines shook his head.
"No, sir. I don't think it does them a *bit* of good; but I
don't think it does them a bit of *harm* either. It's just
a comic book story. It's escapism. Nothing more. Like
movies or television. It's not meant as an educational
tool. There *are* comic magazines that promote this,
but that particular comic is not one of them. It
provides stimulating entertainment, nothing more..."
The senator penciled a note on a yellow legal pad.
"*Stimulating.* Interesting choice of words. I agree with
the word, at least. It's precisely *what* is *stimulated* that
concerns us here."

A break was called for lunch.
Millard Gaines spent the recess in a lobby
phonebooth, trying in vain to locate a physician who
would phone-in a Dexedrine prescription to the
People's Drugs around the corner.
Finally, he abandoned his quest and called his office
instead, where he instructed Al Feldman to hire a
messenger to procure some benzedrine and rush it to
him double-quick.
The bennies worked.
Soon, Millard Gaines felt like a million bucks.
Unfortunately – when the Subcommittee reconvened –
Millard Gaines *looked* like a million bucks.
(Almost literally.)
The benzedrine, combined with his lack of sleep and
dexedrine-withdrawal, imbued his complexion with
an unmistakable waxy, catfish-green pallor.
The senators were genuinely appalled at the
publisher's morbid appearance, and stared in abject
silence as Millard Gaines read aloud from the typed
sheets of paper he'd removed from the textured,

walrus briefcase that'd once belonged to his father
(who'd shot the walrus personally.)
"Gentleman of the Senate, I am here as an individual
publisher. My name is Millard Godfrey Gaines.
My business address is Two Twenty Five Lafayette
Street, Manhattan, New York. I am a publisher of
the Exciting Comics Group. I am a graduate of the
school of education of New York University. I have the
qualifications to teach in secondary schools and high
schools."
Millard Gaines stopped to answer any questions that
might have arisen from such a statement. When none
were forthcoming, he proceeded.
"What then am I doing before this committee? Well,
I'll tell you. I'm a comic book publisher. My group
is known as EC, which is short for *Exciting Comics*.
I'm here as a voluntary witness. You didn't have to
subpoena me. None was necessary. I asked for and
was given this chance to be heard. Two decades ago,
my late father was instrumental in starting the comic
magazine industry. He was proud of the industry he
helped found. He was bringing enjoyment to millions
of people. The heritage he left is the vast comic book
industry – which employs thousands of writers,
artists, engravers, and printers. It's weaned hundreds
of thousands of children from pictures to the printed
word. In other words: it's taught them how to read.
It's stirred their imaginations and given them an
outlet for their problems and frustrations. But – *most
importantly* – it's given them millions of hours of
entertainment. My father was *proud* of the comics he
published. My father saw in the comic books, a vast
field of visual education. He was a *pioneer.* Sometimes,
he was ahead of his time. He published '*Picture Stories
from Science*', '*Picture Stories from World History*',
and '*Picture Stories from American History*'. He also
published '*Picture Stories from the Bible*'. I would like
to offer these as evidence."

Millard Gaines removed a short stack of comic books from his walrus briefcase and handed them to an armed bailiff in a crisp grey uniform.

Senator Kefauver rapped his gavel lightly.

"They will be received for the Subcommittee's permanent files. Let that be...exhibit *number 11*. You may proceed, sir..."

"Thank you. Since 1942, we've sold more than five million copies of *'Picture Stories from the Bible'* in the United States. It's widely used by churches and schools to make religion more real and vivid. *'Picture Stories from the Bible'* is published throughout the world in dozens of translations. But, it's still nothing *more* – nor nothing *less* – than a comic book magazine. I publish *other* comic magazines in addition to *'Picture stories from the Bible'*. For example, I publish *horror* comics. *I* was the first publisher in the United States to publish horror comics. *I* am responsible, *I* started them. Some may not like them. That's a matter of personal taste. It'd be just as difficult to explain the harmless thrill of a horror story to a Doctor Wertham as it'd be to explain the sublimity of love to a frigid old maid."

Millard Gaines coughed – not because his throat was itchy – or because he was congested. He coughed simply because he felt like it.

"My father was *proud* of the comics *he* published, and *I* am *proud* of the comics *I* publish. We use the best writers and the finest artists; we spare *nothing* to make each magazine, each story, each *page*, an honest-to-goodness *work of art*. As evidence of this, I might point out that we have the highest sales in individual distribution. I don't mean highest sales in comparison to comics of *another* type. I mean highest sales in comparison to other *horror* comics. The comic magazine is one of the few remaining pleasures that a person may buy for a dime today. *Pleasure* is what we sell. Entertainment. Reading enjoyment.

Entertaining reading has never harmed anyone. Men of good will – and free men everywhere – should be very *grateful* for one sentence in the statement made by Federal Judge John M. Woolsey when he historically lifted the ban on Joyce's *Ulysses*. Judge Woolsey said, '*It is only with the normal person that the law is concerned.*' May I repeat, he said, '*It is only with the normal person that the law is concerned!*' Our American children are, for the most part, *normal* children. They're *bright* children. But those who want to prohibit comic magazines seem to see them as dirty, sneaky, perverted little monsters who use the comics as a blueprint for action. But perverted little monsters are few and far between. They *don't* read comics, and the chances are most of them are in schools for retarded children anyway. *What are we afraid of?* Are we *afraid* of our own children? Do we forget that they are citizens, too, and *entitled* to select what to read or do? Or do we think our children are so stupid, evil, and *simple-minded* that it takes a story of robbery to set them to robbery? Mayor Jimmy Walker once remarked that he never knew a girl to be ruined by a book. Well...*nobody* has ever been ruined by a comic. The basic personality of a child is established before he reaches the age of comic book-reading. I don't believe anything that has *ever* been written can make a child over-aggressive or delinquent. The roots of such characteristics go much deeper. The *truth* is that delinquency is the product of *real* environment, in which the child *lives*, and not of the fiction he *reads*. There are many problems that reach our children today. They're tied-up with insecurity. No pill can cure them, no law will legislate them out of being. The problems are economic, and social, and they are *complex*. Our people need *understanding*. They need to have affection, decent homes, decent food. Gentlemen, distinguished senators of the Committee, once you start to censor, you must censor *everything*.

You must censor comic books, radio, television, and newspapers. Then, you must censor what people may *say* to each other. Then, you will have turned this country into Spain or Russia. *Thank you.*"
There was a period of silence as the senators stared at Millard Gaines. The only audible sounds were the squeaks of the television-cameras pivoting on their mounts, and the buzzing of the horse-fly.
The senators stared at him for a long time.
Millard Gaines began to feel a tremendous itch on the left side of his anal ring.
But there were cameras trained in his direction. It took everything he had not to scratch at it. He wondered if the Subcommittee knew the pain of hemorrhoid discomfort too.
Millard Gaines hoped that they did.
That was *real* horror.
Senator Kefauver cleared his throat.
"Mister Gaines, do you test these stories out on children?"
"Yes, sometimes..."
"And how do you do that?"
"Well, I hand them a comic book and say, '*Hey, kid. Read this and let me know what you think.*' Then, they let me know what they think."
"And do you sincerely think it does them a lot of *good* to read these things?"
"No, as I stated before, I don't think it does them a *bit* of good, but I don't think it does them a bit of *harm*, either."
"Do you have any children of your own, Mr. Gaines?"
"No, sir. None that I'm presently aware of."
"So...you test them out on children of your friends, do you?"
"Yes. And none have tried to stab me, or begun howling at full moons. Yet."
"Mister Gaines, let me get the limits as far as what you put into your magazine. Is the sole test of what you

would put into your magazine whether it *sells?* Is there *any* limit you can think of that you would *not* put in a magazine because you thought a child should *not* see or read about it?"

"No, I wouldn't say that there's any limit for the reason you outlined. My only limits are the bounds of good taste. What *I* consider good taste..."

"Then, you think a child cannot, in *any* way, shape, or manner, be hurt by anything that it reads or sees?"

"No, I don't believe so."

"So, there would be *no* limit actually to what you put in the magazines?"

"Only within the bounds of good taste."

"Your *own* good taste...and salability?"

"Yes."

Senator Kefauver held up a comic book with both hands.

"Mister Gaines, here is your May twenty second issue of *Tales from the Ditch*. This seems to be a man with a bloody axe holding a woman's head up, which has been severed from her body. Do you think *that's* in good taste?"

"Yes, sir, I do, for the cover of a *horror* comic. A cover in bad taste, for example, might be defined as holding the head a little higher so that the neck could be seen dripping blood from it, and perhaps moving the body over a little further so that the neck of the body could be seen to be bloody."

"But you have blood coming out of her mouth."

"Just a little. For effect..."

"And *here*, there's blood on the axe. I think most adults would be *shocked* by that!"

Senator Hennings interrupted before Millard Gaines could respond to the statement.

"Mister Chairman – if the counsel will bear with me – I don't think it's really the function of our committee to argue with this gentleman. I believe that he's given us about the sum and substance of his philosophy.

But I *would* like to ask you one final question, Mister Gaines. You said that you had a circulation of five million Bible storybooks."

"Yes..."

"Over *how* many years is this?"

"Eleven years, since 1942."

"In other words...in a little over three and a half months, you'll sell more of your crime and horror books than you've sold of the Bible stories in *eleven years?*"

"Yes, sir. Quite a bit more."

"Well, why do they seem to sell better?"

Millard Gaines shrugged and held up his palms like a fat, green, bespectacled Christ.

"I guess kids just don't want to read the Bible anymore. Is that my fault too?"

Millard Gaines collapsed onto the phonebooth stool and breathed heavily as he called his office collect. He was out of dimes.

Vera's nasally voice accepted the charges.

"Vera...I bombed."

"Oh, I'm so sorry, Mister Gaines. It was so hard to see that. You looked so tired."

Millard Gaines held the phone-receiver away from his face and stared at it with shock and disgust.

"Vera, can you please repeat that?"

"I said: I'm so sorry, Mister Gaines. It was so hard to see that. You looked so tired."

"Yeah, that's what I thought you said. So they showed it on the boob-tube, huh?"

"Yes, I'm afraid so."

"Ah, okay. *Perfect.* That's great. Put Feldman on, please."

"Oh, one thing, Mister Gaines. I forgot to mention this to you yesterday. Your doctor called. He phoned-in a new prescription for your diet-pills."

Millard Gaines put his fist in his mouth to shut

himself up. There was a *click* on the line.
"Feldman here."
"*Al*, old chum, I tried. I tried my best..."
"Yeah. We all saw it."
"I guess you know what this means."
*"Yeah. I know what it means, Milly. But it's been a swell
ride though, hasn't it?"*
Millard Gaines dabbed at his forehead with
his handkerchief. He wanted to cry. He dabbed at
his eyes.
His voice began to break.
He was glad his father was dead.
"I guess you're right at that. Say...Al. I got some
money to burn. Let's go to the Palm, my treat. Let's
get some big, thick, juicy steaks. And then let's get
drunk. I mean really, falling-down, shit-faced, stinko,
pickled drunk. And then...maybe a couple of whores.
Whaddya say? On me?"
There was a long pause.
Millard Gaines wondered if Feldman was crying too.
"Yeah. Ok, Mill."

IF THE WORLD OF MEN REJECT ME... THEN I'LL CALL ON THE OTHER WORLD! I'LL CREATE FOR MYSELF A COMPANION OF MY OWN WHIMS...OF MY OWN DICTATES! I'LL BE THE ONE THAT LAUGHS!

IT was a chilly afternoon up on the roof.
Lester held Stella's leather lead tightly as she strained
to get at the pigeons on the red-brick ledge.
He nodded sadly to his friend.
"My brother a *fairy*."
"What do you mean he's a fairy? Like in *Peter Pan* or
something?"
"Nah. He like other boys. That mean fairy too."
The features on Bob Fujitani's wide, flat face screwed
up as he pondered Lester's words.
"So – what's wrong with that? I like boys too. I like
you!"
Lester let out a deep sigh and threw a rusty Pepsi cap
at a row of pigeons.
The flock lifted itself chaotically, shouting avian
obscenities before resettling.
"No, ain't the same thing. He a *fairy*. He funny in the

head. He ain't *right*."

"Gee, that's too bad, Lester. I'm sorry. My brother is dead. At least yours is still alive."

Lester slumped down to the tar-paper, set his elbows on his knees, and let his limp face fall flat into his palms.

Bob Fujitani sighed sympathetically and scratched at Stella, who still strained towards the pigeons. Beneath the plush combed wool, her muscles were as taut as steel.

"Does that mean you're going to be funny too when you grow up?"

Lester shook his head.

"Dunno. Maybe. But I hope not..."

"I hope not too."

Bob Fujitani sighed a second time.

"Lester?"

"Yeah?"

"I have to tell you something."

"Okay."

Bob Fujitani swallowed his saliva and looked up towards the sun for strength. The clouds around it were jaundiced and sickly.

He sighed a third time.

"My mother says I can't play with you anymore."

Lester stared at the roll of fat bulging through the waistline of Bob Fujitani's striped t-shirt. He didn't want to look at his face. He was afraid he might punch it.

"What you mean?"

Bob Fujitani shrugged.

"Well...she says you're a bad boy."

"What she mean by that? How come *I* a bad boy? I ain't no badder than *you*."

Bob Fujitani pointed out a passing cockroach to Stella; who pounced and made loud, crunching sounds as she chewed.

"Well, I *know that*..."

"Then why don't you say nothin' to her? I ain't so bad."
"I *did* say that. But she just shook her head and said
no...that you're a bad boy."
Lester scowled at the tar-paper.
"She mean I'm a *black* boy. And *all* black boys is
bad to her."
"Yeah. Maybe."
Lester shook his head and looked southeastwards
towards the Wall Street skyscraper peaks.
"But...that don't even make no sense. *You Chinese!*"
"We're *Japanese.*"
"Same shit. Don't make no difference. Your
mama think she better than niggers, but she ain't.
Nightriders string her up just as fast as any nigger.
You see."
Bob Fujitani shook his head.
"*Gee,* I sure hope not. I love my mother. She's a swell
cook, even if she is wrong about *some* things."
Lester looked at his friend very seriously.
"Well, what you gonna do? You gonna listen to her?"
Bob Fujitani forced out a laugh.
"What do you think?"
Lester nodded, but he wasn't convinced.
"*Yeah*...We'll see about that..."
Bob rested a hand on his friend's shoulder and
patted it gently.
"*Don't* be like that, Lester. You'll see. I'm your pal to
the end. Straight down the line."
"Oh, you my pal to the end, huh?"
"That's what I said, didn't I?"
Lester turned away from Bob and stared at the
skyscrapers again. He focused on the tall angry spire
of Trinity Church. It reminded him of a stiletto, aimed
at the breast of God.
Lester withdrew a gold-plated Remington pocket-
knife from the hip-pocket of his crisp, new triple-
stitched dungarees. Engraved on one side was the
name '*Butchie*' in cursive and the numbers '*1933*'. On

the other side, in Roman letters, were the words *'To my darling son, A happy family is but an earlier heaven. Love, Daddy'*.
He unfolded the larger blade.
"You know what 'blood-brother' mean?"
Bob Fujitani nodded.
Lester held out the knife.
"Then you know what to do with *this*."

DR. Wertham was tired.
He'd spent the past day and a half in a stuffy Federal building and was in dire need of rest.

When he finally made it back to the sanctuary of Harlem, he sat behind his walnut desk and ordered his secretary to hold his calls. Then, he lowered his head onto his forearms and drifted off to a dreamless black pool of flavorless syrup.

At four twenty seven, Dr. Wertham's intercom awakened him with an ugly, rattling, fly-like buzz.

"Yes?"

"Doctor Wertham sir, there's a woman here to see you."

"Does she have an appointment, Cora?"

"No, sir. But she's very...upset."

"Cora, *what* did I *tell you* about unannounced visitors?"

"Sir, I'm very sorry. She says she's met with you before. It's about her son, sir."

Dr. Wertham sighed, stood up, and made himself presentable with the palms of his hands.

"Send her in."

Seconds later, there was a light knocking at the door, and the doctor crossed the dull red carpet to answer it.

Beyond the threshold stood a short, pretty Puerto Rican woman in her late twenties. Her green eyes were heavily mascaraed and her tight pink blouse barely restrained her breasts.

It took Dr. Wertham several moments to recognize the woman as the mother of a young boy named Luis, a voracious comic book reader.

Despite his mother's prohibition, Luis read whatever comic books he could get a hold of. He'd been referred to the Clinic after some general delinquency.

The doctor smiled as much as he was able to, and nodded at the young woman.

"Oh, hello, Mrs. Fuentes. It's good to see you again. Please, come in and have a seat."

The woman sat in front of the desk and played with her long black hair.

"Doctor...I'm so, so sorry to barge in like this. I just get so worried sometimes that I just don't know what else to do."

In his mind, Dr. Wertham recalled his first session with Luis, a handsome young boy of nine with an aquamarine shirt and a three-inch greased pompadour. He'd struck the doctor as a perfect miniature of the male prostitutes he'd often seen wandering Hell's Kitchen at night.

"And what is your favorite comic book, Luis?"

"'Human Torture'."

The doctor had stared at the the boy quizzically.

"You mean 'Human Torch', don't you?"

"No. Human Torture!"

Dr. Wertham walked over to his filing cabinet and

found Luis's file, which he withdrew from its slot and proceeded to read aloud:

"Luis Grisóstomo Fuentes. Tough little boy. Age nine. Sleeps in one bed with brother Ezzard, age eleven. He gestures with his hands while describing the crimes he fears and enjoys simultaneously. The boy tells me his father was killed by Indians in a logging camp. His mother later reveals that his father has actually died of a heroin overdose after a life spent in and out of prison. 'Strangling is the cat's meow. I think that's my favorite kind of pain.' 'In Nyoka, there is the natives. They tear a guy apart. In two halves. I like that.' 'I like the Green Lantern stabbing the tiger with his magic skull ring. He is the angel of death.' 'I like classic comics too. I like the big white whale killing the bad man. I like Nero fiddling with Rome on fire. The world is garbage. I want it all to burn.' 'I like the Apparition. He wants to kill the girls. Maybe because they want to kiss him all the time.' 'I like the Shining Knight. I like it when the horse flies.' 'I don't remember Batman's name, but the boy's name is Dick. They live together. Sometimes I think that it could be that Batman did something with Dick like I did with Father Scanlon.'"

Dr. Wertham lowered the file.

Mrs. Fuentes looked at the doctor with the saddest eyes he'd seen in weeks. Her stare reminded him of a fallen comrade thirty five years prior – dying in the Belgian muck with an English bullet lodged in his heart. His eyes were green too.

His name was Jurgen. He was only seventeen.

She nodded.

"Yes, that's him, Doctor. He's been caught again. This time, the police picked him up with a switchblade. There was dried blood on it."

"And to whom did Luis say the blood belonged?"

The woman shrugged.

"He said it was the blood of a rat."

Dr. Wertham penciled a note in the file.

The woman's voice wavered and broke as she explained that the State had revoked custody of Luis. She described the sordid details of the youth shelter he was being kept in.

"And when I complained – they just told me that I should just be thankful he's not in the reformatory. That it's even worse there."

Dr. Wertham stared at Mrs. Fuentes from behind his desk as she cried and wiped at her eyes. While he noted her obvious shortcomings, he could tell that she was a decent, hardworking woman who'd given the best care and education to her children that she possibly could. But sometimes, one's best just wasn't enough.

These were *his* people, and he was happy to be there for them.

He tried to console her.

"I know your boy, Mrs. Fuentes, and I believe there is hope for him *yet* with the proper care and guidance. Please...do not despair. The Clinic will take full responsibility for Luis. I will make some calls in the morning. You will get your son back."

Mrs. Fuentes rose from her chair and leaned forward on her elbows across Dr. Wertham's desk, exposing the cleavage behind the gap of her pink blouse. She focused on the doctor's magnified blue eyes and smiled.

"Thank you, Doctor. You're such a saint."

The doctor nodded and remained motionless in his chair while the young mother continued to lean across his desk, still staring into his eyes, her breasts quivering.

Forty five seconds passed.

Dr. Wertham smiled uncomfortably, then made a whisk-broom gesture with his right hand.

"You may leave now."

ON his walk home, Jack Coal made a pitstop along Second Avenue and purchased a dozen pink roses from a cowled woman with an old wooden pushcart that sagged from its burden. She hacked at the stems with a curved rusty blade, wrapped the bouquet in green paper, and snatched at his money with mangled yellow claws.

He smiled stupidly as he walked. The rustling weight of the bouquet pleased him, and his thoughts drifted back twenty years – to the dawn of his quest to strike it rich as a famous cartoonist – when he'd first dragged Dot kicking and screaming to the big city.

Those early days had been awfully lean. They'd lived in a sixth-floor Avenue C walk-up. Their monthly rent had only been fifty eight dollars; but it may as well have been a million.

He'd made the rounds to every agent, editor, and publisher between Coney Island and the Bronx so many times that the receptionists had stopped offering him seats in the waiting rooms; merely yawning and rolling their bored, painted eyes. There were holes in his shoes, his razor had grown so weary that his face was a perpetual Armenian blue, and both pairs of his pants had begun to assume a sickening, greasy shine.

When Dot was forced to take in mending to pay the grocer, it was without a peep. She told her husband that she loved him very much, and that she never wanted to see him toil in a can-factory again. There wasn't enough buttermilk in the world to wash away the stench of sardines he'd brought home nightly. Eventually, the flame of necessity had grown too hot and Jack Coal's syndication hopes evaporated in a wisp of grey steam. He began to draw base, one-panel sex gags for stag magazines, though it'd pained him to do so, for he didn't approve of pornography (which was un-Christian.) But, like God, bills were everywhere, and he'd shucked his morality aside to pour every last ounce of blood, sweat, angst, and bile into his task.

His efforts had been deliciously filthy, Dot herself cackling in his ear and providing much of the gag material. But even those had proved a tough sell. There were a thousand other would-be DeBecks drawing tits back then.

When he'd finally managed to broker a five-cartoon deal with *Peep'n'Pant*, he'd blown the entire $2.50 on a jumbo bouquet of pink roses for Dot.

As he'd beamed with pride, she'd stared at the roses with a mixture of shock, joy, and abject horror.

"But, Dot! Pink is still your favorite color, right?"

Dot looked down to the peeling, rat-chewed linoleum and shook her head.

"Yes, you big dope...but I'd of rather seen that pink in a steak!"

And now, he'd come full-circle. He'd hit the motherload.

Jack Coal lifted his glasses and examined the flowers in the dim yellow light of the Otis. His smile dropped.

Some of the petals were browning at the ridges.
He cringed and a burst of outrage surged through
him. That dirty wop had seen his shattered lenses and
taken advantage of his misfortune.
He briefly pondered reversing the elevator, returning
to Second Avenue, and shoving the defective bouquet
down the thieving gypsy scum's filthy immigrant
throat, but he quickly dismissed the notion.
No. No. Life was too short.
When he told Dot about the new strip, he knew she'd
be too happy to belabor such a petty trifle.
It was time they started discussing things that really
mattered.
Things like JUNIOR.
Yes, by golly, he *was* going to bring it up himself if
she wouldn't. Why *shouldn't* he? A man had a *right*
to discuss these things. Especially a man making
Bushmiller money.
Maybe, he thought, *maybe* Dot was simply just too
afraid to bring it up. Maybe she thought he *didn't even
want* a child anymore. That he'd grown too old; too
used to his own time; and too used to his own space.
Maybe she thought he'd even be *cross* with her.
It wasn't an unreasonable assumption. It'd been so
long since they'd even discussed the matter.
*Well, he couldn't let her think a thing that. No, sir. No
how. He'd set everything straight!*
The doors opened at the tenth floor, and Jack Coal
sang sweetly to Dot's bouquet, sniffing at it as he
danced in slow, luxurious circles down the corridor.
I'd sacrifice anything come what might,
For the sake of havin' you near,
In spite of a warnin' voice that comes in the night,
And repeats, repeats in my ear:
Don't you know, little fool, you never can win?
Use your mentality, wake up to reality.
But each time that I do, just the thought of you
Makes me stop before I begin.

'cause I've got you under my skin!
Jack Coal stopped dead in his tracks.
There was a cigarette butt on his doormat.
He stooped, sniped the butt, and sniffed at that too.
He knew the brand instantly.
Jack Coal very carefully leaned over and placed his
left ear against the front door.
Nothing...
He slid his key into the lock and turned it as gingerly
as he could, trying to suppress any sound.
The lights were out in the living room. Everything
seemed in order, aside from a strange blur on
the couch.
He tiptoed across the room and reached out towards
the blur. It hummed softly as he touched it.
Jack Coal recoiled in disgust and wiped his hand on
his topcoat.
It was a guitar.
He turned his head.
A soft *clink* had come from the bedroom, the sound of
two glasses touching. Then, Dot's laughter.
He pressed his ear to the bedroom door, and clamped
his eyes shut tightly behind the glass cobwebs.
"And how's it going with old Willie?"
"Eh...I dunno. Ok, I guess."
*"He's a shrewd little kike. I'm sure he's squeezing every
last drop of blood out of you that he can. Talented young
guy like you. Watch yourself around him. He's a piece of
garbage!"*
"Ah. He's not so bad. Don't say 'kike'."
*"And you're sure Jack's at the bar with the boys? That's
not like him."*
*"He was gone when I left. So, yeah. I guess so. He's one of
the boys...right?"*
"Well ... sort of. And why is Willie on TV anyway?"
*"I dunno. As long as he pays me on time, I don't ask
questions."*
"Fair enough. A little stoic."

"Can I ask you something?"
"Of course."
"Why'd you ask me over here?"
"You mean, besides to ball?"
"Yeah. Why me in particular? Doll like you could get lots of fellas. Why me?"
"Well. Maybe because I recognized something inside of you. Something ... that I share. A kind of loneliness. Or a hunger."
"You think I'm lonely? Hah! I'm not lonely. I wish I was lonely sometimes."
"You're impossible! Okay ... because you're handsome and I wanted you. Good enough?"
"I got a high forehead."
"You really ARE impossible."
"Yeah. I guess I am."
"And because I like the way you sing."

Jack Coal cringed.
His face cringed.
His muscles cringed.
His organs cringed.
And his testicles cringed.
He was in pain.

He pressed his fingertips to his temples and tried to cave in his skull, but he couldn't summon the strength. His fingers just seemed to seep in knuckle-deep and tickle at his brain. It was as if his skull were made of rubber.

He straightened up with a jerk and the shards in his frames fell soundlessly to the carpet. Almost blind, he groped his way back to the dark living room to retrieve his spares.

In the corner of the room stood an antique mahogany secretary.

Jack Coal had purchased it for Dot at a curios store five years earlier after she'd dropped hints for weeks.

It'd cost him twenty pages pay, but the smile it'd planted across her lips was the prettiest thing he'd seen in 1948.

He loved her so.

Jack Coal thought to himself that he still felt the same way as he gently lifted the secretary's roll-top, which was stiff and slightly off-track.

This is fixable. This is not beyond repair.

Jack Coal slid open the far right drawer, where he kept his spare glasses, and reached around. His fingers brushed against something soft and coiled around it like five hungry pink snakes.

Jack Coal pulled his hand back. It was the velvet drawstring bag he'd been presented at the reading of his father's will.

He reached into the drawer again, this time withdrawing a small, rectangular, cardboard box.

He reached in a third time and finally found his spares. He put them on.

They were an old prescription. Things were still slightly fuzzy, but they'd have to do.

He turned back to the bedroom door.

There was a soft moaning. Then, a creak.

The velvet bag swung back and forth in Jack Coal's hand with a heavy, cruel weight.

The bulge in the bag was shaped like a pistol.

He lowered the secretary's roll-top and took a couple of steps towards the bedroom.

He stopped and shook his head.

No. *No.* That's not the solution.

Junior's in there too.

Jack Coal buried the bag and box in the right pocket of his topcoat, collected the defective bouquet, and glided out of the apartment with the grace and speed of a U-Boat.

Dot Coal peered down through the smoke at her plaything's squinty eyes. They were too narrow to actually look into.

"Can I ask you something?"

"Yeah."

"Do you play golf?"

He smiled.

"No. I'm from Minnesota. We throw axes up there."

"Oh…ok."

"Why would you ask me that? That's a weird question."

"Don't over-think it. It wasn't a trap. It's nothing really. It's just…I've been knitting some head-covers for Jack, but he hasn't taken out his clubs in ages. I just don't want to see them go to waste."

Dot paused, still mounted atop her play-thing, her stiff palms supporting her weight against the balls of his hard, narrow shoulder-points.

She tilted her head.

"Did you…did you just hear something? Like a door?"

He squinted and shook his head.

"Nope. Just you."

The play-thing smiled, blew smoke, and patted Dot Coal's ass.

As it jiggled, his penis throbbed inside of her vagina, and Dot appreciated this. It wasn't very large, but she was thankful for its warmth and sincerity.

"Ok, Wally. I guess it was just my imagination."

IT was dark out.
Jack Coal wandered down Third Avenue and
shuddered from the cold as he tried to focus on
happy, loving thoughts.
*It's okay. Everybody's entitled to a mistake once in a
while. Lord knows, I'm not perfect. Someday, we'll laugh
at all this.*
He noticed Christmas decorations already tacked-up
in storefront windows.
That's awfully silly.
It wasn't even Thanksgiving yet.
Christmas!

He'd always wanted to build a rocking-horse.
Jack Coal touched his stomach. He was beginning to
feel hungry again.
He stopped in front of a travel agency to examine their
display. Sprigs of faux-mistletoe and styrofoam-snow
framed a small cluster of plastic palms that'd been
stabbed through a patch of stubbly Lionel grass.
Above the fronds, a plastic DC-7 dangled from clear
fishing-line. Behind the diorama was a large poster.
It featured an orange sun cleaved by the horizon-line
of a calm blue ocean – ruptured only by a single
leaping silver dolphin. Large letters above the sun
proclaimed:
SAN DIEGO – WHERE CALIFORNIA BEGAN!
Jack Coal felt a sudden, tremendous surge of guilt and
shame. He'd been a stupid, greedy, selfish, callous,
little pig of a man.
This was all his fault.
California!
That was the ticket; the solution; the cure.
He should've taken Dot there in the first place. Just
after school. When they were still young and full of
promise.
The land of golden fertility.
Instead – he'd dragged his sweet, innocent,
rosy-cheeked little girl to a cesspool in cement.
To indecency. To cockeyed values. To unmitigated
moral degeneracy. To lice, blood, rape, rust,
Communists, decay, maggots, vomit, tumors, stench,
Jews, nausea, warts, corruption, disease, niggers,
spics, wops, and rats.
Was it any wonder that after twenty years she'd
become somewhat... *tainted?*
But he could *fix* this. This was not beyond repair.
Things were on the verge...of change.
It wasn't too late.
And he was a flexible, resilient man.
He had the power.

He would prove it to her, and to himself.
Even if the ordeal stretched him to his breaking point
– he would prevail triumphant. Because the good guys
always won.

Jack Coal stared at the poster, smiled, and wrapped
his arms around himself for warmth.

He saw Dot opening the backyard screen-door; a
basket of sun-dried white laundry in her hands; a
small pile of fresh oranges nestled upon it. Junior
tugged at her sleeve.

Her belly was swollen like a melon.

Jack Coal could smell the grove.

He could taste the flesh of the fruit.

A pair of long fingernails pinched his right earlobe
from behind and tugged.

Jack Coal winced. The nails felt like a crab's claw.

He turned around to face a tall woman in white rabbit.

Despite the angry sores around her plush, painted
lips, there was a sad beauty to her.

She looked into his eyes with a strange, expectant
familiarity and waited for him to say something first;
but Jack Coal just stared back blankly.

She gestured towards the pink bouquet, which hung
limply in his hand, facing the pavement.

Jack Coal noticed that the woman's platinum Marilyn-
do had black roots.

Her voice was coarse and masculine.

"Lookin' for a date, fella? How 'bout me?"

Her breath smelled like bleach.

Jack Coal stared at the woman for a moment – unsure
of what was happening. There was a pointy bulge
lodged in the center of her powdered throat, as if she
swallowed a peachpit and it'd become lodged.

"Five bucks, and you won't regret it!"

Jack Coal staggered away from the blonde.

He stretched his legs and began to run, taking
ever-lengthening strides. He wanted to create as
much distance from this thing as quickly as he

possibly could.
It called after him.
"Some Romeo YOU are! God bless your poor wife, creep!"
In his flight, Jack Coal's brown Stetson sailed off of
his head. A wind-current caught the hat and carried it
halfway across Third Avenue.
Jack Coal rotated backwards, stretched out his arm,
and plucked the hat in mid-air, just in front of Chock
Full O'Nuts.

BOB Fujitani had returned to his apartment hours
earlier, but Lester remained on the roof with Stella, to
brood in silence.

He wondered what kind of strange concoction the
Fujitanis were having for supper, and his stomach
grumbled – but he was afraid to go downstairs and
find out what Cornell was cooking.

It was probably just fatback and beans anyway.

He stared at the silvery moon and wished that he
could go back to South Carolina.

He hated New York City.

People weren't right in the head up here.

The white people were even dumber than the niggers.

The Chinese, even worse.

He looked at the gash in his left palm.

There was dried blood caked all around it. Some of it
was his – and some of it was Bob Fujitani's. He smiled
to himself, imagining the dragon-lady's dismay when
she found out that her angelic son now had nigger-

blood pumping through his little heart. They were brothers now.

He'd kept his mouth shut when he and Bob had clasped hands to let their blood flow into each other's veins and spotted the red shoelace tied around his yellow wrist.

Lester wasn't mad at Bob Fujitani.

Bob hadn't known any better.

He wasn't mad at Cornell.

Or even at the fat man.

Lester was mad at God.

He remembered the *'Lawbreakers Suspense Stories'* in his back pocket, which he withdrew and cracked open.

It was hard to read the comic by moonlight. But, by squinting hard enough, Lester managed to make out the heavy blacks in the drawings and most of the Leroy-lettered words themselves.

He turned to a story called *'The Monster They Couldn't Kill'*.

It was about a scientist who'd intentionally exposed himself to atomic energy and been transformed into a misshapen, homicidal giant.

It bored Lester. He'd seen the same basic plot a hundred times before. And there wasn't enough blood, murder, or headlights present.

Even the *comics* had begun to let him down.

Lester thought again about going downstairs. He wondered if Cornell was going to be very upset that he'd seen his johnson. He thought about it long and hard. He'd probably say nothing.

He looked down to Stella, who'd been patiently waiting for him to notice her. She thumped her tail and whimpered at him sweetly.

Lester smiled.

"You hungry, boy?"

Stella wagged her tail harder.

"You want you some food, boy? You wanna go eat some

rats in the park?"
Stella raised herself on her hind legs and hopped
around excitedly. She showed off for her hero – doing
a triple-pirouette, letting her front paws to fall upon
his knees. She looked up into his eyes with deep
adoration.
Lester rubbed the fur on the crown of her head and
studied the dull gun-metal moons in her pupils.
"This all be your fault. You know that, right?"
Stella licked at Lester's hands as he picked her up.
He held her above his head.
She looked down upon him ecstatically.
Her tailed wagged even harder.
She loved her new home.
She loved Lester.
Lester smiled.
"I love you too, boy."
Then, he threw Stella over the roof.

JAGER'S Bar and Grill was a quaint, underlit little tavern with a corny decor that most would identify as 'Black Forest'.

Jack Coal was glad to find it empty.

He asked for three pickled eggs and consumed them within twenty seconds.

He ordered five more.

He felt like his stomach could expand to hold a thousand.

A mug of draught beer was placed in front of him.

He'd not asked for a beer – but was glad it was there. It was exactly what he needed. He downed it in a gulp, and ordered another.

The bartender, a tall, middle-aged man with beetle brows and jet-black hair, eyed Jack Coal's tired pink bouquet skeptically. He spoke with an educated European accent in an almost disinterested, recitational fashion.

"You like that, eh? It's called *'Wurzburger'*. Besides Luchow's, we are the only bar in all of Manhattan to have it."

Jack Coal stared at the carbonation in his second draught, covered his mouth as he belched, and nodded.

"Yes. I *do* like it. It's very good."

"That is from my *hometown*. Where I grew up as a boy..."

Jack Coal grunted as he ate.

The eggs and beer had a very medicinal effect. Soon, all of the tension in his features slowly melted, smoothed, mellowed, and softened. His jowls swung freely once again.

He looked up at the bartender, whose composed, handsome face was a mass of angles and crevices. This was a solid man who'd seen many things. This was a man he could trust.

Jack Coal smiled and stretched a rubbery finger.

"Hey fella, let me ask you something..."

The bartender pursed his lips to indicate he was listening.

"Do you...do you know anything about *women?*"

The bartender nodded and shrugged as he wiped at the immaculate counter.

"As much as any other fellow, I suppose. I know that all they respect or understand is money and position. And power perhaps. Does *that* answer your question?"

Jack Coal looked down and smirked at the wood-grain.

"Ah, so you're a romantic."

The bartender lifted a gleaming pewter stein and began wiping at it. He shrugged again.

"*Ach.* I have not lived entirely without passion."

He stirred slightly, set the stein down, and leaned across the counter until he was peering into Jack Coal's spares from a five-inch distance.

He furrowed his heavy brow. His accent seemed to miraculously fade as he smiled and spoke.

"But sir...listen to me. If there's one thing I *do* know about, it's *people. People,* and their *troubles.* And *you...*

you sir, are a fellow with *troubles.*"
Jack Coal looked into the bartender's cold blue eyes
and shuddered at the sight of his own sallow faces
staring back within them. They bore the same
beaten expression that the Apparition had worn as
he'd pondered his reflection in the window of his
rocket-ship.
But the Apparition had a paper mask to absorb his
tears.
Jack Coal shook his head and wiped at his eyes.
"Okay...okay, yes. But...but what do I do?"
The bartender leaned back, lifted the stein, and
shrugged again.
"There is only one thing *to* do, sir. You must *eliminate*
the source of the troubles."
Jack Coal felt the weight of his father's gun tugging at
the right side of his topcoat.
He thought about the squint, the guitar, and the
wretched blue pencil.
He thought about that awful 'kugel'.
Those greasy boots.
Then, he thought of California.
He thought of Junior. He thought of the long run.
He thought of the long arm of the law.
He thought of the Edge.
From the street came the sound of a man shouting
furiously in Greek. Another replied in Cantonese.
Then: the sounds of a scuffle, a crash, and a scream.
After that: wails of pain.
Jack Coal shook his head.
Babylon.
That was the real problem.
He needed to grab Dot and fly away.
He finished his second beer and motioned for a
third. There was a small television-set above the bar
mounted at a tilted angle. He remembered what Edna
had said, and pointed to the box.
"Can you put on CBS please?"

The bartender looked towards the television-set, reached up, and turned the dial to Channel Two. The picture was slightly scrambled, and he fiddled with the knobs until it was tuned to his satisfaction.

His accent had returned.

"*Hmph!* It looks like another one of these senate hearings or whatever you call them. Every day, it is this McCarthy fellow; him or the other one. Whatever his name is. Every day. Such busy, important men. *Semper Vigilans.*"

Walter Cronkite was speaking.

There were heavy bags beneath his eyes.

"*Earlier today, the Subcommittee heard the continued testimony of Doctor Fredric Wertham, a leading exponent of the psychological impact of comic book magazines. Here – is the man in his own words...*"

Jack Coal stared grimly at Dr. Wertham's gaunt, serious face. He was precisely as he'd imagined him to be.

"*Mister Senators, I will tell you this: children do NOT dislike authority! On the contrary, they have a strong inner urge to find and follow authorities whom they can trust. They may not always understand what is best for them, but they crave our firm guidance. A large part of a child's inner life consists of this search for authoritative wisdom, discipline, and correction...*"

The bartender chuckled.

"*Hah!* Spoken like a true German!"

After a commercial break, the abbreviated testimony of William Meiser was aired.

"*I've been a part of this industry for my entire professional career, and I've admittedly done quite well by it. It's made me a very, very wealthy man. When I began creating comic books, it was my intention purely to entertain; never to corrupt. And this is what I did. Entertain. It's only within the past several years that some ... disturbing ... trends have begun to surface. I don't know...maybe it was the war that changed our appetites, but...the fact is the public has come to crave sex – and*" *violence – in ALL forms of media. The more lurid, the more heinous, the better. At first, I resisted. I'd tried to steer away from these sorts of things, both in my own work, and in the books I produce for other publishers; I'm fully aware that a great percentage of my readership falls beneath fifteen years of age. But – after intense pressure from my advertisers; from my distributors; and from my customers themselves; I eventually had to buckle or risk going bankrupt. I couldn't allow that. I had both my own family and many employees with families who all depended on me to think of. As a result of my indiscretion, I have been the source of ... certain material ... that I now sincerely regret producing. Material that I am now deeply ashamed of..."*

One of the senators, a man with horn-rimmed spectacles and bristling grey hair, pointed to a slide-projection on an easel.

Even through his fuzzy old prescription, the projection looked familiar enough to Jack Coal.

After all, he'd drawn it.

It was the first page of *'Murderous Morphine and I'*.

Jack Coal's testicles began to tighten and knot.

The senator spoke with a soft Southern drawl.

"Now, Mister Meiser. THIS story...which features narcotic-addiction, smuggling, murder, extortion, kidnapping, prison-escape, rape, and suicide...all within nine compact pages...was produced in YOUR studio? Is that correct? Under YOUR watch?"

The camera swung back to Will Meiser, who nodded solemnly.

"Yes, sir, that story was – unfortunately – a product of the Meiser Studio, and I am indeed FULLY responsible. However, I'd like to point out that it was produced upon demand as a sub-contracted job, for another publisher – a man of questionable taste – and was not actually distributed by Meiser Publications."

Thank God, thought Jack Coal.

The monkey in his scrotum began to unfurl its fist.

"So, YOU yourself wrote and drew this, Mister Meiser?"
Will Meiser removed his pipe and shook his head.
Puffs of smoke escaped his mouth in time with
his words.
*"No sir. It was produced by one of my employees. A very
talented artist by the name of Jack Coal."*
The senator nodded and made a note in his ledger
with a pencil.
"I see. Thank you."
The television camera zoomed-in on the easel,
focused crisply, and lingered.
Jack Coal stared at the screen in disbelief.
The monkey clenched its fist again – squeezing harder
with each braying laugh.
On the easel was the enlarged head of a woman. Her
plush mouth was surrounded by angry sores; bags
hung beneath her jaundiced eyes; and a jagged reefer
dangled from her lower lip. Surrounding her were
giant hypodermic syringes, pills, bottles of alcohol,
and dozens of miniature ethnic gangsters zealously
murdering each other with guns, knives, saps, and
nooses.
The woman's blonde hair had black roots.
It was a beautifully-drawn mess. The work of a master.
Jack Coal shut his eyes and desperately tried not to
scream.
The bartender turned the power-switch to the left and
woman's face slowly shrunk until it'd been reduced to
a tiny glowing dot.
"Such filth. Shameful!"
Jack Coal could hear a toilet flush in his mind.
He knew that he could be expecting a second telegram
from Ward Greene almost immediately.
He saw California crumbling into itself and sinking
into the ocean.
He saw Junior in his crib floating helplessly in the
Pacific while a giant bearded green catfish swallowed
him up from behind.

He stood up from his stool. Sitting on his sore testicles
had become excruciating. As he rose, the pain
eased; but something else began to writhe within his
scrotum. It twisted with chaotic, worming patterns –
small, but riotous. He adjusted his pants and shifted.
The bartender was still shaking his head in disgust.
"*Ach!* What kind of swine would create such a thing
for the children to see? I would like to see the face of
such a man!"
Jack Coal looked down into his Wurzburger. There
was no reflection.
He shrugged.
"No man at all. A piece of garbage."
The bartender slapped his damp grey rag against
the counter and glared at it as if it had once deeply
wronged him. He lifted the rag and shook his head. A
stunned, crippled horse-fly staggered on the bar in
wide circles, like a happy drunkard. The bartender
brought the rag down again with a cold finality.
"Sometimes … sometimes I wonder why I ever *came*
to this country. It is nothing but a swarm of blood-
sucking vampires…"
Jack Coal nodded in agreement, ordered a triple
whisky, and asked for the phone book.

IF YOU ARE HAILING A CAB AND GETTING INTO IT, YOU WILL SOON GO ON A LONG JOURNEY DURING WHICH YOU WILL EXPERIENCE MANY COMPLICATIONS AND DISAPPOINTMENTS.

JACK Coal – flush with whisky – stretched out his right arm to hail a cab and let it ripple in long, rubbery waves.

A small, delicate hand grabbed his wrist and wrenched it south.

It was Bert Meskin, coatless and wearing a plaid green Jimmy Olsen bow-tie.

Jack Coal beamed down upon his little friend.

"Bert, m'boy! What're *you* doin' here? How'd you even know where to find me?"

The smaller man shrugged and smiled sheepishly.

"I-I-I-I-I c-c-c-can *always* f-f-f-find you, J-J-J-Jack!"

Jack Coal looped his arm around Bert's shoulders like a creeper-vine and squeezed them tightly.

It was good to see a true friend.

Someone who *understood* him.

"Bert. It's *freezing* out here! You should be wearing a coat. You'll catch your death of cold."

"I-I-I-I...s-s-s-s-saw the t-t-teevee, Jack. I-I-I'm a-awful s-s-s-s-s-sorry."

"Me too, Bert. Me too..."

"B-b-b-b-but w-w-w-where are y-y-y-y-you g-g-g-g-going, J-J-Jack?"

Jack Coal smiled sadly at his poor, disabled comrade
and patted his skeletal shoulder.
"I'm going to eliminate some trouble."
Bert Meskin pointed to the bulge in the topcoat and
shook his head.
"J-J-J-Jack, *d-d-d-don't!* Th-th-think of th-th-the
ch-ch-children! *The children will CRY!*"
Jack Coal winked, made a vulgar clicking sound with
his tongue, and laughed heartily.
"Don'tcha worry, ol' pal. Everything's hunky-dory!
Just sit tight, and I'll see ya soon!"
Bert Meskin sighed as he watched Jack Coal extend
his arm again, wave it like a lasso, and slither into a
yellow cab.
There was nothing more he could do.

JACK Coal bounded out of the yellow cab at West
134th Street at six thirteen that evening.
At six nineteen, he kicked in the front door of the
Lafargue Clinic with superhuman force – which was
unnecessary as it wasn't locked. When the startled
negro receptionist opened her mouth to scream, Jack
Coal stretched his long left index finger against his
chapped lips, and waved her out of the suite with the
blue Colt .44 in his right hand.
He'd loaded the revolver with the Bulldog cartridges
he'd inherited along with the gun – the box
disintegrating into fragments of thick, fibrous dust
as he'd opened its flaps. The tarnished green bullets

were at least fifty years old.

Dr. Wertham answered the dull bouncing thuds at his office door to find a cold barrel pressed tightly against his brow's permanent vertical crease. A quick glance at the sweating, corpulent face behind the gun angered more than scared him.

He loathed the idea of adults throwing childish temper-tantrums. It was the indicator of a true weakling. Even more offensive was the intruder's sagging, shivering jowls – the spitting image of a giant scrotum.

"Sir, exactly who *are* you, and *what* is the precise meaning of this? I warn you, if it is *money* you are after, then you've *certainly* got the wrong office! I am only a doctor...and not a very rich one at that! Most of my work is charitable. Herr *Rosenblatt* across the street is a bail-bondsman. Perhaps it would be prudent of you to visit *him* instead!"

Jack Coal's teeth sunk into his chapped lower lip as he struggled to keep his right arm steady. The blood that flowed onto his tongue was bitter, and he opted to let it drool down his chin and onto the dull red carpet rather than suck it in.

He remembered the bartender's words.
He did not want to be a vampire anymore.

Dr. Wertham made a mental note.

Call carpet suppliers tomorrow. Ask for swatches.

The old man nodded, bobbing the gun with his head. "From the manner in which you brandish this firearm, I trust you were *not* in the military service, no?"

Jack Coal moved forward, the gun tilting the German's head back on its axis, and entered the room.

Dr. Wertham stepped backwards gently, with a dancer's grace.

"You are *obviously* not a conscientious objector. Was this lack of service based upon some physical deficiency? You certainly *look* healthy enough; if a bit obese. No...no, it could not have been that. It may have been some kind of psychological problem or a *nervous disorder*. I am correct, no? Mister…?"

"Coal."

"Mister *Cold*."

"That's COAL, you Nazi swine."

Dr. Wertham chuckled and nodded.

"Ah, Mister *Coal*, I'm afraid you *have* mistaken me for someone else. Someone else entirely, it would seem! Allow me to introduce myself. I am Doctor Fredric Wertham! Most of my immediate family were *killed* by Nazis over ten years ago. I no longer even consider myself a German. I am as American as you, or any other citizen. Would you like to examine my passport? I have it in my desk."

Jack Coal pressed harder with the gun.

"Just shut up and keep your hands where I can see them."

Dr. Wertham raised his open palms and backed up slowly while Jack Coal continued to speak.

"I know *exactly* who you are, Wertham. And I don't give a leapin' lizard whether you call yourself a kraut, a kike, a Yankee Doodle Dandy, or the coronated King of Siam. To me, you are just one thing."

"And this thing is what precisely?"

"*Trouble.*"

The doctor nodded and fretted his eyebrows as he thought.

"Coal…Coal…Coal…*Coal*…I don't suppose you would happen to be *Jack* Coal, would you? *The* Jack Coal? The famous man of the funny-books? That *is* you, correct?"

Dr. Wertham's eyes darted, taking in the whole picture. He noticed the bouquet of pink roses suffocating in the crook of the intruder's left elbow, and allowed himself to smile. It was a calculated move.

"So, while I'm not surprised that a man with your… *talents*…would brandish such a large pistol, I must

admit – the flowers are quite a surprise. Are those for
me? It has been *eons* since anyone has brought me
flowers…"
The intruder blushed, then scowled – angry at his own
embarrassment.
"Don't be cute."
He waved the revolver.
"Get behind the desk."
Dr. Wertham shrugged and muttered to himself in
German as he took a seat and rested his hands flat
atop the cork blotter. He frowned as if something were
bothering him and began to straighten some papers
that'd somehow been allowed to stray crooked. Then,
he picked up a pen and began to write a goodbye-
letter in case the fool's gun should misfire. He
addressed it to the world. Halfway through, he looked
up at the intruder, who remained unmoved, standing
before the desk, staring and holding the gun far too
close to his own face.
"And *what* do you intend to do with me, sir?"
"I'm going to paint this room with your brains."
Dr. Wertham pursed his lips and nodded.
"Aha, I *see*. Mister Coal…may I say *one* thing before
you…begin to redecorate?"
Jack Coal nodded and grunted.
"Sir, while it is *true* that I take issue with the industry
in which you toil, please do not mistake my efforts for
any kind of personal assault upon your character. I
realize that you are somewhat disturbed – but please
– try to understand, this is *not* about *you*, if you can
believe that. I simply want to protect the children. And
I'd like to *continue* protecting them. The children are
everything to me. *Nothing else matters.*"
Jack Coal shook his head.
"Shut up!"
The doctor winced; then shrugged.
"Okay. Sir. Now, I realize that you're upset…and
perhaps you may even have a *right* to be…I have

probably done your chequebook a great deal of harm,
no? But this is merely an unfortunate inevitability.
As you know, the world isn't always fair. Again, I have
absolutely *no* interest in ruining anyone's careers.
There is *no* financial motivation behind my crusade.
As you can see for yourself, my surroundings are very
humble. Most of my work is with the desperately poor.
There is *no* profit in this. I simply want to *protect* the
minds – and therefore the *futures* – of the *innocents*.
That is my *only* concern, and my *only* reward."
Jack Coal began to tremble and his eyes welled with
large, heavy tears.
*"My wife...she thinks...she thinks I'm a fucking joke! I
was gonna fix this. I was gonna fix everything! We were
gonna have a new life. A second chance! But NO! You!
YOU and your pig-headed proselytizing...and now...now
I'm just a fucking joke..."*
Dr. Wertham shook his head mournfully, but not with
sympathy. He detested the wasting of time. At least
three valuable minutes of his life had now been stolen
from him by a fat, simpering fool.
It broke his heart.
"Mister Coal, *please*...show some composure, sir!
If it helps, be rest assured that your wife is indeed
in-correct. You are most certainly *not* a joke. Jokes
make us laugh. Jokes make us happy. Jokes bring us
profound joy! *You* ... on the other hand, are *not* funny.
You...will *not* make us happy. On the contrary – *you* will
only make us sad. You are...a very, very sick man I'm
afraid. And, while there has been extensive research
done in the field of hebephrenic schizophrenia –
much of it my own – I'm afraid that we still..."
*Jack Coal stared at the giant catfish behind the desk as it
babbled on and on.*
*He'd never actually seen a catfish talk before. For that
matter, he'd never seen a catfish wear glasses either.
And he'd certainly never seen a catfish with so many
diplomas.*

Dr. Wertham peered at the gun studiously as it shook. "That is quite an *old* firearm, Mister Coal. An antique in fact. Are you certain it still works? Have you taken it apart and cleaned it? Have you oiled it? Have you kept up with its maintenance at all? I was a soldier once. Would you like me to have a look? I could fix it for you."

"Shut up!"

"Some of my colleagues might even suggest that a gun like that is a replacement for-"

"Shut up. Shut up. SHUT UP! None of your psychobabble you stupid fucking nigger-kike-catfish-Nazi-swine! Save it for Bellevue!"

The old man lowered his spectacles along the bridge of his thin, fleshless nose.

"I'm sorry, sir? Bellevue? I haven't set foot upon those premises since my employment was terminated fifteen years ago. It was not a friendly separation."

"SHUT UP!"

The doctor shrugged.

"And I suppose you'd still think I was being... *'cute'*... if I told you there was a troop of five Girl Scouts standing directly behind you?"

Jack Coal smirked and cocked the hammer of his father's gun.

"Anything else, Kapitän Katfish? Time's up."

A soft, high-pitched voice startled Jack Coal.

"Mister Wertham-sir, your door be broken. We got your cookies, sir."

The intruder's face went blank as he lowered the pistol and buried it within the pocket of his topcoat. He stared at the old man and nodded. His face was smooth again. All of the drunkenness, anger, and confusion had evaporated; only the blood and sweat remained. He looked almost calm.

"Doctor Wertham, would you please just loan me a pen and some paper?"

The doctor handed the deflated cartoonist his bakelite

Pelikan and three sheets of ivory letterhead, then
watched with relief as the man spun on the heels of
his spent Florsheims and exited curtly past the five
uniformed little black girls.
Dr. Wertham smiled and wiped at his forehead with
an FTW handkerchief as the Brownies placed seven
thin sleeves of cookies upon his desk.
"*Thank you*, ladies. You've *really* made my day."
The chubbiest of the troop answered for the rest.
"You welcome, sir. We just sorry to interrupt your
meetin'."
Another Brownie disagreed.
"Don't be sorry, Eudora! That man was *plumb rude!* He
said the *N*-word and didn't even say '*Hello*'
or '*Goodbye*' to us!"
Dr. Wertham took a bite from a Thin Mint and raised a
calming finger.
"Ladies, I would not take that as a personal slight.
I have made a thorough study of that man's work, and
I can categorically assert that you are simply...
not his type."

THE *Cedar Tavern was near Union Square.
It was noisy, crowded, and not the type of place he'd
usually like to be seen in, but that didn't matter anymore.
Nothing really mattered anymore.
Jack Coal simply needed a place to park and write a note.
He ordered a double rye, and then another.
While he waited at the bar for a third, a large, lean
man with a red flattop and green sports coat laid a
heavy arm around his shoulders and squeezed them in a
forward manner.
Jack Coal looked down at the freckled hand as it hung.
There was an odd brass skull-ring on the third finger.
He wondered if this was some kind of homosexual
advance. He wondered if the Cedar Tavern was
a fairy bar.
He wasn't in the mood for love and whispered grimly
into the stranger's ear.
"Slow down, partner. That's how people get killed."
The man with the arm laughed and squeezed him tighter.
Jack Coal squinted at him through his spares.
The whisky was working very quickly. All he could
discern was a smear of freckles and a toothy leer.
The stranger was loud.
"Name's Andrews! Archie Andrews! Put 'er there, pal!"
As Jack Coal shook the stranger's beefy hand, he looked
again at the yellow skull-ring.*

It was pretty. It had red eyes.
The stranger noticed him staring.
"You like that ring? Took it off a dead kraut I found in Hitler's bunker! I was a paratrooper over in Berlin! It was rough over there, lemme tell ya!"
"It's nice."
Archie Andrews squeezed Jack Coal's shoulder once again.
"Tell ya what, buddy. Buy me and my friends here a round...and it's all yours! Honest injun!"
Jack Coal looked over Archie's shoulder and noticed a platinum blonde and a raven-haired brunette smiling behind him. They wore ponytails with bangs, tight, fuzzy sweaters, and pedal-pushers. Besides their hair colors, they were completely identical, both in face and figure.
Jack Coal nodded feebly and Archie ordered three Sidecars from a bald man with a pug-nose and cauliflowered ears. Archie Andrews watched carefully as Jack Coal paid for the drinks and replaced his wallet in his hip-pocket.
"Say – thanks, pal! Didn't catch your name!"
Jack Coal thought about it for a moment. He was having trouble remembering things.
"Oh, I'm sorry. It's Coal. Jack Coal."
Archie motioned towards the girls.
The blonde took Jack Coal's outstretched right hand and nimbly shook it by the fingertips.
"That's Betty! The all-American doll!"
Betty kicked at Archie with an open-toed red pump. Her toenails were bubblegum-pink
"Blackie here's Veronica! Watch out...she bites!"
Veronica winked, hissed through a feline smile, and held up her claws.
They were painted the color of raw beef.
"Ladies, this is my new old pal, Jackie Cold!"
"It's Coal."
"Whatever you say, pal!"
The drinks arrived.

Archie knocked his Sidecar back with a loud slurp and slammed the glass down on the bar. When he released his hand, the glass fell apart in eight different directions.
"Hallelujah! We're alive, and it's time to fucking drink! Barkeep, let's do it again!"
Archie spat on his finger and twisted and turned at the ring until it was finally freed. He handed it to Jack Coal, who studied it in his palm with little sign of emotion.
Archie slapped at his new friend's shoulder and laughed.
"Wear it in good health, brother!"
Betty eyed the flattened pink bouquet, still cradled within Jack Coal's left arm.
"Who's that for, buddy? Your wife? I see that wedding ring!"
Jack Coal glanced down at the flowers.
He'd forgotten all about them.
He looked at Betty and smiled warmly.
"No, dear...they're for you."
Betty beamed, accepted the bouquet, and buried her face in the blossoms.
She pressed her breasts against Jack Coal's chest; crushing the flowers between them.
"Oooooh...MISTER SMOOTH!"
Jack Coal blushed. He was happy.
She tickled his jowls with a fingertip.
"You gonna dance with me, Daddy-O?"
Jack Coal plucked the bouquet from Betty's hands and lobbed it backwards – not caring where it landed. He grabbed her right hand with his left and wrapped his free arm around her twenty two-inch waist.
He whispered into her ear. Her cheeks smelled of lilac-water.
"Come, Desdemona. Let us trip the light fantastic!"
Betty smiled, confused.
"Huh?"
Jack Coal shook his head and lifted Betty off the ground playfully.
"Nothin'. Let's swing, baby!"
As the pair shuffled into the small mass of bobbing

couples, Archie Andrews winked at Veronica and emptied the contents of a stamp-sized, wax-paper envelope into Jack Coal's waiting rye.

JACK Coal performed an improvised dance southwards on University Place that would've made Martha Graham very proud.

He pirouetted, leapt, shagged, spun, and flailed. He even did a fair buck-and-wing on the roof of an ancient LaSalle amidst loud cheers from a gang of Brylcreemed youths in black leather and Buco engineer boots.

When he finally arrived at Washington Square Park, Jack Coal was drenched in sweat, despite the thirty five degree chill.

He collapsed onto a green wooden bench, and smiled to himself at nothing in particular, watching the rats as they watched him. He wondered what they were thinking about. He wondered if they were even capable of thought – beyond hunger or fear.

He envied them.

Their little rat lives were so easy, so free of complication or corruption.

Jack Coal's head was awash with clouds and fuzz. He wasn't quite sure where he was, or why, or how he'd even gotten there. He tried to focus and think backwards; but when he shut his lids – his eyeballs spun like whirling tops.

He sniffed at the air. Something smelled funny; stronger than the usual dried sweat-stench his heavy wool suits carried.

It was a salty, vinegary smell.

He rubbed some of the perspiration off the back of his neck and held his fingertips to his nose.

Piss.

Then, he remembered. He'd awakened face-up on the tiled floor of the Cedar Lounge john, staring at the underside of the urinals. They were disgracefully filthy.

He couldn't remember entering the bathroom though. Nor laying down. It was an awfully queer place to take a nap. The last thing he could recall was...buying another round.

The fourth? The fifth?

Then: *nothing.*

He'd lifted himself up and cleaned himself off as best he could, but – back in the bar – all of his new friends had vanished. Beautiful Blonde Betty. Voluptuously Vexing Veronica. Affable Archie Andrews. All gone.

Way gone, Daddy-O!

The bartender with the flattened nose would only laugh when Jack Coal asked if he'd seen them leave. He couldn't even remember leaving the bar himself. Why had they left without him? They were having so much goddamned fun.

Fuck...

What was the time?

Jack Coal straightened out his left arm and flicked his sleeve back. His Elgin was gone.

He sighed.

That was a shame.

His parents had given him that watch for his high school graduation. It was plated with genuine fourteen-karat gold.

He patted at his hips. His keys were still there, and some loose change, but his wallet wasn't.

And then he remembered Dot.

DOT!

He jostled the tail of his topcoat loose from beneath his thighs and checked the hip-pocket. The .44 was still there.

He was sorry that the thieves, whomever they were, hadn't taken that too.

Now *he'd* have to get rid of it.

He couldn't trust himself to keep it around anymore. Even hidden.

He'd had some truly blockheaded, monstrous notions all day long.

What if another mood struck him?

It simply wasn't safe.

He looked around. There were wire rubbish-bins all over the park. He could wrap the pistol up in some old paper, and just dump it in one of them.

But what if a bum fished it out and hurt somebody?

What if a KID fished it out?

No. That wouldn't do...

He'd throw it in the river.

He'd walk to the Hudson – ignore the queers – and hurl it into the murky green water to lay amongst the crustaceans, the eels, the corpses, and lord knows how many other guns and wedding rings.

Yessir. That's what he'd do.

Jack Coal stood up, took a deep breath, and then collapsed onto the bench again. He needed a few more minutes to right himself. He wasn't quite up to moving yet. His head felt funny.

Worse-comes-to-worse, he could sleep it off on the bench, go home in the morning, and get rid of the gun the following night when it was dark again.

That seemed reasonable enough.

It was at precisely this moment that the two little

green men from Mars decided to make their presence known.

DR. Wertham spent all evening behind his desk, catching up on his backlog. Between the Subcommittee, that Coal fellow, and the police-report, he'd fallen quite a bit behind. When he finally left the Clinic at nine, the Harlem night was windless, cold, and moon-bright.

He breathed in the cool air deeply and felt a deep satisfaction. There was a cleansing quality to it.

He heard a soft, feminine moan.

Out of the corner of his eye, Dr. Wertham noticed a woman sitting on a bus-stop bench, crying.

He recognized her as the young mother he'd spoken to earlier. It was late, and he was very tired, but he approached her anyway and invited her back to the Clinic.

After some time passed, she managed to control her

sobbing; but still, she couldn't speak.

Dr. Wertham gave her some coffee – laced with schnapps – and attempted to console her again.

"My dear...we do whatever we can. I know what you've done for this boy. You've tried so hard. Don't think that it's your fault."

Mrs. Fuentes, suddenly alert, looked up at the doctor and shook her head.

"No! It *must* be my fault!"

She looked down to her lap and smoothed out her skirt as she spoke.

"I heard it in the church lectures. And the judge...he said it too. It's the *parents'* fault that the children do something wrong. He said that's *always* the bottom line, where the buck stops. I asked the judge if maybe when he was very young...maybe he did something wrong too."

"And what did the judge say?"

"He said no, because he had good parents."

Dr. Wertham shook his head sadly and rested his palms on Mrs. Fuentes's soft, round shoulders.

"Mrs. Fuentes, you must cease this manner of thought. It is stupidity, and you are not a stupid woman. You have done all that you could. I have Luis's chart here, and we know it from the boy himself – you are a good mother – and you've given this boy a good home. But the influence of a good home is completely thwarted if it's not supported by the other influences children are exposed to...the comic books, the television crime-programs, and all that other nonsense. Adult influences work against them. We've studied that, and we know good parents when we see them. So, don't worry about yourself. It's simply *not* your fault!"

With the doctor's kind words, the cloud Mrs. Fuentes seemed to have been lurking beneath dissipated into a soft nothingness. She smiled at him with more warmth and gratitude than she'd ever doled to any priest or nun. He really was a saint. It was a tragedy that he rejected Christ. He didn't deserve to burn in Hell.

She stood up to leave.

When she was halfway through the door, she turned around slowly.

"Doctor, I'm so sorry to take up your time. But please...tell me that once again."

"Tell you what?"

She spoke very slowly, almost in a whisper...

Her breasts quivered...

"Tell me again...please. Tell me again that it isn't my fault."

BOB Fujitani and Lester stared at the strange white man on the park bench.

He was a mass of queer tics and reeked of urine. There was dried blood and lipstick on his chin. He slapped at his own face violently with both hands – cackled like a hyena – and then announced that he was about to be vaporized by Martian catfish. Bob Fujitani turned towards Lester and made the circular *'crazy'* gesture with his left index finger. Lester nodded at his friend sadly, and both turned back to stare at Jack Coal. They were completely mesmerized by this smelly, hulking white maniac. Jack Coal covered his face with his palms – interlaced the fingers – and spoke through the fissures in a demented, high-pitched, almost-womanly voice. *"Oh, Wally...Wally, Wally, WALLY! You're so young...so*

handsome...so...so virile ... so powerful ... I simply ADORE your high forehead!"
Jack Coal paused and peeked at the Martians.
"If you're looking for our leader, just head south on
the Jersey Turnpike. Keep going four and half hours
until you get to a big white house. You can't miss it. It's
the one with all the Marines picnicking on the lawn.
The big chief is the bald guy with the Martini breath."
Lester cleared his throat.
"Um. Mister? You okay?"
Jack Coal lowered his hands and let his face unravel
until it was smooth and expressionless again.
"*Gosh*...you fellows are a lot less Martian-y than I'd
expected. Why...why you look just like a couple of
ordinary *kids! Very clever!* Very clever indeed..."
Bob Fujitani stared at the brass skull on Jack Coal's
right index finger and pointed to it.
"Mister, what's *that?*"
Jack Coal looked down at his hand and raised his
eyebrows.
He'd forgotten the ring was there.
In fact, he almost didn't recognize it at all.
It came back to him in soft bursts. He shook his head –
smiled to himself – and chuckled.
"Why, that's my old lodge ring! I'm the Grand
Gooblegooble in good standing of the Secret Society
of Syphilitic Simps. You fellows ever hear of us? We
stage the annual Battery Park beaver-eating contest
every third July ninth. *We accept you!* No sheenies, but
Martians are jake by us!"
Bob Fujitani and Lester ignored the strange
man's bizarre rant and turned to face each other.
They remained silent, and communicated using only
their eyes.
Jack Coal's sickly chuckle tapered slowly and finally
expired with a faint sigh.
"You fellows *want* this ring? You can *have* it if you
want it."

Jack Coal made a serious face in Lester's direction.
"My boy...I'm passing my torch on to you!"
After some coaxing, Jack Coal wriggled the brass ring
free from his knuckles, leaving behind a circle of
green verdigris. He held the ring out in his wide right
palm, his long fingers stretched out flat. Through his
distorted haze, Jack Coal saw his arm extend
a full seventeen feet, bridging the gap between he
and Lester – though the boy was actually only
three feet away.
"Go ahead. Take it, boy! Allah compels you!"
Lester removed the ring from Jack Coal's hand, held it
up above his eyes, and turned it around beneath the
glow of the streetlamp.
"Thanks, mister."
Bob Fujitani frowned.
"Hey, mister! *That's not fair.* You didn't give *me*
anything!"
Jack Coal looked at the little Japanese boy sternly and
stroked his own chin.
"Son, you are a very direct individual – a trait I both
respect and admire. The last of the old-time cowboys.
A real straight-shooter!"
Bob Fujitani did not reply. He had no idea what this
crazy stranger was talking about.
Jack Coal spat out of the side of his mouth and spoke
in a slow, affected drawl.
"What kind of irons you been totin' there, pard?"
Bob Fujitani turned to Lester who shrugged.
Out of Jack Coal's topcoat came the revolver, held by
the barrel. His arm stretched across the park to Bob
Fujitani.
*"Here ya go, pard. Think ya can handle this? Will ya
know what t'do with it when the time comes?"*
Bob Fujitani reached for the gun. Lester grabbed at
the sleeve of his satin baseball jacket.
"No! Don't!"
Bob Fujitani wrested his arm away and scowled.

"*Shut up!* Why not? It's free! What are you...some kind of *fairy?*"

Lester looked at Bob Fujitani angrily. He thought about bopping him with his new ring. It would leave a nice cut.

"*Some kind of FAIRY like CORNY?*"

Lester looked down to the dirt as a rat scrambled past his Keds. He was angry, but wanted to cry too. Blood-brothers were not supposed to treat each other like this. He questioned his faith in everything.

"Mister, can I *really* have this gun?"

"*That's right, pard! One hundred percent gratis! My gift to yuh...to keep them rattlers a'hoppin' on them lonesome trails ahead...*"

Bob Fujitani removed the gun from Jack Coal's hand – gripped it tightly – and took steady aim.

The strange man rambled on.

"*Little Martians, I have here in my hand a list of two hundred and five! A list of names that were made known to the Secretary of Shit as being members of the Garbage Party and who nevertheless are still working and shaping turd-patties in the Shit Department!*"

"Bobby...don't!"

Jack Coal shrugged and fretted at Bob Fujitani.

"*Go ahead already, son! It'll just bounce!*"

APPROXIMATELY twenty minutes after the shot was fired, two middle-aged police officers reluctantly approached the park bench with their guns and flashlights drawn.

They'd been parked on MacDougal Street, eating their bagged dinners, when they'd been alerted to the situation by a jubilant negro named Algernon.

The derelict had been a fairly reliable source of information for the past several years. Unfortunately – suicides were not the type of job the officers liked paying him for. There was no glory involved; it simply meant a mass of paperwork. It'd been very painful for them to surrender the customary five dollar fee that Algernon had come to expect.

The bigger cop sighed.

"I dunno, Joe...do you really wanna deal with this tonight?"

The smaller cop shook his head.

"Not really."

"Yeah, me neither...but, *shit!* If that rummy sells this

to Flanagan too, and then *he* finds out *we* had it first...
then it's *my* ass. His brother-in-law is my friggin'
mortgage broker!"
"But Algy probably wouldn't say nothing. Why would
he wanna hep Flanagan that it's used dope? Then he
couldn't sell it...right?"
The bigger cop studied his partner with hairy eyeballs.
"Because he's a dumb coon who don't know no
better?"
The smaller officer pushed his service cap to the
back of his head and scratched at his bald, liver-
spotted scalp.
"Yeah, I guess you're right."
The pair finished their hamburgers in somber silence
before departing on their tedious chore.
It wasn't easy being a public servant.

As they approached the corpse, the smaller cop
nodded towards his partner.
"Frank...there's a gun down there. It's a *big* one!"
The bigger cop shined his light by the corpse's knees
and saw the Colt beneath its right hand.
"Christ. That's a fucking *cannon*. I didn't think they
even made ammo for those things no more. Joe, can
you do me a favor? Handle this? I don't really wanna
look at this guy's head right now. I...I just ate..."
"Jesus, man...*so did I!*"
"But maybe...maybe he's just sleepin' one off. I mean,
Christ, he smells like a distillery."
"Yeah, and maybe I'm Roland Lastarza! Look at all
that blood! This fucker is dead."
"Okay, okay. So we'll do it together then. Okay
by you?"
The smaller cop nodded, and the partners slowly
approached the corpse.
It was bent forward at the waist as if it were hinged;
its head settled between its urine-soaked thighs.
Blood had seemingly poured from every orifice of the

corpse's face. Even its eyes appeared to be crying red tears onto its spectacle lenses.

A large pool had formed upon the tar between the corpse's cracked, brown Florsheims.

The scent of feces was also present.

The corpse smelled like a big pile of garbage.

Joe put his hand on the corpse's left shoulder and gently shook it. He spoke with the same mindful whisper that he employed to tuck his children in at night.

"Hey, buddy...you okay? One too many drinky-poos?"

The larger cop clucked his tongue.

"This guy is *definitely* dead."

"Yeah, *no shit*. That's what I said!"

"You really think he did it himself?"

"Of *course* he did it himself. There's the fuckin' gun! And look at that green mark on his finger. That's from the fuckin' trigger, right?"

"I dunno...I never seen a trigger leave no mark like that."

"Of *course* it's from the trigger. *Or*...it's a lot of fuckin' paperwork."

"It's *already* a lot of paperwork."

"Is it? *What is?* I didn't see nothin'. Did you?"

"*Nah.* I didn't see nothin'. Nothin' at all..."

"Could you eat another burger?"

"Yessir. I believe I could."

"Then c'mon. Let's get the fuck outta here. *Quick!*"

As the officers walked away, a triumphant bloody horse-fly emerged from the corpse's left nostril like a newborn infant and discreetly followed them back to MacDougal Street.

MICHAEL Rat scurried off with the piece of paper
gripped firmly between his sharp yellow teeth.
It was a very good find indeed, and Wilhelmina would
undoubtedly be pleased.
He would mate with her at least fifteen times that
night in celebration of their good fortune.
Perhaps even twenty.
Not only was this paper of the thicker variety – which
was more difficult to shred, but provided a far warmer
insulation – it was utterly drenched with the sweetest,
fattiest blood on Earth: *HUMAN.*
Usually, when Michael Rat found human blood, it
was in the form of droplets or puddles and could not
be transported. He'd be forced to drink it then-and-
there, and only speak of its wonders later; which
sounded like just so much bunk to his audience.
Wilhelmina and the children would laugh at him
and his wild imagination. He'd feel like a fool and
sulk in a corner.
But not this time. This time, he could actually share
the wealth, the magic, and the wonder. And – perhaps
in the future – he'd even be treated with the respect he

deserved.

There was some writing on the paper in blurred ink.

"Dear Mize,

When you read this I shall be dead. I cannot go on living with myself hurting those who love me. I am finished. What I did has nothing to do with you or your testimony. You were only doing what you had to do. There are no hard feelings. You have been the best guy I've ever worked for in all these years. I'm only sorry I leave owing you two bits for a sheet of bristol I lifted a couple weeks ago, but dear Dorothy will repay you when the insurance policy is settled. I'm very sorry about that. It was an impulsive move on my part, and I deeply regret it. I wish you nothing but the best in the years to come. Also, my best regards to all the fellows, especially Bert. Thanks again for everything Willie. You're a good guy and a fine American. Kindest regards, -Jack."

(But Michael Rat did not know what writing was, so none of this mattered.)

When he arrived home at his nest beneath the roots of the Hangman's Elm, he was dismayed to find Wilhelmina eating the litter of babies she'd given birth to only the night before. She barely took notice of his entrance and offered him zero assistance dragging the paper through the narrow hole.

Michael Rat stared at Wilhelmina for a while with the paper still clamped between his teeth.

It shivered and swayed. The dirt began to taint the blood, ruining its subtleties.

He wanted to weep.

All he'd ever tried to do was make her happy, but nothing was ever good enough. And, deep within his muridae heart, he knew that nothing ever *would* be good enough.

Michael Rat was spiritually lost.

All that was left to do was to surrender to the void.

He let the paper fall to the dirt and joined Wilhelmina by her side. She was utterly engrossed in her meal and still hadn't acknowledged her mate's presence.

He stared at the blue and purple viscera dangling from the corners of her mouth. There was just enough moonlight in the hole to make it really shimmer. Her whiskers were slicked with bile. He took a deep breath and held it in. Wilhelmina was the most beautiful rodent Michael Rat had ever seen, and suddenly he felt very, very fortunate.

There was no guilt as he bit into the thigh of one of his nameless infant sons. The baby squealed in agony, but he tasted too damned good to pay much mind. Even his bones, which were still only semi-formed and floppy, were absolutely delicious.

But that's just the way things were.

Life was hard and sometimes you had to eat your own children to survive.

THE END.